ONE STOLEN MOB PRINCESS...
TWO MEN WHO WILL STOP AT NOTHING
TO GET HER BACK.

As the daughter of Russian mob royalty, Risa lives on the outskirts of Philadelphia society. True friends are hard to find. Women ignore her unless they want her money. Men pursue her for her ice-queen looks and her father's favor. She might as well be a born-again virgin, since the only two men she desires want nothing to do with her and one-night stands have lost their appeal.

When a new friend invites her out for a night, Risa jumps at the chance to unwind and have a few drinks somewhere no one knows her. She enjoys the freedom and forgets, for a split second, that she's got a target on her back whether she deserves it or not.

Now, kidnapped and put up for auction to the highest bidder, Risa needs a hero. She gets two.

Gens has wanted Risa for years. But her father took him in after his parents were murdered and Gens owes him everything. He's buried his love for Risa behind brotherly affection but never stopped wanting her.

Tony left behind the Philadelphia underworld when he

became a cop and moved west. But after a shocking betrayal, he returns to Philadelphia disgraced and unemployable. Until his boyhood friend Gens gets him a job as a body-guard...and Tony falls hard for his mobster boss's daughter.

And when they have her, Gens will give her whatever she wants to help her heal...even if that means pushing her into the arms of his best friend. But Risa wants them both. And she's not going to take no for an answer.

AN INDECENT DESIRE

AN INDECENT DESIRE

STEPHANIE JULIAN

MOONLIT NIGHT PUBLISHING

Don't miss updates about new books and sales. Join Stephanie's newsletter on her website at www. stephaniejulian.com.

Don't miss any of the books in the Indecent series:

An Indecent Proposition
An Indecent Affair
An Indecent Arrangement
An Indecent Longing
An Indecent Desire

1

"You're going out?"

Larisa Antonoff stopped in the foyer of her father's home, wondering if she could simply ignore the man who'd asked the question.

It wasn't his question itself that she objected to. It was simple enough on the surface.

But her relationship with him was anything but simple. At least, to her.

Gennady Markov, she was sure, thought differently. He believed she owed him an answer. As her father's right-hand man, Gens made sure he knew everything that went on in their home. That meant he wanted to know every aspect of her life.

Swallowing a sigh, she turned and faced the man she'd fallen in love with at fourteen, when he'd come to live with her and her dad. He'd been sixteen and he'd sparked something inside her she had no context for at the time.

Her chin lifted as she gazed at him with what she hoped was a cool expression. "Yes, I am. Is that a problem?"

Of course, it wasn't. At least, not for her. And since Gens was nothing more to her than her father's employee, it shouldn't be for him.

Liar. He's much more. He just doesn't want to be.

"You don't look dressed for a night out. Where are you going?"

Gens leaned against the wall, crossed his arms over his chest, and waited. Like he deserved an answer simply because he'd asked. And that pissed her off. For all the wrong reasons.

Damn him, she wanted him to care where she was going. Just not because he worked for her dad. She wanted Gens to want *her*.

"Out with friends."

His brows rose over warm blue eyes that made her own look dishwater gray in comparison. "Oh yeah? Who?"

Her chin tilted up. "I didn't know my social calendar was under your jurisdiction."

If she'd hoped to get a response from him, she was disappointed.

He lifted a shoulder. "It's not. Just making conversation."

Which was total bullshit. She and Gens no longer made conversation. There'd been a time when all she'd wanted to do was make conversation with Gens. The man fascinated her. He had since he'd moved in with them after his parents' deaths. He'd been quiet and wounded, perfect first-crush material for a girl who'd never had one.

Those blue eyes along with his light brown hair, cut short but not too short, made him appear approachable, which was more wish on her part than reality.

Flashing him a fake smile, she continued on her way to the front door, where Daniel was waiting for her in the car.

"Have a good night, Gens."

"Risa."

She thought about ignoring him. But that would make her a bitch, wouldn't it?

Turning, she waited.

"Be careful."

Her brows arched. "When am I not?" She paused when Gens didn't respond, her gaze narrowing. "Or is there something you're not telling me?"

He shook his head. "No."

Stifling a sigh, she turned and reached for the doorknob. Pulling open the door, she sucked in a sharp breath as she came face-to-face with Anton Blankenship.

"Hello, Risa."

Her heart kicked into high gear again, pissing her off.

Damn it. She should've told Daniel she'd meet him in the garage. And damn the rush of emotion making it hard for her to breathe.

Slightly taller than Gens, Tony looked like he should be working security for her father. Broad chest, thick arms and thighs, tightly shaved dark hair, and dark eyes to match. He looked like the kind of man you didn't want to meet in a dark alley.

In reality, Tony was a former cop who'd been her sister Dorrie's bodyguard until recently. Dorrie had told her Tony was looking into options now that she'd moved in with her two men and they'd taken over her protection.

Her sister had gotten lucky.

Risa, on the other hand, wanted the two men who seemed most likely to *never* date her.

"Hello, Tony."

"Heading out?"

She gave him the same fake smile she'd given Gens. "Amazingly, yes."

When he didn't immediately step out of her way, she gave him a look that had been known to make other men cower, their balls shriveling into raisins.

Tony didn't blink. Except his gaze did take a quick trip from her face to her feet and back again. She knew why his eyebrows were slightly elevated when he got back to her face.

Yes, she was wearing old Converse sneakers and jeans, worn-soft and washed until they were pale blue. Her top was a plain navy t-shirt, and she had her hair braided in a thick rope that fell over one shoulder. Barely any makeup. Simple silver hoops in her ears and a thin silver chain around her neck.

No, she didn't look anything like she normally did when she left the house to meet friends. Then again, she didn't have a lot of friends who… Well, maybe she should just leave it at didn't have a lot of friends.

"Date?"

She blinked. Had he seriously just asked her if she had a date? Did he even care? It was on the tip of her tongue to ask. She bit back the urge.

Another fake smile. If she truly smiled at him or Gens the way she wanted to, they'd know how she felt about them. And that was unacceptable.

"Excuse me. Daniel's waiting."

Then she sidestepped him and walked out the door.

Good thing she wasn't driving herself. She had a feeling she was going to need a few more drinks than she'd already had planned.

* * *

"I'm not comfortable with this, Ms. Antonoff. Your father specifically told me not to leave your side."

Maintaining eye contact with the hulk standing in front of her, Risa raised her perfectly shaped eyebrows and crossed her arms over her chest.

The hulk visibly paled.

"I know exactly what my father said, Mr. Sokolov. But I'm not my father, and I'm telling you to stay in the car. You will not be comfortable in that bar, and I will be uncomfortable all night watching all the cops look for any excuse to arrest you. I told you, it's a cop bar. My friend's brother owns the place. *No one* will touch me."

At six-foot-two and a solid two hundred ten pounds, Daniel Sokolov was one of her dad's most trusted guards. He had to be if he was on her protection detail. Daddy never took chances with his daughters' lives.

Which was why Daniel was refusing to back down, even though he'd been with her long enough to realize she wasn't going to lose this battle. She'd learned from an early age how to hold her own against the men in her dad's employ.

Staring back, she waited him out. Ultimately, she knew she'd win. Her dad had never intended for her to be a prisoner and he knew she was never disagreeable only to be contrary. She wasn't stupid enough to believe she should go out at night without a bodyguard. She really did know better.

But tonight, she wanted a few hours to simply be herself with friends who looked beyond the fact that her father was the head of Russian organized crime in Philadelphia.

She wanted to laugh, drink, have a good time. So her friends had suggested this bar, where she'd be surrounded by cops.

With a barely concealed sigh, Daniel shook his head. "You have your panic button?"

And she'd won this round.

"Of course." She never went anywhere without it. Again, not stupid. But she also knew if anything happened to her, it would be Daniel's head on the chopping block and she didn't want that. She liked Daniel. He always seemed steady.

A few more silent seconds elapsed before he sighed, a little louder this time. "I'll be in the car right outside the door."

She smiled, trying to look grateful, not triumphant. "I know. Thank you, Daniel."

He nodded, ice-blue eyes narrowed, mouth a tight line. "Text me when you're ready to leave. I'll have the car ready to go."

"I will."

"Do not walk out of that building before you call me."

"Of course."

Before he could get out of the car and open her door, she pushed it open herself and slid out. Heading straight for the entrance to the bar, she didn't hesitate. Because, if she were honest with herself, she did have a few reservations. Not about her safety. She hadn't been lying about that.

No, she was actually nervous about spending the night with these women. And that was so very stupid, she couldn't help but shake her head every time she thought about it.

It'd been a damn long time since she'd been out with friends. It'd been so long, she couldn't actually remember the last time. Probably in college, more than seven years ago.

And even then, she hadn't had many close friends. She'd learned at an early age that most people wanted something from her because of who her father was.

"Risa! Hey, you made it."

The redhead waving at her from a booth in the back drew a smile as she adjusted course. The mostly male, Friday-night crowd at the neighborhood bar parted as she headed for the table where Mary Alice Dubrosky sat with Isabella DeMarco and Damaris Contino.

"I did. Thanks again for the invite." Sliding into the booth next to Mally, Risa turned her smile on Izzy and Maris. "I'm happy to be out of the house."

"Oh, I know what you mean." Izzy rolled her eyes and held one hand up. "I swear I've been chained to my desk at the office twenty-four-seven this week."

"You're chained to your desk every week." Mally rolled her eyes. "You need more than one night out a month to cure your workaholism."

Izzy made a face and flashed her middle finger at Mally. "Hey, I gotta eat and Maris gets pissy if I don't pay my share of the rent. Especially now that you moved out to be with your men," Izzy stretched out the word to at least three sylla-bles, "and left your friends behind to fend for themselves."

And, wow. It'd only taken one whole minute before Risa began to rethink her decision to come tonight. She was an imposter here, an intruder. She had absolutely nothing in common with these women. She'd never had to work a day in her life, though she did have a job. Mostly to keep busy. She wanted for nothing. Her dad paid for everything. Why the hell had she thought—

"Hey, I don't get pissy." Maris rolled her eyes. "You're the one who's always pissy. You need to get laid."

Izzy's face screwed up in an adorable frown, her long, brown hair pulled up into a ponytail and her dark eyes glinting with laughter. "Hey, I do—"

"Oh no. Toys don't count." Maris talked over her roommate. "Only real human contact with an actual male penis is acceptable."

Risa's mouth curved into a grin as she shook her head. Okay, maybe she did have more in common with at least one of these women than she'd thought.

Mally sighed. "Well, that devolved quicker than I thought it would. I'm so sorry, Risa. We're not normally so crude."

Izzy looked across the table at her and grimaced. "Actually, yes, we are. But we're really not bad people. We're just—"

"Nutcases," Maris finished. "We're all pretty much crazy. But you've met Mally, so you already know that."

"Hey, I'm not crazy." Mally looked offended, though the twinkle in her eyes gave her away. "I'm…"

As Mally searched for a word, Izzy's eyebrows rose.

"You're having a relationship with two men," Izzy said. "That's the definition of crazy. Seriously, how do you manage not to kill them? They're both so overprotective. I can't imagine how you put up with both of them."

Since Risa knew Mally's men, Max Burdanov and Jesse Kanatawa, she had to agree with Izzy on this point.

"Hey, those are my guys you're talking about." Mally scowled. "No dissing them."

Izzy's mouth curved in a slight smile. "I'm not dissing them. I was just testing your listening device. Must not be working properly. They didn't jump out of the woodwork to defend you."

As Mally rolled her eyes and Maris laughed outright, Risa just shook her head.

"Actually, I'm surprised because I do know Max and Jesse, and I'm with Izzy," Risa took the opportunity to join the conversation. "I wouldn't be surprised to find Max sitting in his car on the street watching through the window."

Which was exactly what her bodyguard was doing. But of course, she wasn't going to bring that up now, was she?

Izzy turned to her with a wide smile and raised hand, which Risa took to mean she wanted a high five. A little awkwardly, she slapped the other woman's palm and grinned when Izzy then balled her fist and waited until Risa did the same and they knocked knuckles.

She probably looked like an idiot, but she felt...normal.

For the first time in a long time, she felt just a little less isolated from the rest of the world. So she took a deep breath and tried to relax into the easy conversation between the women.

And tried to forget about the encounter with Tony and Gens earlier.

The conversation was still a little awkward on her part, only because she didn't really know Izzy and Maris. But in the past few weeks, she and Mally had become unlikely friends.

Risa wasn't quite sure how it'd happened, but Max had had a lot to do with it. She and Max had been friends for years. With the exception of her sister, Dorrie, whom she could never reveal was her sister, Max had been the only other person in her life she allowed close enough to be considered a friend.

And when Max had fallen for Mally, Risa had needed to decide for herself if this interloper was worthy of him. After their first, tension-filled meeting, she and Mally had slowly developed a relationship that had become a friendship.

At first, Max had forced it on them. He'd invited Risa to dinner with him and Jesse and Mally and practically twisted her arm to get her to say yes. She'd pretty much told Max no way in hell.

Max had countered with, "Get off your haughty ass and get over here for dinner or I'm going to think you're jealous."

It'd been a challenge and, since she was a little jealous, but not for the reasons anyone would believe, she got off her ass and joined them for dinner at a downtown restaurant that was more dive than destination.

The first time had been teeth-grindingly awkward to the point that she'd wanted to leave after half an hour. And she was pretty sure Mally had felt the same. Jesse had tried his damnedest to keep the conversation flowing while Max had gotten increasingly frustrated.

Risa had left that night vowing never to go back. She'd actually cried herself to sleep because she'd figured Max would never talk to her again. He'd called the next day and invited her back the following the week. Glutton for punishment that she was, she'd agreed.

And it'd been better. Not much, but enough. She and Mally apparently had come to the same conclusion. Neither of them wanted to upset Max so they had to do better. And from that shared realization had sprung a call from Mally to meet for lunch. Surprisingly, Risa had agreed.

That'd been two months ago. The lunches had continued once a week every week. At first, Risa had wondered if Mally had realized just how lonely Risa was and had taken pity on her.

But when Mally had asked her to join her and her friends tonight, she'd finally let herself be convinced that Mally actually liked her. And that Risa returned the feeling.

Mally was fierce, unafraid to speak her mind, and had a huge heart. Risa didn't consider herself any of those things. Opposites attract, right?

"So after I turned him down for the *third* time, he actually said I was frigid and I should loosen up or I'd end up old and alone and living with thirty cats." Izzy shook her head. "I told him I'd be better off with the cats. At least they weren't assholes."

Izzy had been explaining why she was currently single as Mally and Maris continued to needle her.

Risa just nodded, choosing her response carefully. "Izzy's right. Better to have a few pussies around than be stuck with an idiot just because he has a penis."

All three women turned to look at her with wide eyes.

Shit, had she overstepped? Maybe she should've kept her mouth shut—

Mally threw her head back and laughed so loud, Risa

figured people in the next state could hear her. Then Maris and Izzy joined in and Risa was pretty sure every man in the bar took a step away from their table.

When Mally finally stopped laughing enough to talk, she looked across the table at Risa and grinned, the warmth of friendship shining in her eyes and making Risa breathe more easily again.

"I knew there was a broad in there waiting to get out." Mally's smile softened. "See? I told you. You won't have any trouble fitting in here. You just needed an incentive to loosen up."

Risa raised her half-empty martini glass. "Then I'm ready to be incentivized."

2

Two hours later, Risa had had at least two more martinis and a couple shots of cotton candy-flavored vodka.

She shuddered thinking about that abomination, but Mally had insisted everyone have at least one shot and, since Risa was fitting in so well, she figured she'd just go with the flow.

That'll teach you.

"You look like you're contemplating world domination. Or you're just really pissed off about something."

Risa turned to face Mally. They were the only ones left at the table. Izzy and Maris had moved to the bar a minute ago to talk to Mally's brother, who owned the place and was serving as bartender tonight.

Tommy had kept an eye on their table all night. It'd made Risa feel strangely comfortable. She was used to being constantly under the watch of either her bodyguards or her dad.

"Not pissed off and not planning world domination. Just...enjoying the night out."

Mally smiled, looking pleased with herself. "I'm glad you came. I was pretty surprised that you showed up alone, though. I figured you'd have a guard with you."

Risa's mouth twisted. "I do. He's in a car across the street. I figured any man who worked for my dad wouldn't be welcome in a cop bar. Besides, I can't imagine anyone would be stupid enough to harm me here."

Mally rested her elbow on the table then rested her head on her hand. She looked only slightly buzzed, though she'd had just as much to drink as Risa. Izzy and Maris...Well, they'd started slurring their words about half an hour ago. Since none of them were driving, Risa figured it didn't matter.

She herself was pleasantly mellow. It felt good.

"Max told me you and Dorrie had a scare a few months ago." Mally's eyebrows rose. "Wanna talk about it?"

"Nothing to talk about really. Nothing happened. People like to talk big but, in the end, most don't have the balls to go through with it."

"You sound pretty laid-back about someone potentially trying to kill you."

"I'm not." Risa shrugged. "But if I worried myself sick every time someone made a threat against me, I'd never leave my house. And frankly, I'm sick of sitting around waiting for something to happen."

Mally smiled as she tapped her shoulder against Risa's. "Good for you. You know, I really didn't like you first time I met you."

Risa wrinkled her nose. "You weren't supposed to. I had to make sure you were worthy of Max."

Mally made a face in return, looking even more adorable than she already was. "I realized that later, but I really hated you for a little while."

"Well, the feeling wasn't mutual. You stood up to me. Not many people do. Either my resting bitch face or my Russian crime lord father scares them off. Or it could be the fact that I don't really like many people and I don't have to pretend because I have enough money and connections to make them disappear."

Mally was laughing by the time Risa finished, which made Risa smile in return.

"See, that's what I like about you, Ris. You're not afraid to own your life."

If only that were true.

Mally's head cocked to the side and Risa realized she'd said that aloud. Maybe she'd had a little too much to drink.

"Would you change things if you could?" Mally's gaze sharpened. "I mean, would you want your dad to be an accountant or a mechanic? You know, just some everyday average Joe with a nine-to-five and a pension?"

Risa took a moment to think, but not about the answer to Mally's questions. "Do you know you're the only person to ever ask me that? Not even—"

She snapped her mouth shut before she finished that thought.

"Not even what, Ris?" Mally leaned even closer. "I know we haven't known each other long, but you can trust me."

Risa nodded. "I know. It's just... It's tough after all these years of not being able to talk to anyone about it." Anyone except her sister, who she couldn't even acknowledge as family. "I guess sometimes, yes, I've thought about it. But only because..."

The words died on the tip of her tongue.

"Because what?" Mally prompted.

"Because my life will never be normal." Shaking her head, she sighed. "Do you know I've never done this before?"

Mally's gaze narrowed. "Done what?"

"Had drinks with friends. Something that seems so... normal. I've been to more cocktail parties than I can remember. I've organized dinner parties for hundreds of people. I've managed a foundation for the past five years."

"Really?" Mally's eyes widened. "I didn't know that. What's it called?"

"The Madelaine Foundation. We go to great lengths to keep it away from anything connected to my dad. We fund several charities through it, some you may have heard of, some you haven't. Runaways, drug addicts, battered women, LGBT abuse. I handle everything. Some of the money's legitimate. Some of it's," she shrugged, "not. But I tell myself it's going to a good cause so I don't...oh, I guess I don't make myself crazy over it. I could, but it wouldn't help. So..."

Slowly, Mally nodded. "You are. Doing good, I mean. We can't help who our family is."

No, you couldn't. And she loved her dad unconditionally. But...

"Did you know I've never been on a date?"

Mally's mouth dropped open. "Say what now?"

She nodded, knowing it wasn't only the alcohol that'd loosened her tongue.

"Max may try to tell you otherwise, but it's true. I've

never been on an actual date. I went to all-girls schools. We had mixers in high school with all-boys schools, but I never went. I had very few friends and I didn't exactly *mix* well. I spent breaks with my dad. After my mom died, he was all I had." Until Dorrie. But that was a secret she couldn't tell. "Except for Gens."

"And who is Gens to you?"

Risa thought carefully about her answer. "He's the son my dad never had. His parents were killed when he was sixteen and he came to live with us until Dad sent him to college. Now he's my dad's personal...assistant, I guess you'd call him."

Mally's gaze narrowed for a brief second before her expression set in determined lines, as if she were about to broach a tough subject. And apparently, she was.

"Have you always known what your father is?"

Risa felt her walls begin to slam closed. She never discussed this. Not with anyone, not even her sister.

And Mally had already begun to shake her head. "Sorry. So sorry. That was... I'm normally not so rude. Please put that question down to too much alcohol. And totally ignore it."

Just as Mally seemed on the verge of asking another question, Risa forced herself to answer.

"No, I didn't. Has Max or Jesse ever said anything about my mom?"

At the pained look on Mally's face, Risa could tell she'd heard something.

"Only that she was...troubled."

"Bipolar, actually. Severely. The meds kept it in check. Sometimes. When they worked. And when she took them.

When she didn't..." Risa shook her head. "Things got problematic."

And that was a huge understatement.

"For the first seven years of my life, she held it together. She took her meds, went to the doctor. She baked cookies. And she sewed. She used to make these tiny little dresses for my Barbies that were miniature works of art. Before she married my dad, she studied to be a designer in Paris. She had an entry-level position with Chanel. Of course, my grandfather bought it for her, but she had talent. A lot of talent, actually. None of which I inherited."

As Mally's gaze narrowed, Risa realized how that must have sounded and she grimaced, waving a hand in front of her face as if she could wave the words away. "Anyway, she gave up her life to marry my dad because her father forced her to."

"Sounds like an arranged marriage."

"It was. My mom understood that. So did my dad. The problems started when my mom fell in love with my dad and he didn't return it."

Mally's expression stilled. "Ris. I'm sorry. You don't have to—"

"No, it's okay. I never really get to talk about her anymore. It's kind of like she...disappeared off the face of the earth after she died. I think that's the hardest part."

Reaching across the table, Mally took her hand. Such a little gesture but one Risa didn't exactly know how to return. The only people she touched with affection were her dad and her sister. Occasionally Max. It didn't come easily but she wasn't ready to pull away either.

"I can't even imagine how hard that has to be." Mally shook her head. "I'm so sorry."

"What's worse is knowing she tried to take me with her."

Mally's eyes widened. Apparently, Max hadn't relayed that bit of news.

"Jesus, Ris. That's…" She shook her head, unable to find the words she wanted. Maybe due to the amount of alcohol they'd consumed. That's what Risa was blaming for her own lack of a filter. It couldn't possibly have anything to do with the fact that she was miserably lonely and feeling sorry for herself.

"I think the word you're looking for is sad. My mom wasn't happy, and I think she didn't want me to suffer the same fate." As Mally's eyes widened, Risa continued. "I'm not making excuses for her, but she was ill. And I was the only person in the world who loved her unconditionally."

Mally continued to shake her head. "Obviously, she didn't succeed."

"No. She mixed bennies in my soda but I only took a sip. It didn't taste right. I realized she wasn't acting right so I poured it into the wastebasket and told her I drank it. Then she passed out and I got my dad."

"I'm so sorry." Mally squeezed her hand.

"It was a long time ago." She shrugged but squeezed Mally's hand in return. Then she took a deep breath. "Anyway, before she passed out, she told me my dad was a criminal and I should be happy I wouldn't be part of it. Until then, I didn't really have a clue. After she died, my dad and I didn't talk for months. It was…difficult. I got over it. He's all I have. And over time, I've realized he has more scruples than some legitimate businessmen I've met. Life isn't as cut-and-dried as we'd like it to be, is it?"

Mally shook her head. "No, it really is not. I'm sorry. I didn't mean to bring up such bad memories."

"I've learned to deal with it. It's taught me to be tough."

"No one should have to be *that* tough."

Risa dropped Mally's compassionate gaze. "We all need to be that tough." Then she looked up again. "It was a long time ago. I'm still here. She's not."

"Are you a virgin?"

Blinking for several seconds, Risa then began to laugh. "No, I'm actually not. That would make me a complete loser, wouldn't it?"

Mally's smile was a little wicked, but Risa knew she'd changed the subject deliberately.

"So how'd you manage? I mean, having a bodyguard all the time would make it hard to find privacy, wouldn't it?"

"If I meet a man I want to go to bed with, I tell my guard to wait for me in the car. It's become code for, 'yes, I'm going to have sex.'"

"Ooh, how awkward is that drive home?"

"I can count on one hand how many times that's happened so..."

Mally's mouth dropped open again. "You've only had sex five times?"

Risa had to smile at the incredulous look on Mally's face. "No. I did go to college. I had a female guard who shared a room with me. I'm sure you'll be happy to know I did occasionally pick up guys."

"But you never had a date?"

She shrugged. "I have high standards."

"Honey, there's nothing wrong with standards." Mally's gaze narrowed, and Risa swore she could see the other woman's gears working in her brain. "Soooo, are you in the market?"

"For what?"

Mally rolled her eyes. "For a *man*."

She hesitated a second too long and Mally's eyes widened.

"Wait, are you seeing someone?"

"No." Risa could answer that truthfully. "Definitely not."

"But you have someone in mind."

She actually had two men in mind. She'd settle for either. But since that would never happen, she needed to move on.

"No, I don't."

Mally didn't respond right away, but Risa knew the other woman was about to suggest a man for her. She should shut Mally down right now. If she couldn't have either of the men on her list, she didn't want anyone. And yes, maybe she was being ridiculous. Maybe she was going to end up an old maid.

"How would you feel about being set up?"

She shook her head. "Mally—"

"Don't say no immediately. Hear me out." When Risa kept silent, she continued. "What if I can guarantee you the guy I'm thinking about is handsome, has all his teeth, and can be taken out in public without fear of embarrassment?"

Shaking her head, Risa sighed. "That's a ringing endorsement."

Mally leaned in closer, as if she didn't want anyone to

overhear them, even though there was no one around. And the music would preclude people at the next table from hearing them.

"What if I vouched for the man myself?"

"You want to set me up with a friend?"

"I want to set you up with my brother."

Risa's mouth dropped open in shock. "You want to what?"

Mally rolled her eyes and waved her hand in front of Risa's face. "You heard me. My brother Tommy. The one behind the bar. He's just like you. He never gets out, he's a workaholic, and I can tell you right now, he's a nice guy."

Still a little shocked that Mally wanted to set her up with her brother, Risa turned to look toward the bar.

The man standing behind it was tall, dark-haired, and conventionally handsome, if you liked guys with beards and flannel shirts and blue eyes. He looked...like a nice guy. The kind of guy you took home to your parents. If your parents weren't crime lords.

"I'm not sure that's such a good idea."

"I think it's a great idea. Tommy needs someone like you."

Curious, Risa raised her eyebrows at Mally. "Someone like me?"

"Someone tough. Who doesn't take any bullshit. Someone who'll shake up his life a little."

Is that how people saw her?

That's how you want people to see you, isn't it?

Fierce. Tough. Untouchable.

Alone.

"So? What do you think?"

Mally looked at her with wide-eyed enthusiasm, like she'd found the answer to a lifelong mystery.

"I think...maybe...I might say yes."

3

"Have you given him your answer yet?"

Tony tipped back his head and let the rest of his drink spill down his throat.

Yeah, he was avoiding the question, but Gens knew Tony didn't want to answer.

Of course, he knew Gens wouldn't let the subject go, either.

"You know, it's not like he's gonna make you disappear if you don't say yes. You're allowed to say no."

The problem was, Tony didn't want to say no. He just wasn't sure he should say yes.

"I'm not sure it's a good idea."

"Because you want her?"

Yeah, that was part of it. But it wasn't the biggest part.

Tony turned and looked directly at Gens. "Don't you?"

It was a rhetorical question and Gens knew it, but Gens still shook his head.

"Never gonna happen and you know it. She wants you, man. I say go for it."

"And you know *that's* never gonna happen. I don't belong in her world."

He didn't *want* to belong in Larisa's gilded cage.

He'd kept himself out of the gangs growing up. Became a cop, duty sworn to uphold the law.

And look where that got you.

The irony that he'd lost his career because of a crooked cop wasn't lost on him. Neither was the fact that he could afford to drink at the swanky bar in Haven Hotel because of the money he'd made as a bodyguard for a crime lord's secret daughter.

In the past year, he'd made friends with Haven's owners, a pair of brothers he had nothing in common with but whom he genuinely liked. He and Tyler, especially, had hit it off. Tony wouldn't be surprised if Tyler joined them later for a drink.

"Christ, you gonna start singing Disney songs now?"

Tony shot Gens a what-the-fuck look. "What the hell are you talking about?"

"What? You never saw that Disney movie, *Aladdin*?"

"You seriously think I'm quoting Disney movies?"

Gens shrugged and tipped his glass Tony's way. "Point taken."

"What I want to know is how you know it?"

Gens's gaze slipped away. "It's one of Risa's favorites."

And that, right there, was why he wouldn't ask Risa out on a date.

He and his best friend wanted the same woman. And neither of them would ever have her.

So, they drank. Every week, they chose a bar and had

dinner and drinks. Sometimes they talked for hours. Sometimes, they couldn't manage more than a few sentences.

When Tony had returned to Philly from San Antonio, he'd been a little…antisocial. Gens had just called him a fucking cave dweller and badgered him until he agreed to meet for drinks. And their weekly date had been born.

Considering neither of them had *actual* dates with women just made it more pitiful.

"You ever call that woman from the bar two weeks ago?"

Gens frowned, his gaze unfocused as he dug through his memory, which pretty much answered the question.

Tony snorted. "Don't be getting on my ass about dating, man. You're just as bad."

With a shrug, Gens gave him the finger. "Maybe I'm just not interested in dealing with all the bullshit right now."

Tony gave Gens a more thorough look and noticed the bags under his eyes and the fatigue that seemed to press down on his shoulders.

"You wanna tell me what's wrong? You look like shit."

Gens huffed out a laugh, which he drowned with a swig of beer. "Been a few long nights lately."

Since Gens worked for the head of the Russian crime organization in the city, Tony's stress level immediately jacked. "Something going on? Is Dorrie in danger?"

Is Risa?

Tony's hands clenched into fists before he consciously relaxed them. For the past eighteen months, Tony had been Dorrie's bodyguard. Gens had gotten him the gig when he'd returned to Philly, unable to find work, his name blacklisted in every law enforcement office from coast to coast.

"No, Dorrie's not in any danger. It's nothing, just a lot of shit going down."

And that was total BS. Gens was a consummate liar, but Tony's bullshit detector was infallible.

"Thanks, asshole. Now I'm even more worried." Tony turned to face him, watching Gens carefully. "What's going on?"

Tony wasn't sure Gens would talk, but finally, he shook his head and leaned closer, even though they were at the far end of the bar, the closest person out of hearing distance.

"There've been a few rumblings from different factions. One in particular. Nothing specific. And that's it. But...Karel's been restless lately. Dorrie's incident didn't help."

That "incident" had happened while Tony had been recovering from a gunshot wound. The shooting had had nothing to do with Dorrie or her father. They'd just happened to be in the wrong place at the wrong time, which pissed him off even more.

A second later, he realized he'd brought his hand up to rub against his side.

Gens's gaze narrowed. "You still having pain?"

"No. Just force of habit." He forced his hand back to the bar. "I'm fine. Tell me more about what's going on."

Gens didn't immediately comply, just watched Tony with a steady stare, until Tony finally sighed.

"Jesus, I'm fine. You're worse than my mother, I swear."

"Did you even tell your mom you were shot?"

He rolled his eyes. "Of course not. I wasn't dying. No need to worry her."

Gens shook his head, his eyes closing for a brief second. "Right."

"Oh for fuck's sake. It wasn't a big deal. I lived."

"Yeah, but you haven't been the same since."

No, he hadn't. But he hadn't realized anyone had noticed. His mom, now retired to Florida, only heard what she wanted to hear. That he was fine, and everything was going well with his private security firm. His dad heard nothing at all, ravaged by the later stages of early-onset Alzheimer's.

He should've known Gens would notice. There was a reason he was Antonoff's most trusted lieutenant. And Tony's closest friend since grade school.

Maybe it was the dim lighting or the soft music or the fact that Tony felt so out of his element here. Whatever it was, the words were suddenly on the tip of his tongue.

"I think maybe it's time for me to move on."

Gens didn't speak right away, simply stared at Tony for several seconds.

"Why?"

"Because I'm not needed here anymore."

Gens lifted his brows. "And what about that job offer from Oleksy?"

Now that was tempting. A local private security firm had offered him a job. They wanted to expand and needed men they could trust. For some reason, that included Tony.

"Maybe I want a change of scenery."

"You get a job offer somewhere else?"

He shook his head. "You know I haven't."

"Then why are you running?"

Tony's jaw clenched. "I'm not."

"Yeah?" Gens snorted. "What do you call it?"

He had to think for a few minutes. "Seeking new opportunities."

Another snort. "Uh-huh."

Tony's jaw clenched. "What about you? I thought you wanted out, wanted to do something...else."

Gens's gaze fell to his glass. "Maybe this is where I want to be."

Tony took another hard look at Gens. "Is it? What happened to the guy who wanted to be in control of his own life? The guy who wanted to go to college and be a fucking marine biologist?"

Gens shrugged. "I did. Wasn't for me."

"Really? The guy who aced every damn biology test and blew the curve for the rest of the class? The guy who wanted to save the damn rain forest and the whales?"

Gens' jaw tightened. "That guy grew up."

"And that guy wants to tell me that I shouldn't leave and look for something else some*where* else?"

Gens huffed and took another swig of his beer. "Then I guess we're both idiots."

Tony lifted his glass and Gens shook his head as he tapped his bottle against it.

"Are you seriously thinking about leaving?"

"There's not much holding me here."

Gens's gaze slipped away to stare out over the bar, and Tony could've punched himself in the head for being a dick.

"Shit, I didn't mean it like—"

"I understood exactly what you meant."

"Fuck, Gens. You're the only damn reason I'm still here."

Which wasn't totally true.

"Bullshit." Gens smirked at him. "But if you wanna play it like that, go right ahead and keep kidding yourself."

"Goddamn it, what the fuck do you want me to say?"

Tony struggled to keep his voice subdued. "It's never gonna happen. Why do you keep—" He paused, trying to rein in his frustration. "Just leave it."

Gens took another swallow of beer, shaking his head. "Apparently, that's exactly what you're planning to do."

Tony sighed hard. "Do you *want* me to hit you? It might be worth getting thrown out."

Gens went silent, staring at him until Tony wanted to fidget. Instead he held himself completely still. His nickname Blank wasn't only a short form of his last name. He'd been told he had a damn good poker face. It'd come in handy when the shit had been raining down on his head three years ago in San Antonio. Now it'd become his default setting.

With a sigh, Gens reached into his pocket, pulled out a wad of cash, and threw a few bills on the table. Tony was pretty sure they were all fifties.

The sight of them jacked his blood pressure even higher.

"Let's get out of here. You're right. We need somewhere private for this conversation and I know a place."

Because Gens was right, Tony followed him out the door, attempting to breathe through the anger. He had no idea where this rage was coming from, but it'd been building for a few weeks now. Maybe months.

As he and Gens made their silent trip to the garage, he tried to remember when he'd first noticed it. After he'd been shot? No, it'd been before that.

The night he'd seen Risa at the hospital fundraiser. He'd been there with Dorrie, watching her back as always. But he hadn't been able to ignore Risa. Sleek, cool, beautiful Risa. Waist-length blonde hair in perfect waves down her naked back exposed by a pink dress that'd made his heart race.

From the front, it'd covered her from collarbones to the tips of her toes, but the back was nonexistent.

Some magic kept it from sliding off her shoulders and he swore every time she moved, he swallowed his tongue.

She wasn't built like a supermodel. She was a little too round in all the right places. Her breasts captivated his attention for their sheer perfection. Her ass was built for his hands to pet and that haughty expression she wore most of the time only made his dick that much harder.

That had been the first night he'd noticed how tightly wound he was becoming.

It hadn't frightened him at first. But when it'd continued to escalate, as it'd done in San Antonio, he'd become worried. And after he'd been shot...

It'd gotten a hell of a lot worse. To the point that he knew he needed to make a change. And the only change he could make that would have any chance in hell of working was to move.

Away from her.

"So where are we going?"

Tony finally broke his silence as they slid into Gens's car and he headed out of the parking garage.

"The gym. We both need to blow off some steam."

"Lifting weights ain't gonna—"

"Do I look like I'm stupid?" Gens shook his head. "We're going to the hole."

Yes. That was exactly what he needed.

Tony cracked a smile for the first time in what felt like weeks.

"Are you sure you won't change your mind? It's still early. I know my brother makes awful daiquiris, but we'll do more shots. He can't screw those up."

From the wicked look in Mally's eyes, Risa wasn't sure if the other woman was kidding or not, so she simply laughed and shook her head.

Standing by the front door, Risa had already texted Daniel that she was leaving. He'd replied to say he'd be waiting.

She'd had fun tonight, more than she'd expected. But it was close to midnight and she'd had a long day. Her eyes burned, and she'd been battling yawns for the past half hour.

"As good as that sounds, I'm really tired and I can't keep my eyes open any longer."

Mally's pout was cute and it probably got Max and Jesse to do anything she wanted. But it didn't work on Risa. At least, it didn't yet. Maybe someday.

Finally, Mally snorted and threw her arms around Risa's shoulders for a hug. Risa barely had time to tense from the unexpected contact before Mally pulled away.

"Fine. Leave us. But I want a promise that you'll come out with us again. If you didn't find us too terribly boring."

Risa shook her head, her lips twitching into a smile. "No one would ever call you boring."

Which was the god's honest truth. When they hadn't been talking about sex, the women had talked about everything from politics to movies to sports.

Risa hadn't always had something to add, but the other women had never made her feel left out. There hadn't been time. The conversation had moved at the speed of light.

Mally's smile reappeared. "Then I'm glad you had a good time. You look like you could use more downtime, Risa."

She shrugged. "I like being busy." Kept her mind from getting stuck on a particular problem. Or a particular man.

"Well, there's busy and there's avoiding. But I'm a little drunk and I probably shouldn't be talking anymore."

Mally's expression made Risa laugh, and she was still laughing when she stepped out of the bar seconds after another, less awkward hug from Mally.

Risa stopped for a second to suck in warm fall air, which had begun to clear out the rancidness of summer.

Still standing in the doorway, she looked to her left, expecting to see Daniel. And she did, no more than twenty yards away.

Unmoving.

She took one step toward the car before she realized something wasn't right.

The next second later, she felt a prick on her neck and everything went black.

4

"Gens, Larisa is missing. Daniel was shot. He's at Dorrie's and I need you back at the house. Now."

It took his brain a second to realize exactly what the message from Karel said. Then every muscle in his body seized for a heartbeat.

In the next, Gens reached for his shoes and socks. "Risa's missing. We need to go."

Beside him, Tony froze for several seconds before he shoved his arms into his shirt.

They'd spent the past hour in the boxing ring, pounding on each other. Best therapy in the world and Gens had been feeling a hell of a lot better. Getting hit in the face a few times by a good friend would do that. Now, he felt like he'd taken a sucker punch to the gut.

"What the fuck happened?"

Tony sounded like he felt. Stone-cold terrified and pissed off.

"That's all I know."

"Where was she?"

"Don't know."

"Who was she with?"

Gens practically growled. "What part of 'don't know' don't you understand?" *Shit.* "Sorry. All Karel said was Daniel was shot and I need to get back to the house."

"I'm going with you."

Gens looked up at him. "Could get dirty."

Tony stared back. "I'm going."

Gens didn't ask twice. Since he didn't know what was going on, he'd be glad to have Tony at his back.

The drive to Karel's home was silent. Gens didn't bother to turn on the radio. It would've grated on his nerves. He broke every speed limit and never once saw a cop. Luck was on his side because he wasn't sure he would've stopped.

By the time he and Tony got to Karel's Main Line mansion, there were already four cars parked on the curved driveway. He recognized all of them but one. But he had a feeling he knew whose car that was.

Pushing through the front door, Tony on his heels, Gens headed straight for Karel's office at the back of the house, where he heard voices. There were already six men in the room.

"Gens." Karel motioned for him from his desk, flicking a quick glance at Tony before nodding. "Someone took her off the street in Northern Liberties. She was at a bar with friends. No one should've known she was there. We still don't know who has her."

To the rest of his men, Karel looked stone cold and in charge, confident and slightly pissed. Karel had the same blond hair and pale blue eyes as Risa. But where Risa had a cool beauty, Karel looked harsh, ominous. If whoever had taken her could see him right now, they'd know they wouldn't get out of this alive.

"What the hell happened?"

"Someone got the drop on Daniel, shot him in the chest. He's lucky they didn't go for the head shot. He'd be dead. Risa disappeared after she left the bar. Her friends said she left around midnight."

Gens looked at the clock on the mantel of the huge stone fireplace. One-thirty.

"Were you two in a fight?"

Karel's question didn't compute right away, and Gens looked at him with a frown. "What?"

"You and Blank look like you've just come from a fight."

Ah. "Boxing. We're fine. Have you checked with Tosto?"

Karel nodded. "This isn't him."

"Cartel?"

"For what purpose?"

Gens ran a hand through his hair. "Leverage?"

"Possible." Karel's jaw clenched, his only outward sign of emotion so far. "But so far no contact."

Which meant no ransom demand. *Fuck.*

"Who do you have working the street?" Tony asked.

"Adam, Tristan, and Jesse." That answer came from Max Burdonov. "Risa was out with Mally tonight."

Gens wasn't surprised to see Max. He and Risa had been friends for years. He and his best friend, Jesse Kanatawa, had an unconventional relationship with Mary Alice Dubroksy, one that Gens had thought would never work. Except it was working. And it was working for Adam

Oleksy and Tristan Donovan, too. The two friends owned a private security company and had offered Tony a job, a legitimate way to earn a living and distance himself from this life. And if Tony got out, maybe he could take Larisa with him.

Gens had been thinking about that himself lately. About getting the hell out. About getting Risa away. If anyone hurt her, he would kill them. No remorse. He'd put a bullet between their eyes and be happy for it.

"And no one in the bar saw anything?"

Max shook his head, his expression grim. "She left by herself."

"Sonuvabitch."

Tony's curse sounded more like a growl.

"No way." Gens shook his head. "She knows better."

Karel's voice remained steady. "The facts remain. Daniel is dying and Larisa is missing."

Gens nodded, his mouth set in a flat line. "Then I'm gonna go knock on a few doors."

And possibly knock a few heads.

He'd get answers. He couldn't believe otherwise.

Risa woke with a pounding headache and an overwhelming sense of fear.

No, not fear. Terror.

She had no idea where she was. It was pitch black and the air held a slightly musty odor. Definitely not home.

Trying not to move, she took stock. Nothing hurt, except her head. She didn't feel any restraints around her body, but she was afraid to move. The surface beneath her was hard and cool, but she didn't think she was on the floor.

Her lungs started to contract, like someone had put them in a vise.

Breathe. Think.

What did she remember? Keeping her eyes closed, she thought through the pain in her head. She'd gone to a bar with Mally and her friends. They'd had drinks. Had she gotten drunk and ended up asleep on Mally's couch?

No. She knew that'd never happen. She wouldn't allow herself to lose control like that. Besides, she remembered leaving the bar. She'd walked outside after texting Daniel and...

And then nothing.

No, wait. She remembered a prick at her neck. Her hand rose instinctively, and she realized now that her neck ached at the injection site.

She drew in a ragged breath, her heart beginning to pound against her ribs like a trapped animal.

Don't panic. Don't panic. Keep it together.

If anyone could do it, she could. She was the queen of cool. She just needed a clue as to what was going on.

Drawing in a deep breath, she sat up. And lights flickered on overhead. Blinking against the harsh glow, she pushed her hair over her shoulders. Someone had taken the elastic out of her hair. She looked down at herself, relieved to find that was all they'd removed.

Another breath.

She was in a room with four walls made of cinderblock. No windows. The door across from her was metal. The only furniture was the metal cot she sat on.

Basically, she was in a cell. Her heart beat a little faster and her mouth dried. Swallowing hard, she sucked in more air.

"Hello. I'd like to speak to someone."

She almost added "in charge," but she'd been taught never to give anyone the upper hand. Even when you certainly were not in charge. Then it was even more imperative that you act like you were.

She raised her voice only loud enough to be heard over, say, a vacuum cleaner. She had no idea if the room was equipped with speakers or microphones.

When no one responded after what seemed like forever, but was probably only a minute or so, she swung her legs over the side of the cot and sat on the edge. Using the techniques she'd learned in yoga, she kept her breathing level and tried not to let her fear show in her expression.

She knew better than to show fear, even though her mind was racing, and her terror had only grown.

After an excruciating amount of time, where she swore her muscles hardened into marble, she heard someone at the door, the screech of metal on metal, then finally the door swung open and a man walked through.

He wore a dark suit with a white shirt. No tie. He looked to be in his forties. Not overweight. Not thin. Dark hair cut short. Nondescript features. You could pass him on the street and never remember you'd seen him. She couldn't recall ever seeing him before.

He smiled, but it didn't reach his dark eyes.

"Hello, Larisa. I'm Neal Turner. How's your head?"

Stopping just inside the door, he thrust his hands in his pants pockets and let his gaze walk over her from her feet to the top of her head. Checking her out but not in a sexual way. No, he looked at her like she was a commodity. That look made goosebumps rise all over her body.

"It hurts. Who are you?"

"A businessman. You're here because I've had several requests for your...company. Your father may have the opportunity to bid for your release, but there are other interested parties. Apparently, you're in high demand. You'll be sold to the highest bidder two days from now."

Her breath caught in her lungs. Her brain buzzed with white noise and her tongue stuck to the roof of her mouth. His words hammered at her already throbbing brain, made her sick to her stomach. This man wasn't screwing around. Obviously, he knew who her father was, and he was either too stupid to be afraid to use her as a bargaining chip in negotiations. Or too good.

After unsticking her tongue, she asked, "And what do you want?"

"That's not something you need to worry about. Keep quiet. Don't give my men any hassle. And hopefully you'll leave soon." He paused and her blood went cold. "If you cause trouble, there will be consequences."

The look he gave her left her in no doubt of what those consequences would be. He would have no problem hurting her. He might even enjoy it.

Her heart raced a little faster.

"Are you hungry?"

It took a few seconds for her to process his words, and when she did, she nodded. It would do no good to starve herself. She needed to keep up her strength. Because she wasn't sure he was telling the truth. He had no reason to.

"I'll send something in."

He turned and walked through the door without another word.

Leaving her alone with her fear.

"This is getting us nowhere. We need to start cracking heads. Maybe that will get some answers."

Gens paced the floor of Karel's office, shaking his head, his expression a mix of fear and frustration. It didn't look good on him.

Tony figured he looked the same.

Karel looked as if he'd aged ten years overnight.

It'd been a full twenty-four hours since Risa had gone missing and they'd heard nothing. Not even a rumor or a whisper of who might have taken her. No ransom demands.

And there'd been no body.

Standing at the window looking out over the expanse of the backyard, Tony felt like he was holding himself together by sheer force of will. Occasionally, he had the urge to put his hand through the wall. And while he knew it wouldn't help, he figured it would release some of this pent-up energy.

He hated feeling useless. Even more, he hated feeling like he'd run out of options.

He refused to give up, though. Not until they found her. But he knew the longer it took, the more likely it'd be that they wouldn't find her alive.

His blood pulsed hot through his body; chills ran up and down his spine. He didn't want to think about the alternative.

But he'd worked as a cop for far too long to ignore the odds.

Karel had said less and less after Tony and Gens had returned to the house this morning a little after eight a.m.

They'd been out all night, personally speaking to every high-ranking member of the criminal underworld in Philly. Karel had called the heads of their organizations personally to let them know what was going on.

Every one of them had claimed they didn't have a clue. Someone had to be lying. But Tony had watched everyone they'd interviewed with laser focus. He'd seen nothing that indicated they had any idea what was going on.

Which had frustrated him even more.

If she hadn't been taken by someone they knew, they had an even bigger problem. And not a clue where to look.

"We do that and we start a war."

"Isn't that what they want? Why the hell hasn't anyone made any demands? Jesus, what the fuck is going on?"

"Anton." Karel's use of his given name got Tony's attention faster than anything else would have, especially spoken in that tone of command. "Suggestions."

Surprised that Karel had singled him out, Tony looked straight at Risa's father. "I agree with Gens. It's time to use force."

Karel's eyebrows rose. "And who do you suggest we start with?"

"Street dealers. Work our way up. They know more than you think. And I want to talk to her guards again. Go through her schedule for unusual meetings. Talk to employees at her favorite shops. Did anyone come in and ask about her? Was she ever seen with anyone?"

He paused, his back teeth aching as he ground them together. "Are you sure she wasn't seeing anyone? Maybe she just didn't tell you. We need to talk to Dorrie again."

Karel nodded. "I'm sure. And yes, Dorrie was busy with Daniel last night but she's awake now. You and Gens handle Dorrie. I'll set up the other interviews."

Which was a fancy way of saying he'd assign some of his thugs to beat on the street dealers.

Tony didn't feel even the least bit remorseful. If they knew anything about Risa, he'd find it.

And Karel was right to send him and Gens to Dorrie. If he let Gens lose on the street, who knew what would happen. Tony wasn't sure he'd be able to keep himself in check.

A half hour later, he and Gens sat in Dorrie's office in her medical suite downtown. She looked like she hadn't slept for days. Dark circles under eyes, shoulder-length dark hair messy and pulled back in a rough bun.

Ian stood behind her, leaning against the glass wall that overlooked the city. Benji leaned against the door that led into the medical suite. Dorrie had spent more than six hours working on Daniel and had refused to go home to rest.

"You're telling me you don't have a clue? That *no one* has a clue where Risa is?"

Gens looked like he wanted to smash his fist into the wall. Ian and Benji watched his every move. Tony had no doubt that if Gens gave any indication he was about to get violent, they'd have him subdued in seconds.

Tony understood exactly how Gens felt. Which was probably why Ian had been watching him, as well.

"Yes," Tony answered. "But we're not giving up. That's why we're here. We need to talk to you about anything Risa might have said recently that might indicate she thought she was in danger. Did she say anything about strange emails or letters or phone calls from strange numbers? Did she meet anyone new recently?"

Dorrie shook her head continuously.

"The women she was out with tonight...have you met them? Mary Alice Dubrosky, Isabella DeMarco, or Damaris Contino?"

Dorrie's gaze sharpened. "You think Mally had something to do with this? No way."

"No. Not Mally. But we don't know Isabella or Damaris. And we need to."

"You do know Izzy's aunt and uncle are Frank and Grace DeMarco, right?"

Yes, he knew that. Frank and Grace were local legends. Former decorated CIA operatives now running a security firm in Philadelphia. Upstanding citizens held in the highest regard by everyone from presidents to criminals. He'd never met them, but he sure as shit knew who they were.

"That doesn't mean Isabella isn't wrapped up in something she shouldn't be. Or that Damaris doesn't owe favors to someone with a grudge against the Antonoffs."

Dorrie sank her teeth into her top lip, but she continued to shake her head. "I can't help you there. I just don't know."

"Was she seeing anyone new?"

Dorrie's gaze sharpened again and now she looked between him and Gens. "Do you mean was she dating anyone? Or was she sleeping with anyone?"

Tony's jaw locked and he had to restrain the urge to grab Gens so he wouldn't put his hand through a wall.

"Either."

Dorrie's eyebrows rose in a silent challenge that wasn't lost on him. "You sure you want the answer to that?"

"If it helps us find her, yes."

Dorrie sighed hard. "No. She hasn't mentioned anyone. And I would be the only person she'd tell."

Conflicting emotions threatened to derail Tony's train of thought, but he reined himself in. He didn't want to be happy that she wasn't seeing anyone. That she wasn't dating, wasn't living, wasn't—

"But I do know she was sick of being alone." Dorrie stared at Tony for several long seconds before she pinned Gens with a glare. "She wasn't going to wait around anymore."

Fuck. He didn't want to know that.

"Do you think she slipped out with someone and Daniel's shooting was random?"

Gens's question was exactly the same one that slipped through Tony's mind and he found himself holding his breath, waiting for Dorrie's answer.

After a few more seconds, she shook her head. "No. She's lonely, not stupid. Risa's the smartest person I know. She doesn't take unnecessary risks. Wherever she is, she's in trouble and you better fucking find her soon."

As far as Risa could tell, based on the pattern of meals she'd been given, she'd spent an entire day in this cell. Combined with the hours she's spent sleeping off the drug they'd given her, she'd been gone almost two days.

When she'd asked, they'd allowed her to use the bathroom across the hall. There'd been no windows in the long hall but several other doors. She'd heard nothing and no one from the other rooms.

She spent the rest of the time sitting on the bunk or pacing the floor. She hadn't seen Neal Turner again.

She'd tried to sleep several times, but she figured she'd had maybe four hours of sleep at best over the past forty-eight hours.

What the hell was going on?

If he'd asked her father for money, he would've been paid. She couldn't imagine there was anything her dad wouldn't give to get her back. People who didn't know him might think he was a cold-blooded killer with no human emotion. She knew better. There were three people in this world Karel Antonoff would give his life for. She was one.

And what if this is something other than a simple kidnapping and ransom demand?

As the hours dragged on, that thought took up more space in her brain. Why should she take at face value anything that man had said?

Now, doubt started to eat away at her. Until fear had built in her blood like poison. The next meal they brought, she could barely eat, afraid she might not be able to keep it down. She couldn't sit still for more than a few minutes at a time.

Is anyone even looking for me?

That was stupid. Of course, they were looking for her. The problem was they hadn't found her yet, and that brought up a whole slew of other questions. Other fears.

The next time the door opened, she flinched, then stiffened her back. She hated being this terrified. Hated being a prisoner kept in a concrete box. Hated feeling like she had no control over her life.

And when Neal Turner walked into her cell, every bone in her body wanted to turn to jelly.

"I understand you've been good," he said, his voice that same monotone as before. "I appreciate that. I wanted to let you know that you won't have to wait much longer. The sale is set for tomorrow night. All you need to do is not cause trouble until then."

His face had the same unemotional expression from the other day. He reminded her of her dad when he dealt with business. Her skin broke out in goosebumps.

Rising from the bed to face him, she stood her ground.

"And then what happens?"

"You'll be sold to the highest bidder."

Her stomach flipped and she felt her blood rush from her cheeks. She knew she must have gone pale as a sheet but that couldn't be helped.

"I'm sure my father will pay whatever you ask."

"I wouldn't be a very good businessman if I only entertained one offer."

She swallowed hard. "This isn't about money, is it?"

His lips curled in a slight smile. "Beauty and brains. And the fact that your father is Karel Antonoff makes you an almost priceless commodity. I had no idea how many other businessmen would want to be involved in your sale."

Her lungs constricted in her chest and her stomach knotted. "I didn't realize I was being sold."

"That's what I do, Miss Antonoff. I buy and sell."

"I've never heard of you."

"We don't exactly run in the same circles." He let his gaze

run down her body, sending another chill through her. "I have a potential buyer coming in a few minutes. Remove the sweater or I'll have someone do it for you."

He turned and left. The door closed behind him with a snick.

She stood there staring at the door, frozen in shock.

5

"I think I got something."

Gens looked up from the food he'd been pushing around his plate for the past ten minutes. He had no appetite, but he knew he had to fuel his body or it would give out on him. And he couldn't afford that.

It'd been two days since Risa had disappeared, and the tension in the house coated everything in a thick haze that made him want to punch walls, scream, and throw furniture through windows.

He watched Tony stalk into the kitchen, phone in his hand. His grim expression didn't give Gens much confidence, and he braced himself for bad news.

He hadn't let himself consider anything other than the fact that they would eventually get her back. But in the past few hours, it'd gotten harder and harder to believe that.

"What is it?"

Tony sat down across from him at the table. "Made contact with the guy from the Romano family. Told me he heard a rumor of an auction tomorrow night. A big one."

"What the hell are you talking about? Why—"

"An auction for sex slaves."

Gens's gut clenched and the little he'd eaten threatened to come back up.

"Jesus Christ. Are you telling me—"

Tony held his hands up in front of him. "I don't know anything other than that, but he told me the guy running it's being cagey and that struck him wrong. I've got no information other than that. But at this point, we have to look at everything."

"Did you say anything to Karel?"

Tony shook his head, his mouth a flat line. "We need to check this out first."

Gens saw the wisdom in that. Karel had gotten increasingly icy in the last twenty-four hours. He looked brittle enough to break under the slightest pressure.

Nodding, Gens shoved his chair away from the table. "Come on. Let's go to Adam and Tristan's office and make some calls. Adam may have some contacts we don't. Call Max and have him meet us there."

Half an hour later, six men sat around a conference table, listening in to Jesse's conversation in Spanish. After five minutes, Jesse put his phone down on the table and exchanged a glance with Max before he looked at the others around the table.

He stopped at Gens and spoke directly to him.

"My source says the auction's being held in Center City tomorrow night. Million-dollar bond gets you the location of the sale. Merchandise held off-site. Delivery guaranteed. Seller has a good reputation. No one questions his methods."

Gens unclenched his jaw enough to ask, "So who the hell is he?"

"Name's Neal Turner. Holds these auctions all over the world, never in the same place twice. No one knows if he's the mastermind or works for someone behind the scenes. Potential buyers give this guy a wish list. If the guy can deliver, the buyers are given notification of the auction."

"So someone must have been planning this for months." Adam shook his head. "Has anyone ever heard of this guy?"

Everyone shook their head.

"Shit." Tony shoved away from the table and started to pace like a caged animal. "So we're still no closer to finding out where she is. *Sonuvabitch*."

"The good news is they still have her in the area." Max knocked on the table, trying to get Tony's attention. "She has to be close."

Gens was having a hard time focusing himself. He wanted to pace with Tony but he knew if he did, it would only agitate him more. Gens was barely holding it together as it was.

Whoever laid a hand on her would lose that hand, slowly and painfully, before he fucking killed them.

And if they'd hurt her...

Christ, if he and Tony had just—

Fuck.

Gens shoved that thought aside. He needed to keep focused. They needed to find her and get her back. That was all that mattered. He couldn't afford to think of the alternative.

"All right. We have a name." Gens looked at Adam and Tristan. "We need to track it down."

"I'll call my uncle," Adam said. "See if he knows anything about this guy."

"I have contacts in the ATF and CIA." Tristan stood. "We'll find something. In the meantime, why don't you and Tony make another sweep of the families in the city? We have a name now. See if it rattles a few brains."

Without a word, Tony got up and headed for the door. He didn't shove his chair, didn't bang open the door. But the air of leashed violence coming off him heightened Gens's anxiety.

"Is he gonna be a liability?"

Max's quiet question made Gens grit his teeth. "He's fine."

"Doesn't look fine." Max held his gaze. "Neither do you."

Now his molars began to grind. "We're both fine."

"Good. Because if Mally were missing, I'd be pretty fucking not fine."

But Mally wasn't missing. She was safe at home. At the home she shared with Max and Jesse. Gens didn't have the same relationship with Risa and, right now, that grated like salt in an open wound. He knew Tony felt the same.

When they found Risa, and they would find her, he and Tony needed to talk. But that would be after they found her.

He caught up to Tony at the car. Tony sat in the passenger seat, staring out the front window. Gens got into the front seat of his Volvo but didn't start the car right away.

After at least thirty seconds, Tony turned his head just enough to be able to see him.

"What?"

Gens stared back at him. "You okay?"

"I'm fine."

"Are you gonna be able to do this without bashing someone's head in?"

A muscle in Tony's jaw started to twitch. "I should ask
you the same thing."

"I need to know you're not gonna—"

"Seriously? You need to ask me that?"

"Yeah, I do. Because I'm fucking worried about myself,
okay? And I need to know you're gonna be able to keep me
from killing someone if I pull my gun."

That seemed to break through the ice surrounding Tony.
Over the past few hours, Gens had started to worry that Tony
was going to crack. A former inner-city kid who'd grown up
to be an inner-city cop, Tony was just as tough as any gang
member Gens had ever known.

But when Tony had returned from San Antonio, he'd
been...different.

"Why would I stop you?"

"Because you're always the stable one." Gens meant
every word. "Why do you think you became a cop and I went
to work for Karel?"

"The cop thing didn't work out so well, did it?"

"Because you still have morals."

"No, because I just stopped caring."

Gens knew that wasn't true but now wasn't the time to
argue about it. "Doesn't matter. Right now I need to know
you can rein me in. Make sure I don't cross any lines."

"Why would I want to stop you if you get answers?"

"Because we don't want this to become a bloodbath."

Tony turned to look out the front window. "I'm willing to
shed a little blood if we get her back."

"And I appreciate that. But I need to know you're not going to let this get out of hand."

"I'll let it go as far as it needs to go to get her back."

Gens couldn't fault him for that logic. He started the car and got them on the street, headed to their first stop.

"Where are we going?"

Tony finally broke the silence that had fallen but Gens's mind wasn't on their upcoming meeting. It'd skipped ahead

"When we get her back, we're going to need to talk."

Tony continued to stare straight through the windshield. "No, we don't."

"Because you're going to walk away."

"There's nothing to walk away from."

"So you can honestly tell me you don't want her?"

Gens stopped for a red light, though he didn't care if he broke every fucking law in the city right now. But he wanted to see Tony's face when he answered.

Tony continued to stare straight through the windshield. "You already know the answer to that question."

Yeah, he did. But he needed to hear Tony say it. Needed to know without a doubt. Because when they got her back, he was going to make sure she was safe. And he needed Tony for that.

"Just fucking say it."

"We're not having this discussion. Not now. Light's green."

Gens didn't move. "When this is over, you need to tell her. And then you need to get her the fuck away from this shit."

Tony's jaw looked like it was going to break if he opened

his mouth. Gens knew he was pushing but he couldn't stop. Not now.

"Take her and keep her."

The car behind him tore out around him and the other driver shouted obscenities through the closed window. Gens barely registered it. His entire attention was on Tony.

They'd been friends years ago, growing up on the same block in a rough neighborhood. His dad had already worked for Karel, though he hadn't been in charge back then. Tony's mom had worked two jobs to make ends meet, which had left Tony and him a lot of time to get into trouble. Nothing bad. Nothing illegal. Just kid stuff.

Gens had been skinny and frail back then, but everyone could see that Tony was going to grow into a hulk. People wrongly thought Tony would be a thug.

He'd been a damn good cop. Until his crooked superior had tanked Tony's career. He'd gone down for not following a direct order. Except the order had been to shoot an unarmed man and Tony wasn't corrupt.

When the dust had settled, one man was dead and Tony had been out of a job. And when he hadn't been able to get another job in law enforcement, Gens had gotten him the job as Dorrie's personal security.

No, Gens had become the thug, even though he wore a thousand-dollar suit.

And he would never be safe enough for Risa.

"We're not discussing this now." Tony finally spoke though he didn't look at Gens. "We need to move."

They did need to move. But Gens had a plan and *when* they got Risa back, he'd make it happen.

"Hey, Blank. Are you okay? What are you doing here? Is something wrong? Did something happen?"

Jumping up from behind her desk, Dorrie practically ran toward Tony as he slipped into her office.

Fuck. He wanted to kick his own ass. What the fuck had he been thinking, coming over here without warning Dorrie he was on his way?

"Sorry. Nothing's changed. Damn it, I didn't mean to get you worked up. I just...needed to get out for a while."

While her expression cleared of most of the fear, Dorrie wrapped her arms around Tony's waist and hugged him. The fact that they were alone allowed him to return the affection without fear.

Not fear that Ben or Ian would kick his ass for touching their woman, but fear of revealing just how worried he was.

"You want a drink?"

He almost said yes, before he remembered it was only nine in the morning and he needed to keep his head clear. Needed to be ready for anything.

"No, I'm good."

Dorrie pulled back and looked up at him with a look that clearly expressed her doubt.

"How about a Xanax?"

He huffed out a quick laugh but shook his head. "We may have a lead about the auction. Can't take anything that'll screw with my head."

"Way to bury the lead." She smacked him on the chest. "What do you know? And why didn't anyone tell me?"

"Gens went to talk to your dad." Still weird to say it, even though he'd known Dorrie and Risa were sisters for months now. "I came here."

Her eyebrows rose. "Is that the only reason you're here?"

Dorrie had always been way smarter than anyone else in the room. And they'd become friends during the time he'd worked as her guard. He considered her the little sister he'd never had. She'd considered him the annoying big brother she really hadn't wanted. He should've known she'd pick up on his vibe.

"If I'd paced around Adam's office any more, someone might've shot me. I had to get out."

Besides, he needed a distraction from thinking about what Gens had told him earlier in the car.

With a wry smile, Dorrie gave him a shove toward the couch she occasionally napped on then settled beside him.

"Tell me what's happening. What lead did you get?"

"We think we know where the auction'll be held tonight. Max, Jesse, and Adam are tracking that down now. Gens wanted to go but Tristan and Adam thought he'd be a distraction. Or he could tip off anyone watching that we have a lead."

"You think someone's watching?"

Someone had to be watching. Otherwise, what was the point of taking her?

"They wanted a way to get to Karel. Taking Risa was the most effective way of doing that."

Dorrie nodded, her cheeks losing the little color that'd remained in them.

"Shit. I didn't come over here to make you feel worse. I should go—"

Dorrie grabbed his arm when he made a move to stand.

"You sit your ass right there and don't move until I tell you to. I'm not weak, Blank. I can take whatever you need to say. Tell me about this lead."

"We got it from Tosto."

She swallowed hard, her lips flattening. "Does that bastard have something to do with this?"

That bastard had sent men after Dorrie several months ago, wanting to use her to get to Karel. "No. But he was approached by someone two months ago who wanted to know if he'd be interested in bidding on a tool to use against Karel. When Gens and I talked to him last night, he remembered thinking the use of that word was weird. Bidding. He gave us the name of the man who approached him. Fake, of course, but there was a trail. It led us to another name and another name and finally we found someone who thought maybe he had an idea of where to look for this auction."

"It's a start."

"Yeah, but we need to find out where she's being held, not where they're holding the auction. Apparently, they're not the same place, which makes sense." He sighed heavily, shaking his head. "Jesus, I hate this."

"Hate what?"

He tried to think of the right words before he realized there were no right words. "I fucking hate knowing there's nothing I can do. I hate knowing that she's out there terrified and alone. Daniel was supposed to be in the fucking bar with her, not in the goddamn car. But I know she told him to stay outside."

"How do you know that?"

"Because she was at a cop bar. And she knew Daniel would've been a distraction."

"So you blame Daniel?"

"Fuck no. Daniel did what she wanted."

Dorrie's expression never changed. "So this is Risa's fault?"

"Of course not. Risa's not stupid.

Dorrie's mouth quirked in a sad little smile. "You should tell her that when we have her back."

"I won't be around long enough to tell her."

Now her gaze narrowed. "What are you talking about?"

"I've been thinking about leaving for a while. Somewhere new. Now that you don't need my services, I've been trying to figure out what to do with my life."

"I thought you were going to join Adam and Tristan?"

They'd asked. He'd given it some thought but he hadn't made a decision yet. After they had Risa back, he'd figure it out.

"I can't think that far ahead. Not now. After…"

Dorrie nodded, but she looked more worried than she had before he'd come in. And that hadn't been his intention. He needed to get her mind working on something else.

"How's Daniel? Can I talk to him?"

"Better. And yes, but only if you're not going to yell at him."

"No yelling. Just want to see how he's doing, bring him up to speed."

"Okay. You can have a few minutes. If he wasn't practically strapped to the bed with tubing and wires, he'd be out there trying to track down Risa. He's taking this really hard."

"I'll make sure he knows no one thinks this is his fault."

"Then go right ahead." Dorrie waved her hand at the door. "But, you and I, we're not done with this conversation."

He nodded and stood, headed toward the door. But before he opened it, he turned.

"You and your men..." He paused when her eyebrows practically disappeared into her hairline. "Everything going well there?"

Her lips parted for several seconds before she answered, as if she were shocked. Then her smiled softened.

"Yes. Everything's great."

"Good." He nodded. "That's good."

Then he headed out the door.

6

Risa had spent most of her time alone in her cell. She saw two men besides Neal Turner. They didn't speak to her, did nothing more than give her food. She refused to cry or beg for anything. She took the food and ate every bite.

To make the rest of the time pass faster, she did a lot of yoga. It didn't exactly help reduce her stress, but it kept her muscles from getting stiff. If she got the opportunity to run, she wanted to be sure she could.

Sitting on the cold floor didn't help with the stiffness, but keeping her body moving was crucial. They had to transfer her at some point, if what Turner had told her was true. Someone would buy her and someone would take her away from here for whatever purpose they had in mind.

She tried not to dwell on what that purpose was, but it'd been harder and harder not to think about it. Trying to clear her mind to meditate proved impossible, but she did manage a few minutes of peace.

Otherwise, she would've been a raving lunatic by now.

Was her father close to finding her? Had Gens hurt anyone searching for her? What was Tony doing? Was he helping?

Poor little rich girl. Nobody loves you.

She'd allowed herself a few minutes to whine, silently. She had no idea if she were being watched. She assumed she was, so no breakdowns from her.

Even if you're in the worst possible position of strength, act like you're at the top of the food chain. If nothing else, it will give your opponent pause.

Smart words from her dad. Probably how he'd been able to rise to the position he held now. And why she was occupying this cell.

Her heart raced and her lungs contracted as fear washed over her like an acid bath. She tried to contain it, but her coping mechanism finally seemed to desert her.

Tears rushed to her eyes and she sucked in air but couldn't seem to get enough. She curled into a ball on the bed and concentrated on her breathing. But she fucked that up and started to pant. Hyperventilation became a real fear. She knew if she lost it completely, she might not be able to control it.

Control was everything. Control was the difference between possibly getting out of this situation and being sold to the highest bidder.

Control had served her well for many years. It'd kept her safe. And alone.

Would she ever see her dad again? Her sister? Tony and Gens?

The pain in her chest amplified, a sharp biting ache that made it even harder for her to breathe. Her brain spun, unable to find an anchor, something that would make everything calm, at least for a few seconds.

Thinking about her dad didn't do it. Even though he wouldn't show it, he'd be frantic. So would Dorrie. Tony and Gens would be pissed. Furious that someone had taken her. Maybe a little angry with her. Probably ready to strangle Daniel for allowing her to go into the bar alone.

She hoped they didn't blame Daniel. This wasn't his fault.

The more she thought about Gens and Tony, the more she found her heart rate slowing and her breathing coming back to normal. They were searching for her. She knew they were. And they wouldn't stop until they found her.

They became her anchor, her rock. Which was stupid because, for so long, she'd kept them at arms' length. Now she was dreaming about them saving her. Because she sure as shit couldn't save herself. And that thought had the power to set her off again.

"No. No. No."

She had no idea how long she lay there fighting off sheer panic by just repeating that one word and telling herself Gens and Tony wouldn't let her down. They'd come for her. And if she got the opportunity to run before they showed up, she'd take it.

Of course, she would.

Coward.

She had been a coward. All this time, letting them dictate how she felt about them.

Letting them keep her at arms' length.

When she got out of here, she was finished doing what they wanted, how they wanted.

If you get out of here.

Fear began to rise again, nearly choking her.

Was it time to fight? So far, she'd put up no resistance. Her father had always told her that if she were taken, unless they threatened to hurt her, she shouldn't put up a fight. That he would come for her. That he would always come for her.

But what if he couldn't find her in time?

No, she needed to find a way out, needed to make an attempt to get herself out of this mess, at the very least. She was sick of sitting and waiting for someone to rescue her. Foolish or not, whether she took a beating or not, she'd know she'd attempted to save herself. Besides, they needed her alive.

Someone was paying good money for her. They wouldn't want her damaged too badly. So what the hell did she do?

Her brain began to race but this time she had a focus, a goal. Should she attempt to run the next time they brought her food? Or should she wait until they moved her?

She had no idea of the layout of the building, so it'd probably be best to wait. Then at least she could identify an exit and make a run for it. Maybe she got out, maybe she didn't. But she'd be damned if she'd continue to sit passively and panic.

Fuck that.

Her breathing began to level out now that she had a plan. Might be a shit plan, but at least it was something other than her sitting here terrified.

She didn't have to wait long for the chance to put her plan into action because maybe an hour later, she heard the lock on the other side of the door give way.

Sitting up slowly, she turned to face it, hoping her expression didn't give away her thoughts.

She was expecting one of the guards. She was hungry so it was probably time for dinner. She'd already had breakfast and lunch.

But it wasn't. It was Turner.

Her heart stuttered but she refused to be thrown off her course.

"My men tell me you've been no trouble." Turner's mouth curved up slightly, into what she took to be a smile. Which just freaked her out. "I'm glad to hear they haven't had to use force. Better all around. It's time."

She swallowed hard, unable to control her reaction. Then she took a breath and held it before answering.

"Time for what?"

"Your sale."

You can do this.

"Has my father been informed?"

"He will be. Let's go." He waved for her to head out the door. "This will all be over soon."

She didn't move. "And then what?"

"And then you'll leave here."

"Are you giving my father the chance to bid on my release?"

He didn't answer right away, his gaze raking over her like she was a piece of art he was appraising.

Finally, his gaze met hers again. "No. He wasn't included in the original arrangement. He can negotiate with whoever wins your auction."

"You'll make more money if you go to him directly. He'll pay you whatever you ask."

And there was that smile again. She shivered and drew back, even though he was across the room from her. "I've found it's not good business to deal with family members in this situation. No more stalling. Let's go."

When she didn't stand right away, because she wasn't sure her feet would hold her, Turner motioned behind him and two of the men who'd been delivering her meals entered and headed straight for her.

"Please don't start giving us any trouble now. It's really not in your best interest."

The men grabbed her arms, and they weren't gentle. Yanking her to her feet, they dragged her out into the hallway, strong hands wrapped around her upper arms so tightly she knew they'd leave bruises. She also knew if she tried to get away, they'd make it hurt even worse.

The gnawing pit in her stomach came back with a vengeance, almost blinding her to what was going on around her. Instinctively, she resisted, her knees locking and her heels digging in.

The men corralling her locked their hands even tighter around her arms and frog-marched her down the hall. She began to pant, her lungs working overtime as she struggled. She couldn't help herself now. She had to get free.

But every time she pulled away, they tightened their grip until she was pretty sure they were about to break her arm.

"You need to calm down or we'll give you something to make you calm. I don't think you'll like that option."

Her entire body went rigid, her stomach flipping over on itself to the point that she thought she might throw up.

And when they pulled a blackout hood over her head, she couldn't help herself. She started to fight.

"Oh, for fuck's sake. Pick her up. Give me the syringe."

Struggling in earnest, her mind blank with fear, her instinct to run took over. She tried to yank her arms away, barely feeling the punishing grip around her forearms until the pain became a sudden and sharp blast.

As she sucked in air, the fabric of the hood pressed against her lips. Combined with the fire in her arm and the uncontrollable panic, she thought for sure she was going to black out.

And when she felt the stick of the needle in her arm and the burn of whatever drug they'd pumped into her, she almost welcomed the immediate fog that blanketed her brain.

In the next second, the world blinked out.

7

"I think we have their holding facility."

Gens's head snapped up off the back of the couch as Max shoved through the door into Karel's office. He'd closed his eyes seconds ago, trying to ease the constant ache in his forehead. It hadn't been working.

"Where?"

"Warehouse in Chester near the river." Max hustled across the office, trailed by Jesse and Tony.

"Credible information?" Karel asked.

Gens looked at Karel. The lines on his face seemed to have multiplied in the last couple of hours. Gens had started to worry that Karel might actually stroke out if they didn't get a lead soon. He'd become increasingly quiet and had been unable to sit for more than a few minutes at a time.

"Former coworker so, yes, credible." Jesse headed straight for Karel's desk and started typing. "Told me he'd heard rumblings about an unknown player in Chester renovating an abandoned building. No one'd had time to check it out yet but since there'd been no activity, they didn't give it a lot of thought. Contacted me as soon as he heard about Risa. Adam and Tristan are on their way there now to check it out. Here."

Gens came around behind Jesse to look at the Google Earth map he'd pulled up on the screen. Tony stepped up next to Gens, attention laser-focused on the screen. "I know this area. Had an uncle who lived not far from there."

"Then you're driving."

Gens and Tony were practically out the door when Karel called out to them.

"Get her back. By any means necessary. I'm sending backup. They'll be right behind you."

Gens noticed Tony didn't hesitate to nod before heading for the small room off the kitchen. Gens called it the stock room. Most people would call it an armory.

They didn't speak as they grabbed extra clips for their weapons. Tony had been wearing his Glock since yesterday and was about to cross a line he couldn't uncross.

"I can take this myself."

Tony shot him a glare so hard, it could cut glass. Gens lifted his hands in the air in surrender.

"I'm trying to give you an out."

"I don't want an out." Tony paused. "You need me."

Truthfully, Gens didn't trust anyone but Tony right now. Not Adam or Tristan. Not Max or Jesse or any of Karel's men. He had no doubt Tony would do whatever it took to get her back. Same as Gens.

"Then let's go."

Tony said nothing as they pulled away from the house and headed for Chester. Traffic was a bitch this time of night and it took them longer than they'd anticipated. By the time they got to the address, tension had eaten away at the lining of Gens's stomach.

Glancing at Tony, Gens watched the muscle in his jaw clench.

"She's smart. She won't do anything stupid."

"You trying to convince me or yourself?"

"Does it matter?"

Five minutes later, Tony slowed, pulled the car to the curb more than a block away, behind a truck that looked like it'd seen better days. He left the engine running but turned off the lights.

"Straight ahead." Tony nodded. "That's the one."

The building looked deserted, though that could be a trick of the flickering streetlights. Boards covered the second-floor windows, the graffiti on the walls a mix of old and new. The three bay doors lining the street looked like they hadn't moved in years. Same for the entrance door farther down the block.

"We need a closer look."

Tony shook his head. "No traffic on this street. We drive by, it'll tip them off."

"I can't just sit here."

"Give it a few minutes. Wait for another car then we can follow it down the street."

Gens knew Tony was right, but it still pissed him off to have to wait. He felt ready to crawl out of his skin.

"And if there's no other car?"

"Then we'll circle around back and come around from the other side. For now, we sit."

"I don't sit well."

Tony slid him a narrow-eyed glance. "This is why it won't work."

"What the hell are you talking about?"

"Risa. Me. What you said earlier. It won't work."

Gens's hands curled into fists before he could stop them. He had to make a conscious effort to unclench them.

"We'll talk later."

"No, we won't. But you should take your own damn advice and get the hell out. Take her and run."

"Not the time—"

"It'll never be a good time. Haven't you figured that out yet?"

Tony was right but it didn't matter. Gens wasn't going to leave Karel's side. Not as long as Karel needed him. He didn't know if Tony didn't understand that or just didn't care. Gens owed Karel more than he could repay. Tony would tell him he didn't owe Karel his life. Gens would argue that wasn't true.

But when they got Risa back, he would make damn sure nothing like this would happen again.

"Movement."

Tony sat forward, gaze locked on the slowly opening bay door at the far end of the street. A panel van emerged and turned toward them, heading up the street at a pace that would make any grandmother proud.

"Looks like they've got something to hide in there." Tony turned toward Gens and away from the van as it drove by. "Tell Karel's men to set up surveillance here. We're following the van."

Tony waited until the van turned the corner then pulled a U-turn and raced up the street. More traffic now, giving them enough cover to stay a little closer. They followed the van through Chester and onto I-95. Toward the airport.

"Shit." Tony's voice rumbled through his chest like a growl.

"We can't let them get to a fucking hangar. She'll be gone."

"We don't even know she's in the damn van."

Tony shook his head. "If she is, we're gonna lose her. I'm not willing to take that chance."

"Agreed. Force them off the road. Now before they get to the next exit."

Tony floored the gas pedal, weaving in between several cars before pulling up alongside the van. The highway wasn't as crowded as it would've been earlier, so they didn't have to worry about much collateral damage, but that meant the van had more room to maneuver.

Tony had a response to every move the van made. And though he was trying not to cause an accident that could hurt Risa, they both knew they were going to have to chance it by forcing the van off the road.

The van managed to elude them for a couple of miles but with the exit in sight, Tony muttered, "Hold on," and jerked the steering wheel to the right.

The front end of Tony's sedan rammed into the side of the van, making the car shudder and the van skid along the shoulder. At the speed they were going, a less-skilled driver could've lost control. Gens had absolute trust in Tony. Bracing one hand on the dashboard and the other on the door, he leaned into the swerve as Tony jerked the wheel to the left and took them back into their own lane.

The van corrected back into their own lane and poured on the speed. Tony was ready for that and stomped on the gas pedal, keeping pace. The engine revved as he nudged the van off the side of the road again.

This time, the van turned into their car, but Tony refused to back off. The van weighed more than the car, but Tony had the experience to force the van back to the side. Gens had a split second to realize what Tony was about to do. He sucked in a breath and tried not to stiffen.

In the next second, Tony yanked the wheel again sent them into the side of the van. Unfortunately for the other driver, he had nowhere to go. Tony had the van pinned against the guardrail.

They skidded for yards, metal grinding on metal, until finally, they came to a halt. Gens had no time to shake off the pain from his right shoulder slamming into the door at exactly the wrong angle. Tony was already out of the car, weapon trained on the van by the time Gens muscled open his door. With the van pinned against the guardrail, the passenger door was blocked so whoever was in the van had to come out the driver's side. But Risa wouldn't be in the front.

Gens headed for the back of the van, grabbed the handle, and pulled the door open. He kept his weapon up, ready for anything.

"Do anything stupid and I'll shoot her."

The voice was male and sounded wrong, like he was in pain.

Darkness shrouded the interior of the truck, but Gens could barely make out two figures. When approaching car lights illuminated the gloom, he got a glimpse of what he needed to see.

A split second later, he pulled the trigger.

8

Tony heard a shot fired and his heart dropped into his stomach.

Fuck.

Giving the darkened windows of the cab one final look, he ran to the back and saw Gens holding his gun steady, the smell of gunpowder sharp in the air.

"Gens—"

"Careful, I shot one." Gens spoke low and steady, his voice flat. "She's in there. I'll cover you."

Grabbing his phone out of his pocket, Tony took a few precious seconds to turn on the flashlight. He only started to breathe again when he saw her. It had to be her. He couldn't let himself think otherwise.

Two bodies lay on the floor, one on top of the other. The man on the bottom was bleeding from a head wound. The smaller body on top of his wasn't moving at all.

Tony shoved his gun in the back of his pants and hopped into the back. He grabbed the woman and got the hell out of the van. They needed to get the hell away because, though no one had stopped yet, their luck wouldn't hold much longer.

But he had to know.

"Is it her?"

Gens tugged off the hood covering the woman's face.

Risa. Unconscious.

Thank fuck.

Tony had to lock his knees against the relief that wanted to make him weak.

"Let's get the get the fuck out of here." Gens spun and headed for the car. "Give her to me and let's go."

Tony had a split second to think fuck no, he wasn't giving her up. Then he came to his senses. He shoved Risa's limp body into Gens's arms and ran for the driver's seat. Gens slid into the back and barely had the door closed when Tony sped away.

In the backseat, he heard Gens calling Antonoff.

"We've got her." Pause. "Okay. Yeah. No. Yeah. Okay."

Gens hung up a second later. "We're taking her to Dorrie."

Tony nodded, afraid if he opened his mouth, something stupid would come out. Because what he really wanted to do was take her and run. Get her the hell away from here because she wasn't safe.

Stepping on the gas, he accelerated down the highway, getting off at the Broad Street exit and weaving through downtown until he got to the building where Dorrie had her medical suite.

Since it was close to nine at night, only a few cars sat in the underground parking garage, but he knew from being

Dorrie's bodyguard that the building had an extensive surveillance system.

It was one of the reasons she'd taken the space. One of the reasons her father had wanted her to take the space here. He also knew Karel paid the security company a hell of a lot of money to make sure whatever Karel wanted to hide was scrubbed. So he wasn't worried about anyone finding out Risa was here.

He was worried that she still hadn't opened her eyes, even though Gens had tried numerous times to wake her.

Slamming the car into park in the space nearest the elevator, he practically ripped the back door off its hinges to open it.

Gens handed her over when he reached inside for her then followed Tony to the service elevator. He'd learned fairly soon after taking the job that Karel's men didn't come through the front door.

Silence held as they ascended, though Tony could practically hear Gens grinding his teeth. When the elevator finally dinged and the door opened, he let Gens lead the way, gun out. They saw no one, heard nothing. Deserted.

Tony tried not to think about how she felt like so much dead weight in his arms, tried not to dwell on the fact that she hadn't moved since they'd rescued her.

The door opened before they got to it and Gens had his gun aimed at Ben for a split second before he lowered it. Ben didn't blink.

"Take her back. Dorrie's waiting."

He brushed past Ben, Gens at his heels. Ahead, he saw Ian at the door marked private that led to the surgical rooms.

He didn't stop until he saw Dorrie and he finally remembered to breathe.

"In here." She motioned him through the door and hurried ahead to the table. "Set her down."

He laid her out on the table, but he couldn't get his feet to move. He could only stand there, staring down at her.

Across the table, Dorrie pulled her stethoscope from around her neck with shaking fingers and started to check her sister.

"Was she responsive when you found her?"

Tony couldn't seem to get his jaw unlocked to answer.

Luckily, Gens didn't have the same problem. "No. She might've banged her head when we forced the van off the road but I'm not sure."

"I don't see any visible bruising but I'm not going to rule it out." She moved around the table but when Tony wouldn't move out of her way, she put her hand on his arm.

"I need you and Gens to wait outside." She didn't yell at him. "Actually, I need all of you to get out. My nurse is on her way in and you all hovering over me isn't going to make me help her any faster."

Tony's gaze snapped up, ready to tell Dorrie there was no way in hell he was leaving. She'd have to drag him away. Out of the corner of his eye, he saw Ian and Ben take a step closer.

It took him a few beats of his heart and a few deep breaths before he stepped away from the table. Away from Risa. Then he looked at Gens, whose expression probably looked pretty damn close to his.

"Guys, I need you to—"

"We're going." Tony nodded at Dorrie, whose eyes looked a little too wide. Then he looked down at her hands and saw she'd stopped shaking. The fact that she'd been able to pull herself together helped him gain back a little more of his own composure. "We'll be outside if you need anything."

Dorrie's lips flashed a smile that disappeared in a flash. He and Gens were making this worse for her. And it was already bad.

He didn't look at Risa again as he left. He couldn't. If he did, he wasn't sure he'd be able to leave. It took every ounce of his willpower to brush past Ian and Ben. He had to fight against the urge to go back every step of the way.

He didn't head back to the waiting room. He slammed his back against the wall and slid down onto his ass on the hallway floor.

Seconds later, Gens emerged from the room, hands clenched into fists by his side, Ian close on his heels.

Silence held except for the sound of Gens sucking in air then releasing it on a huge sigh.

After a few seconds, Ian leaned back against the wall, hands shoved in his pockets.

Then they waited.

9

"Hey, Ris. Open your eyes. It's Dorrie. Come on, sis. Wake up."

Dorrie's voice. Seemed so close. Was she dreaming?

And why the hell did her head *hurt*?

She remembered...

Everything. Being taken, being confined. Being terrified. The last thing she remembered was trying to run and then... Nothing.

Had they sold her? She didn't want to open her eyes for fear she wasn't really hearing her sister's voice. They'd drugged her. She remembered being stuck with a needle, could feel the throbbing spot on her arm where they'd stuck her.

"Risa. Wake up. Now."

Oh. God. Was that Gens? Was he here? Was he really here or was this just some cruel side effect of the drug they'd given her?

Her brain still felt foggy and her body heavy.

"Is she awake?"

And now she heard Tony.

Goddammit, she was afraid to open her eyes. Because if she did and they weren't there…

Tears welled, and she slammed her lids shut against them. She fucking refused to cry. She hadn't cried through this entire episode and she refused to now. She just had to find the courage to open her eyes.

"Guys, give her a little room. Risa, open your eyes. You've been asleep for a while and you need to wake up. Before Gens blows a gasket and Tony paces a rut in my hallway. You're safe. I swear. Just open your eyes."

Listening to the command in her sister's voice, she blinked but the light hurt her eyes and she snapped them shut again.

A huge, warm hand grabbed hers and squeezed.

"Risa. Goddammit, open your eyes."

The sheer bossiness of Gens's voice drew an immediate response.

"Don't tell me what to do."

This time, when she opened her eyes, the light was dimmer. Or maybe her eyes had adjusted better this time. Whichever it was, she could make out dark forms looming over her and she instinctively recoiled.

But she had nowhere to go. A split second later, Dorrie had her arms around her shoulders, hugging her.

"Jesus, Ris. I was so worried."

"Dorrie?" She blinked, her eyes still struggling to focus even as her arms curled around her sister's back. "Oh my god. Am I really here?"

As soon as the words left her mouth, she wanted to take

them back. Of course, she was here. That was such a stupid thing to say.

But fear continued to grip her by the throat, making it hard to breathe. Until she let her gaze travel around the small room. She knew this room. It was the same one she'd visited Tony in when he'd been shot.

Now he stood by one side of the bed, looking down at her with a fierce expression that made her stomach hurt just to look at him.

She turned and saw Gens on the other side of the bed, his expression an almost comical echo of Tony's.

"Ris." Dorrie had actual tears in her eyes when Risa finally tore her attention away from the two men she'd been praying to see again. "How do you feel?"

Her gaze strayed to the two men again, watching her like a bug under a microscope. Neither of them touched her.

She burst into tears.

Five minutes later, Dorrie had ordered everyone else out of the room and Risa lay on the bed, one hand over her eyes.

Dorrie had spent most of the time they'd been alone together testing her reflexes and her memories.

"The drugs should work their way out of your system in a couple of hours, but you're going to have a headache. I'll give you some aspirin to help with that. Are you sure you don't have pain anywhere else?"

Risa knew what her sister wanted to know. "Other than my neck where they injected me, nothing hurts. I wasn't raped. I wasn't beaten."

No, but she had been held against her will, unable to save

herself, and every time she thought about it, she wanted to puke. So far, she'd won that battle.

"The bruises on your arms—"

"Are from where I was grabbed from behind. Nothing else. I'm fine, Dorrie."

The relief on her sister's face was plain, but Risa knew Dorrie didn't completely believe her. Luckily, her sister didn't push. Risa might have completely lost it if she had.

"Okay, good. I'm glad. Dad will be here in a few minutes." And finally, Dorrie's face lost her cool doctor expression. "Jesus, Risa, I was so scared. Do you remember what happened after you left the bar?"

Dorrie grabbed her hand and squeezed as she sat on the edge of the bed. Risa held on for dear life. She wasn't honestly sure she'd be able to let go.

"I don't remember all of it. I remember having drinks with Mally and her friends. I texted Daniel when I was ready to go. He texted me back. I walked out and then everything went black. Oh my god." Her stomach flipped. "Daniel. Did something happen to Daniel?"

Dorrie grimaced and Risa felt every muscle in her body tense.

"He was shot, but he's going to be fine," Dorrie added immediately as Risa drew in a sharp breath. "I won't lie to you, it was touch-and-go for a while but he's going to be okay."

Risa started to shake her head then couldn't stop. "God, this is all my fault. He wanted to come in with me and I told him to wait outside. I just wanted one night. Just one night to be...normal."

"I know." Dorrie's gaze narrowed into a fierce stare. "I

totally get it. None of this is your fault, Risa. This is totally the fault of the asshole who thought taking you was a good idea. When Dad finds him..."

He'd kill him. Risa had no doubt about that. She just didn't want to think about that now.

Dorrie sighed. "I don't know whether I should talk Dad off the ledge or hand him a gun. And I thought I was going to have to sedate Gens and Tony, along with Dad."

At the mention of the men who'd saved her, Risa felt swallowed hard. "They couldn't leave fast enough when I fell apart a few minutes ago."

She hadn't meant that to sound as bitter as it had and Dorrie just shook her head.

"Don't be too hard on them. They were terrified. If they hadn't found you soon, there'd be a lot more dead bodies in the streets. They're the ones who rescued you. They left a hell of a mess on I-95 for the police to clean up. Pretty sure that's gonna cost Daddy a few bucks to fix."

Dorrie was trying to get a smile out of her but Risa wasn't there yet.

"They would've done the same for you."

"True." Dorrie's brows rose. "But they haven't left your side since they brought you in."

"I can't think about that now. Will Dad be here soon?"

Dorrie nodded. "Should be any minute now. I told him not to come in until you woke. I was worried if he was here, someone might try to retaliate and..."

So much trouble. All of this. So much trouble.

Was this what she had to look forward to the rest of her life? Being in danger from men who wanted to sell her to the highest bidder as a bargaining chip against her father? Never having friends for fear they got caught in the cross fire? Never having a normal relationship with a man?

Never having either of the two men she wanted most in the world?

"Ris?"

She looked into her sister's eyes.

"I'm sick of this."

Dorrie's eyes widened. "Sick of wha—"

"Sick of living like this." She shook her head. "I hate that I can't acknowledge that you're my sister. That I can't go to a bar and have drinks with friends without a bodyguard. Did you know my previous guard has a degree in business because she went to every single class with me? Dad set her up with her own business when she wanted to leave."

"Ris—"

"I made three friends in college. I met hundreds of people, but after a few days, or a few hours, they found out whose daughter I was. Then I'd get the distant smile when I saw them next time. And I knew what that meant. They'd found out who I was. Who my father was. And they didn't want to know me. High school was hell. A few times, I actually wondered if my mom had been right."

"Oh God, Ris—"

"But that was the coward's way out. I told myself it'd get better. It never did. It never will. I will never get married. I will never have children because I don't want to worry that I'll lose them to some psycho with a grudge. I'm going to die an old maid who has mindless sex with nameless men who don't give a shit about me. I'm never going to be happy. I have to come to grips with that now or I'll go crazy. Like my mom."

When she finally stopped, Risa realized her lungs hurt from not breathing. Sucking in air, she released it in a rush. She looked down to find her hands shaking in her lap and balled them into fists.

Damn it. *Damn it.*

Why the hell couldn't she keep her mouth shut? Glancing at Dorrie, she saw horror mixed with pity on her sister's face and wanted to take it all back. No one needed to know any of this. Especially not her sister.

Christ, she wanted to crawl into a hole, somewhere in the mountains where no one knew her and where she'd never have to face anyone again.

"Risa."

Fuck.

Gens. How the hell had she not noticed he'd come into the room?

She forced herself to look up and found him by the door. Along with Tony.

Her heart stuttered in her chest, her lungs frozen. She felt a blush burn her cheeks, but she refused to look away.

Had they heard? Did she care? She refused to be embarrassed. This was how she felt, and she was done keeping it all inside.

"No, Gens." She shook her head at him, her gaze pinning him in place. "You don't get to say anything. Not one damn word. I don't want your goddamn pity. I don't want you to tell me everything will be fine. I'm grateful to you. I'm thankful you and Tony rescued me. But I am sick and tired of feeling like I don't exist to you, other than as some untouchable virgin in a goddamn tower. I'm so fucking sick of wishing for something I'm never going to get."

Gens looked as if his jaw could crack at any moment. "Risa, what the fuck—"

"No." She slashed her hand through the air, making the IV tubing sticking out of her hand swing and pull. "No. I don't want to hear anything from you. From either of you. Not that I *actually* expect you to speak to me, Tony."

Her gaze nailed Tony as he stood behind Gens. Always behind Gens. The two of them united. Which left her nowhere.

She felt the burn of tears in her eyes and furiously wished them away. She would not cry. Not now. Not in front of them. It was a weakness she couldn't afford.

"I'm done hoping. I'm just done. Leave. Please. I can't be in the same room with you."

Gens made a move forward, but Tony grabbed his arm, stopping him cold.

"You're upset." Tony's hand tightened on Gens's arm. "And we're making it worse. We're going."

Gens looked like he was going to fight Tony's grip. If he had... If he'd made any attempt to come near her, she might've started to scream. She wasn't sure she'd have been able to stop.

Gens looked torn. Tony looked furious.

And she just wanted to be left alone to cry. But her dad was on his way and she couldn't let him see her break down. She was stronger than that. He'd raised her to have a backbone.

"We'll be back." Tony's words sounded like a promise and her aching heart longed for him to mean those words. For so long, she'd wanted something neither of them seemed willing to give her.

Now… She couldn't look at them. It hurt. And when they finally left the room, she sucked in air. And again. And she couldn't stop.

"Risa, you're going to hyperventilate. Do you want me to give you something?"

Her heart pounded as if it was trying to escape her chest and her ears rang until she thought she'd go deaf.

"Risa. You're having a panic attack. I'm going to give you something to calm you down, okay? Just nod. That's all you need to do."

She didn't know when she'd reached for Dorrie's hand but now she couldn't release it.

Damn it. She didn't want the drugs, hated the drugs, but she forced herself to nod because she was afraid she wouldn't be able to cope otherwise.

"Okay. Good choice." Dorrie's voice had dropped into doctor mode, which alternately pissed off Risa and calmed her down.

She clutched at Dorrie's hand when she loosened her grip on Risa but forced herself to let her go.

"Don't worry," Dorrie said as she reached for a syringe already lying on the table next to the bed then shot it into the trap in her hand. "I'm not going anywhere. It's gonna be okay. I swear. "

No, it really wouldn't.

That was her last thought before she felt the fake calm of the drug wash through her and she closed her eyes.

10

"We need to get out of here. If we don't, your head's going to explode."

"I'm not leaving. You heard her. We left her alone too long. We fucking left her alone and we almost didn't get her back."

Tony rubbed a hand over his head, buzz cut scraping against his palm. "She doesn't want us here. We're making it worse for her."

In the waiting room of Dorrie's office, Gens slammed his back against the wall next to the door and banged his head hard enough to make the picture next to him shudder.

"Which is why we're out of her room. But I'm not fucking leaving."

Watching Gens fume was enough to give Tony some perspective. One of them had to keep his head. Apparently, it was Tony's turn. He could handle that. For now.

He'd been handling it since she'd gone missing. He'd handled the rage and the fear. He'd managed to keep Gens from going off the deep end. He only needed to keep it together a little longer. Karel would be here in a few minutes and he'd take over.

Then Tony would get the hell away from here. He'd head to a dive bar in south Philly, somewhere no one knew him. Far from his townhouse in Kensington.

Then he'd drink himself into a fucking coma and sleep for two days. And when he woke, he and Gens would take care of whoever had taken Risa.

"We both could do with some sleep." Tony figured he'd attempt rational discussion first. Probably the one thing that wouldn't work on Gens right now, but he figured he had to give it a try.

"You can catch a few hours here." Gens's gaze narrowed. "I need to talk to a few people."

"And then what?"

"Then we'll go find the bastard who took her and kill him."

Tony didn't bother to contradict the last part of Gens's statement. He'd been a cop for years. He'd drawn a hard and fast line in the sand when he'd taken the job guarding Dorrie. Deadly force only when needed.

He was pretty damn sure that would go out the window when they found whoever was responsible for Risa's kidnapping. When you dealt with criminals, sometimes you had to stoop to their level. This was probably one of those times.

"Until then, we need to get some sleep."

Not that he thought he would. Like Gens, he was running on adrenaline. He'd eventually crash, but for now, he'd make damn sure no one got near her again. Including either of them.

He was about to tell Gens exactly that when the outer door opened, and Risa's father walked through.

Karel looked like hell. He'd put on a good face for the last two days but now he looked like he'd aged ten years. The bags under his eyes looked darker. His hair looked as if he'd been running his hands through it. His slumped shoulders and wrinkled shirt said more than any words could.

Tony had never seen the man look anything other than completely put together.

He actually felt sorry for Karel. His relationship with Risa's father had always been problematic, and if he'd had any other option when he'd returned to Philly two years ago, he never would've taken the job guarding Dorrie.

But...

He would've missed out on his relationship with Dorrie. He never would've met Adam and Tristan, who were offering him a new career and a new lease on life. He wouldn't have reconnected with Gens, who'd become more than a brother to him.

And he never would have met Risa.

Maybe that would've been a good thing.

The rest of him told that part of his brain to shut the fuck up.

Karel nodded at Gens and Tony as he walked through the room, but he didn't speak. Tony didn't take it personally. The guy had been through hell. But there was a part of him that wanted to get in Karel's face and scream that his daughter wouldn't be in this situation if he weren't a fucking criminal.

A criminal who gave you a job when no one else would.

Yeah, yeah. Life sucked. Get over it. Shoving those

thoughts out of his head, Tony caught Gens's eye and jerked his head toward the door.

His jaw tight, Gens followed him to the other side of the room.

"Why don't you rack out for a while? I'll stay for a few hours, wake you then head back to my place."

Gens shook his head. "I don't think I can sleep."

"You need downtime."

Gens's mouth curled in a sneer. "What I need is to find the bastard who took her."

"What you need is to get some sleep before you make a mistake you can't fix."

Gens stared at him for several, long seconds. Tony saw fatigue, rage, and sorrow in his friend's eyes. He recognized them because they were the same emotions he'd been shoving down inside himself.

But he'd sworn an oath when he'd become a police officer to serve and protect. It was a hard oath to break. And so far, he hadn't.

If and when he crossed that line, he'd deal with it. Right now, he needed to keep Gens from dragging him over it before he was ready to make the leap on his own.

Finally, Gens let his head fall forward, eyes closed.

"Give me two hours. I don't know if I can sleep..." He sighed, long and heavy, looking back up at Tony. "But then you need to do the same."

Tony nodded. He knew he needed to rest and reset. Knew he needed a breather, away from here. Away from her.

With a curt nod, Gens pushed away from the wall and brushed past him, headed for the entrance to the back rooms.

Tony watched him until he disappeared behind the door. Then he stared at the door for several seconds before he released the breath he'd been holding.

"Do you want to join him?"

Max's quiet question made Tony sigh. "We're not—"

"Let me rephrase that before you jump to a conclusion." Max's mouth curled into a slight smile. "Would you also like to get some sleep? I could—"

"No." Tony grimaced at the edge in his voice. "No, I don't think I could sleep. But...thank you."

Max shrugged, shoulders shifting beneath a white dress shirt. He'd obviously been home to shower and change in the past day, something Tony needed to do as well.

"I understand. Just wanted to extend the offer."

Tony nodded, figuring their exchange was finished. He and Max hadn't spent a lot of time together, and he figured that wasn't going to change any time soon. Max and his business partner, Jesse, didn't have a lot in common with Tony. They didn't run in the same circles.

But Max and Risa had been friends for years. And Max and Jesse's girlfriend, Mary Alice, had been with Risa the night of the kidnapping. The guy wasn't just some bystander.

Hell, Max probably had more of a legitimate claim on Risa's friendship than he did. Didn't mean Tony was going to stand down and let Max replace him.

"You do know I was in a similar position."

Tony sank into one of the stiff-as-a-board couches in the waiting room as Max took the seat across from him.

His confusion must have shown on his face because Max

actually smiled this time. Tony didn't think he'd ever seen the guy do it before.

"I don't know—"

"Three-way relationships can be exhausting. They're fraught with problems you never see coming, not to mention the emotional seesaw of trying to deal with the differing opinions of three people and not just two."

Tony had started shaking his head the moment Max said "three-way" and hadn't been able to stop. "We're not—"

"But the benefits far outweigh the negatives." Max continued on, ignoring Tony as if he hadn't spoken. "At least for us. The biggest benefit is that, when I can't be at Mally's side, Jesse can. And vice versa. It works because we find a way to make it work. Out of the three of us, Mally's the strongest. She has to put up with two men."

The wall Tony had put up to keep his emotions from getting in the way of what he'd needed to do over the past few days had done its job. But the more tired he became, the more unstable that wall became.

Every word out of Max's mouth knocked another chink from Tony's defenses. But as much as he wanted to tell Max to mind his own damn business, Tony knew the guy wasn't busting his balls. If Max saw parallels to his own situation… he wasn't wrong. But Tony wasn't in a position to do anything about his situation now. Or maybe ever.

Max had to know that. So Tony figured if he just let the guy get this off his chest, he'd leave him in peace that much sooner.

"Mally wants to see Risa. I told her I'd bring her over in a couple days." Max's smile broadened. "Actually, she told me she'd be visiting tomorrow unless Risa told her to stay away."

That drew a reluctant smile from Tony as well. "Mally doesn't take any shit, does she?"

"No. And trust me, neither does Risa." He paused. "You might want to remember that when you tell her you're planning to leave."

Stunned, Tony's eyes widened in shock before narrowing. "Who the hell told you I was leaving?"

Max didn't flinch at the menace in Tony's voice. "No one. You're easier to read than you think. And I'm not stupid." Then he paused. "But I love Risa like a sister and I don't want to see her hurt. If you're going to leave, do it now."

Having someone say the words out loud made every muscle tense until he vibrated. And when Max continued, Tony's hands curled into fists.

"Leave before she thinks she can rely on you. Before she thinks you're going to be here for her while she works through this."

"You don't know what you're talking about."

Max shrugged. "I don't know you that well. And yeah, maybe I need to mind my own damn business. But I know Risa. She's going to say she's fine. Maybe she will be. For a while. But eventually she won't be. And she's going to need people she can count on to be there for her. You should figure out where you plan to be for the next few months before she starts believing she can count on you."

Tony's jaw clenched against the urge to tell Max to fuck off. The words were on the tip of his tongue, but he managed to bite them back. He didn't need to get in a pissing war with Max. Not now and definitely not here.

So he nodded and hoped like hell that Max would move the fuck away and leave him the fuck alone.

But Max wasn't done.

"On the other hand, if you're gonna stay, man the fuck up. She's going to need someone to help her through this. Hell, she's going to need all the help she can get. Her safe world's been shattered, and she isn't going to know how to deal with that. She's going to want to hide and ignore and that's going to be the worst thing she can do. Because I know Risa, and I know she's going to keep it all inside. Until she can't. And then she's going to break. And that could destroy her."

Every word out of Max's mouth made Tony's jaw clench a little tighter, until he was afraid his back teeth would shatter from the pressure.

Sighing, Max finally stood but didn't move away.

Tony stood as well, meeting Max's gaze because he couldn't not. He had to show Max... What? That he wasn't afraid of him? That he wasn't an asshole? That he was going to be here for Risa when she needed him?

How about all of the above?

Sonuvabitch.

"I'm going to grab some food. If he asks, tell Karel I'll be back in a couple of hours."

Not trusting himself to speak, Tony nodded then took the hand Max stuck out.

"And think about getting some rest," Max said. "She's going to take one look at you and know exactly what you're planning to do. And that's not gonna help her."

Gens had every intention of taking a room in the back and getting some rest.

He really didn't think he'd be able to sleep, but he was willing to at least give it a shot if it meant Tony would do the same.

He was seriously worried about Tony snapping under the pressure. The fact that he hadn't was a good sign, but Gens didn't want to take any chances. He also didn't want Tony to make any rash decisions. Like deciding to disappear.

Risa had been right about one thing. He and Tony had treated her like shit. That stopped now.

He'd fix this.

On his way to a room in the back, he had to pass the door to Risa's room. And he knew he wouldn't get any sleep. So, he propped himself against the wall. And waited.

He heard the murmur of voices from inside the room, heard Karel, heard Dorrie, but couldn't make out the words. He didn't hear Risa at all.

He wanted to go inside, wanted to make sure she was okay. Wanted to force her to go to sleep and wake up the next morning, the past few days wiped out of her memory.

Then he'd do what he hadn't until now. He'd show her just how much he wanted her.

And he'd bring Tony along because that's what she wanted.

He'd make sure she got whatever she wanted, whatever she needed to feel safe. He'd make sure she was never hurt again and he'd fucking kill anyone who tried.

Minutes passed. His muscles began to protest being held so tightly but he couldn't bring himself to move. Instead, he closed his eyes and tried to breathe through the acid burning through his chest.

He didn't know how long he stood there, but his knees ached by the time the door opened and Karel walked out. Risa's father didn't see him right away and Gens watched the rage Karel must have been suppressing while he was with Risa flood his face.

His pale cheeks flushed red and his lips flattened. He stood at her door for several seconds before he turned and looked straight at Gens.

"You're going to take her away. I don't want to know where. I want her away from here. And then I'm going to clean up this mess."

Conflicting emotions tore at Gens.

"Send her with Tony. I'll stay here with you and take care of this."

Karel shook his head. "I want both of you with her. If things go sideways and there's retaliation, I want her protected. I trust you. I know you won't let me down. Her safety is the most important thing. And if anything happens to me, I want your promise that you'll make sure she's safe. Whatever it takes. Do you understand?"

Gens wanted to argue but he was torn between competing emotions. The desire to protect Risa and the ingrained need to fight in Karel's place battled for prominence. He'd trained since he was eighteen to protect Karel. To make sure nothing ever happened to the man who'd given him a home and a purpose after his parents' murder.

Karel had never asked Gens for his loyalty. Hell, Karel had sent him to college and to get a white-collar job. Some cushy position in a company that imported or exported or bought and sold. Karel had pushed Gens to get out of the business.

Gens hadn't wanted out. He considered Karel his family. He wanted to stay with his family.

And Risa?

His. He considered her his. He had for years. His to keep safe. To watch over.

But he'd never considered crossing the line that separated them...until she'd almost been taken away.

Now, he was going to cross that line. And hope like hell it wasn't too late.

"I understand."

Karel nodded and turned, his gaze on the door. But before he moved away, he stopped and looked at Gens.

"She's not going to want to go. Give her a reason to."

Then he left, leaving Gens staring at the door to Risa's room.

After several long seconds, he moved until he could see in the small window in the door. Risa clung to Dorrie's hands, staring down at the bedspread like it had something fascinating to say to her. He couldn't see Dorrie's face, but he knew she was speaking because he could hear the low murmur of her voice.

After several minutes, Dorrie leaned forward, put her arms around Risa's shoulders, and hugged her tight. Risa wound her arms around Dorrie's neck and clung. Risa never clung, not to anyone. That someone had managed to make her do it now...

When Dorrie finally pulled away, Gens stepped to the side of the door, where Risa wouldn't be able to see him.

With his back against the wall, he waited for Dorrie to step out.

She didn't seem surprised to see him.

"She needs to sleep." Dorrie stared straight into his eyes. "Your presence isn't conducive to sleep."

"I'm not going in. But I'm not leaving."

"I didn't think you were. Why don't you take the room next door? Get some rest if you can."

"When will she be ready to leave?"

Dorrie's brows rose. "She's not physically injured. She could leave now but I convinced her to stay overnight. Tomorrow, she's coming home with me."

He shook his head. "We'll be leaving tomorrow."

Dorrie brows rose and she blinked, just once. And he knew he'd made a serious error in judgment.

"I thought Risa made it clear she doesn't want you around right now." Dorrie's voice was calm, composed. "And it would be better for her mental health to be somewhere she doesn't feel threatened. She's going to stay with me for a few days. Ben and Ian won't let anything happen to her."

But they weren't him or Tony. "Your father made it clear—"

"My dad will understand when I tell him moving Risa now will do more harm than good. You do know that if you force her to do anything she doesn't want to do, she'll hate you, right?"

He shook his head. "I don't care, as long as she's safe."

"And she will be. With me. But," she held up a hand to stop his immediate rebuttal, "I'll say something to Ian and Ben. Maybe they'll take pity on you and put you up for a few days. We bought the townhouse next to ours when it went up for sale a few weeks ago. It's kind of a mess. We're using it to store the furniture from three apartments while we figure out what to keep and what to toss, but there are beds and the security system was installed by Adam."

One thought raced through his head. "Tony—"

"Do you think I'm stupid?" Dorrie rolled her eyes. "The invitation included him."

It took a second but, finally, Gens's mouth curved in a hint of a smile. "You're a tough one, aren't you, kid?"

Her eyes rolled as she huffed. "I'm hardly a kid, but don't piss me off and you'll never have to find out how tough I really am."

He nodded. "I appreciate the offer. But if she agrees, we're taking her away."

"I would never stand in the way of what Risa wants but," she sighed heavily, "I think she's going to have a tough time for a while. She's already pretending everything's fine. She's going to need to talk about it, and if you can't handle that—"

"I'll handle it."

Dorrie stared at him for several long seconds before she nodded. "Get some sleep, Gens. We'll figure out the rest tomorrow."

11

Risa woke with a start, sucking in air and stifling a scream just as she realized where she was.

In her sister's medical suite.

Safe. But not alone.

Gens sat in the chair facing the bed, asleep.

He had to be uncomfortable, slumped to the side, one arm propped on the arm of the chair and his head propped in his hand. His neck was going to hurt like hell when he woke, depending on how long he'd been there.

Glancing at the clock on the table next to her, she calculated she must have slept about twelve hours. Whatever her sister had given her had allowed her to sleep without dreaming. But already, her heart was speeding up its pace as fear began to creep back in.

No. She was safe.

But are you really?

That was the fear talking. She had to banish that fear before it became a beast that wouldn't leave her alone.

She'd done it before. She'd do it again.

But what did she do about the man in the chair?

She'd freaked out on him and Tony earlier and managed to make everyone think she was weak. Terrified. She'd told them to leave her alone.

Of course, Gens hadn't listened. She wondered if Tony had or if he was still here, too.

Her gaze slipped to the door then to the bathroom. Could she get out of bed without waking Gens?

Of course not.

As soon as she started to slide out of bed, Gens's eyes opened and she sat up straight.

"Hey. Where do you think you're going?"

The tone was so like the Gens she'd known four days ago that relief flowed through her. Until he opened his mouth again.

"Let me help you." Rising from the chair, he closed the distance to the side of the bed and reached for her arm.

Instinctively, she pulled away, which made him freeze in place.

"I don't need your help to get out of bed." Her voice sounded level, but she heard the slight tremble just below the surface. "I need to use the bathroom."

Gens didn't move away from the bed, just continued to stand over her, staring down at her.

Staring over his shoulder, because she couldn't bear to look in his eyes and see his pity, she waited for him to move. When he didn't, she felt tears start to form at the corners of her eyes.

Which made her angry. But the anger also fueled her anxiety. Which fueled more anger.

Frozen on the bed, she wanted to rage and cry and throw

things. And she wanted him to hold her. And she wanted him to leave.

And she wanted to be back in charge of her life. She wanted to go back to four days ago when she'd been pissed off at him for refusing to be with her. When she'd been pissed off at Tony for treating her like she was radioactive.

"Risa—"

"I really need you to leave."

The words came out much more pathetic than she'd wanted, and she began to shake her head.

"I'm not leaving." His arms crossed over his chest. "Not this time."

Now her gaze shot to his and her lips parted in shock. A little of that shock must have taken the edge off her panic because she glared at him for several seconds before blinking and dropping her gaze again.

Her lips flattened, and she gained a little steel in her spine. "Fine. Stand there."

Shifting to the other side of the bed, she swung her legs off the side of the bed, but when she went to stand, dizziness hit her like a bat to the head.

Gens was at her side before she had a chance to wobble.

"Damn it, Ris. You're going to hurt yourself."

Then he shocked the hell out of her by picking her up and walking to the bathroom. She opened her mouth but her brain short-circuited. Words wouldn't form. So, she snapped her mouth shut and let him carry her to the bathroom.

For a second, she thought he was going to carry her inside and then she would've told him to put her down. But he stopped just outside the door and released her legs so her feet could touch the floor. He didn't release her completely, not at first. He waited for several seconds, probably to make sure she wasn't going to keel over.

Or…maybe…just because he wanted to hold her.

As the heat of his body soaked into her, she wanted to stay right here, one hand on his shoulder, the other curled around his neck. With her breasts pressed tight against his chest, she drew in his scent with every breath. It lodged in her chest, spreading through the block of ice that'd taken up residence there. She felt that ice begin to crack.

No. No, damn it. No emotion. She didn't want to feel anything. Not now.

Releasing her hand from around his neck, she used the other to push him away. This time, she didn't sway. Keeping her gaze averted, she stepped into the bathroom, turned, and closed the door behind her.

And hoped like hell he'd be gone when she was finished.

Minutes later, she took a deep breath and blew it out before she opened the door. She should've known he'd stay. At least he wasn't right by the door.

Gens leaned against the bed, his gaze clear and steady on hers when she opened the door. Those blue eyes that she'd always thought were so sharp made her feel naked now.

Frustration wanted to creep in, but she wasn't going to let it. Emotion of any kind right now might break her tentative grip on her control.

"I thought I told you to leave."

Pleased to hear her voice sounded steady, stable, unemotional, Risa walked back to the bed, then stood by the side. She realized she didn't want to get back in.

She wanted to be in her rooms at her home, curled into a ball on her couch, watching a movie.

Alone.

No, not alone. She didn't want to be alone. She wanted to be held by someone who cared about her. She frowned at the image that popped into her head, of Gens on one side and Tony on the other. Her head rested against Tony's arm, Gens's hand on her thigh.

Shaking her head, she forced the image away.

Stupid. Unattainable.

Fuck this. Looking around the room, she spotted her weekend bag on the other side of the bed on a table and headed for it, ignoring Gens for the time being.

She felt his gaze follow her every move as she reached the bag, opened it, and breathed an audible sigh of relief at seeing fresh clothes. *Her* clothes. Washed soft jeans and a pair of yoga pants. A few t-shirts, a sweatshirt, underwear and a couple of bras, including a yoga bra.

Dorrie must have put this together for her. Her father wouldn't have thought to put in her comfort clothes.

Without a word to Gens, she grabbed the bag and retreated to the bathroom again. He watched her every move without comment. When she emerged again, dressed in yoga pants and a camisole covered by a loose, comfortable sweatshirt, she felt some of the crushing weight on her chest lift enough for her to ask a question.

"Why aren't you with my father?"

He didn't answer right away and, finally, she looked up to find him watching her intently. Probably waiting for her to break down again. Which wasn't going to happen.

"Gens?"

"Are you ready to leave?"

His question didn't make sense for a second until her brain made the leap. "I'm going to Dorrie's—"

"I know. I'm taking you."

Okay, she could deal with that. As long as she got the hell out of here. Instead of answering, she shoved her feet into canvas slip-ons, grabbed her bag, and headed for the door.

Gens made it there before her, opened the door, and checked the hall before allowing her to walk out. The routine of it chafed now, reminding her that her life was far from normal and never would be. She'd thought she'd come to grips with that and maybe she had. And maybe everything she'd come to grips with had been blown away in the space of three days.

Thoughts for another day.

With Gens at her back, she moved down the hall, trying not to freak out at the silence. Jesus, how was she going to handle the noise of the city if she couldn't handle the silence of an office?

Forcing her feet to move her closer to the door, she stopped well enough away that Gens could open it without having to get close to her.

Now that she had freedom in her grasp, she wasn't sure she wanted to leave.

"Risa?"

She knew what he was asking. Gens had known her for years. He might actually know her better than Dorrie, simply because they'd shared the same home for years.

"We don't have to leave—"

"Don't." Her tone could've cut ice. "Don't say anything else. Just...take me to Dorrie's."

Gens kept his mouth shut, holding the door open as he

waited for her. When she finally got her feet moving, she walked out the door. He was instantly at her side.

And a little bit of that crushing anxiety lifted from her chest.

The elevator ride gave her a few seconds of heart palpitations but luckily, it didn't take long to get to the underground garage. Gens had parked his BMW in the handicap spot right at the elevator.

Anger quickly followed on the heels of the relief that she wouldn't have to walk across an open space to get to it. Together, they created a toxic stew that tied her stomach in knots.

But she forced herself to keep moving forward, knowing Gens watched her every step.

She reached for the door, but Gens was quicker. Her fingers brushed against his hand, sending a shock up her arm. Snatching her hand back, she took a step away. Gens was so close, she swore she felt him tense, but she couldn't help herself.

He didn't say anything, though, just opened the door so she could climb inside and shut it with a quiet snick when she was safely seated.

Their silence held as he pulled out of the underground garage and onto the street. The light of day hit her hard, making her blink.

"There's a pair of sunglasses in the glove compartment if you want them."

Why did his low growl of a voice make her feel tingly and warm inside? She didn't want it to.

Instead of answering, she opened the little door in front

of her and grabbed the case on top. Sure enough, sunglasses. Settling them on her face, she felt instantly better.

The drive to Dorrie's wouldn't take long, but every minute she sat this close to Gens felt like an hour. And as the silence stretched on, she grew more and more restless. Until finally, she couldn't take it anymore.

"You didn't answer my question earlier. Why aren't you with Dad?"

"Because he wants me with you."

That made sense, because her dad trusted Gens implicitly. "And where's Tony?"

The words were out before she'd even thought about them. Now she wished she could take them back. Then again, maybe Gens wasn't going to answer.

Finally, he did. "I'm not sure."

Her eyebrows rose. "Really?"

"We're not attached at the hip."

"I didn't mean... I know that. I just..." *What?* "Never mind."

"If you want him, you know how to reach him."

Something in Gens's tone made her turn to stare at him. Was he jealous? She couldn't tell from his expression. He wore sunglasses, as well, and stared straight out the front window.

"I don't want—" Damn it. The urge to scream welled in her chest, and she shoved it down hard. She wasn't going to let him rile her. Couldn't let him rile her.

Sucking in air, she held it in until she couldn't any longer then released it on a silent sigh. Biting her tongue all the way to her sister's might require stitches so she closed her eyes and reached for the meditation breathing she used during yoga.

After her mother's suicide, one of her therapists had suggested yoga as a way to handle stress. It had been a last-ditch effort on the part of the therapist to help Risa get through the icy rage. She'd had a hard time letting go of that emotion. At the time, it'd been the only thing holding her together. If she hadn't had that, she might have splintered into a thousand tiny pieces and she would've broken her father's heart.

"Don't want what, Risa?"

Turning to look out the side window, she ignored Gens, focusing instead on her breathing. But the words she wanted to say to him wouldn't go away, and finally, she turned back.

"Do you want me to tell you I want him? Will it make you feel better if I do?"

A muscle in his jaw tensed and, out of the corner of her eye, she thought she saw his hands tighten on the steering wheel.

"I want you to be honest." His voice sounded low and growly, which made her feel better because he sounded more like himself. "If you want Tony, tell him. Otherwise, you're going to lose him."

"And if I decide to come on to Tony, to seduce him into my bed, you'd be okay with that?"

Now she definitely saw his hands clench hard enough that his knuckles went white.

"I'm saying you should tell him how you feel."

"And does the same go for you? Should I tell you how I feel, too?"

"Risa—"

"No, Gens. You wanted to talk. Now I'm going to talk and you're going to answer. What if I want something neither of you are willing to give?"

He didn't respond immediately, and she shook her head, figuring he wasn't going to. Until at least a minute later, he did.

"Why don't you tell me what you want, Risa? Just lay it all out. Can you even do that?"

Her mouth opened before she'd actually thought of an answer, so she snapped it shut before she said something she'd regret. Instead, she considered her words carefully.

"I'm tired of being alone. I want a lover, a partner. I want what my sister has. Someone who's just mine."

A few beats of silence.

"Then you're going to have to choose, Risa. Because I'm not sure Tony and I are going to be able to give you what your sister has."

"Why do I have to choose?" Her voice came out sounding pathetic and weak and that pissed her off. "Why can't I have both?"

"Because we're not Ian and Ben. We're not Max and Jesse. I don't know that I could share you. I think it would eat me up inside to watch him touch you. And I'm pretty sure he'd feel the same way about watching me touch you."

With every word, Gens hammered a nail in the fantasy she'd been nurturing. The one she'd only thought about when she was alone.

His tone held so much pent-up frustration, she wanted to cry. And she never cried, damn it. Just something else to hold against the man who'd thought to use her as a pawn against her father.

"Then I guess I know what I have to do."

"And what's that, Risa? Are you going to go to some function and pick up a stranger for a night?"

Was he jealous? He definitely sounded jealous and that made her happy. Which was petty but, at the moment, she didn't care.

"Do you care, Gens?"

"Of course, I fucking care. I don't want you to be hurt. I don't—"

"Oh, that's rich, coming from you."

"What the hell is that supposed to mean?"

"It means that you're the one who's been hurting me for the past decade. I would have given you whatever you wanted, Gens. I would have given you anything. And you chose to ignore me."

"I thought I was doing the right thing. Your dad gave me a home and a job and I—"

"You weren't going to give that up just for a piece of ass."

"Goddammit, that's not fucking fair."

Now he was pissed. She saw it in the stark line of his jaw and the way his hands curled even more tightly around the steering wheel.

"No, you know what's not fair, Gens? It's not fucking fair that I'll never get to kiss you the way I want to. That I'll never kiss Tony. That I'll never have either of the men I've been dreaming about for years."

"Risa—"

"No, I'm done." She turned to look out the front window. "You made your point. I made mine. Nothing more to talk about."

"Bullshit. If you think that's the end of this—"

"That's exactly what I think. We're done."

To her surprise, he kept his mouth shut, though she knew he had more he wanted to say.

Maybe he'd realized she couldn't take any more. Because she couldn't. If he'd opened his mouth to say one more thing, she would've screamed at him. And with him navigating city traffic, that wouldn't have ended well.

Now, she just wanted to get to Dorrie's so she could get out of this damn car. She physically ached to get away from him. The silence that descended held so much tension, it felt like a physical pressure against her skin.

When Gens finally pulled up to the curb at the home Dorrie and her men lived in, she had the door open before he put the car in park.

She could barely restrain herself from running for the front door, which opened right before she got there. Ian stood to the side, watching her with narrowed eyes, which he turned on Gens as he came up behind her.

Turning in the entrance, she forced herself to stand and face Gens, and block him from entering.

"Thanks for the ride, but I hope you understand why I don't want you here. I'll tell Dad not to send you back. Tell Tony not to come, either."

Then she turned and walked deeper into the house and didn't look back.

Gens watched Risa disappear, frustration making his hands clench into fists at his sides.

His fucking fingers ached like hell and itched to hit something. His teeth ached as well, the molars grinding against each other.

And when he realized that Ian stood there staring at him with his arms crossed over his chest, he wanted to punch the guy. He managed not to give in to that impulse because, in the mood he was in now, he might actually hurt Ian.

"Do I need to know what happened?"

Gens's immediate reaction was to tell Ian to fuck off. He reined in the urge, knowing it wouldn't do anyone any good to get into a fistfight at Ian's front door. Especially not Risa.

"No."

He wanted to tell Ian to make sure nothing happened to her, make sure she didn't do anything stupid, like go out of the house alone. Wanted to threaten the man with bodily harm if she so much as broke a fingernail.

He also realized he didn't have the right. She hadn't given him any right to be concerned about her safety.

"Any leads on the guy who took her?"

Gens shook his head, his gaze still on the last place he'd seen Risa. "No. I've got a few leads to chase down today. Then I need to…"

He needed to see Risa again, to make sure she was okay. He figured the closest he was going to get to that was sitting out front on surveillance.

"Gens?"

"Yeah?"

Out of the corner of his eye, Gens saw Ian shake his head, which drew his attention.

"Why don't you come back in a few hours?" Ian said. "Maybe she'll be willing to talk then."

Not likely but he wasn't going to say no to the invitation.

"Thanks." He paused. "I'll try to convince Tony to stop, too."

"You're both welcome. But if she doesn't want you here…" Ian shrugged.

Yeah, Risa could be a brick wall when she wanted to be. Impossible to reason with. Impossible to get to change her mind.

Reminded him of someone he knew well. Someone he needed to talk to. Because if they were going to fix this, he and Tony needed to come to an agreement.

Half an hour later, he was at the door to Tony's apartment. He let himself in without bothering to knock. Their years of friendship had given him the right, as did the key Tony had given him.

"Tony? You here?"

The reply came several seconds later.

"In the kitchen."

He should've guessed. Now Gens could smell the garlic and onion. Tony had always been good in the kitchen. His grandmom had had a restaurant in south Philly for years and Tony had spent a lot of his childhood working there.

Walking through the small place, Gens took a look around. He hadn't really noticed before that Gens didn't have a lot of stuff. A chair, a television, and a table in the living area. A desk and a small square dining table with two chairs in the dining area.

Stopping in the entrance to the kitchen at the back of the apartment, he leaned against the wall and watched Tony chop something before adding it to the sizzling skillet on the stove. Tony took up most of the space in the tiny kitchen, like a giant in a dollhouse. But the man knew what he was doing.

Whatever he was cooking smelled delicious. And going by the size of the pot, there'd be a hell of a lot of whatever he was making. Enough to feed an army. Or two hungry men.

"We need to talk."

Gens figured now wasn't the time to beat around the bush.

"Yeah? About what?"

"Risa."

"Nothing to talk about."

Tony flipped the pan, expertly tossing vegetables and meat into the air before settling the pan back on the stove. Not a single piece escaped but Gens saw the way Tony's hand tightened on the pan handle before he released it and reached for something on the counter.

"Karel wants us to take her away from the city."

Tony flipped him a quick, narrow look. "Us? Not happening."

Gens crossed his arms over his chest, trying to stop the frustrated anger from spilling out.

"Are you telling me you don't want to make sure she's well-guarded?"

"She will be. With you."

"She will be with both of us."

"It's not going to work. The three of us. It's never going to work. You've had a hard-on for her for years."

"And you haven't? At least I'm not a goddamn coward. I'm willing to fucking try because it's what she wants."

"After what she went through, she doesn't know what the hell she wants."

"Oh, that's fucking bullshit, Tony, and you know it.

You're taking the coward's way out if you keep telling yourself that."

Slapping down the wooden spoon he'd just picked up, Tony braced both hands on the counter and took a deep breath. "It won't work."

"It's working for Dorrie. It's working for Max. Why the fuck can't it work for us?"

"Because I'm not sure I want to share her." Tony lifted his gaze and looked Gens right in the eyes. "Not even with you. And that will come back to bite both of us."

Gens held Tony's gaze for several seconds before he nodded and pushed away from the wall.

"Then you're right. You need to get the hell away."

He didn't wait for Tony to respond, didn't need to hear anything more. He walked out and didn't look back.

12

Risa woke with a start, a scream halfway up her throat. She managed to stifle it before it escaped, snapping her teeth together so hard her jaw hurt.

Shit.

Her gaze flying around the room, she finally latched on to the picture on the nightstand. A picture of Dorrie and her mom, at least twenty years old. Dorrie looked so serious, not smiling, but her mom wore a huge grin that seemed so natural.

Risa's mom had never smiled like that.

Risa couldn't remember the last time she herself had smiled like that. Definitely not in the past few years, anyway.

Damn it.

With a sigh, she threw her legs over the side of the bed and, this time, didn't need help to stand. Not that there was anyone around.

But she was positive there was still someone somewhere in the house. No way would they leave her alone.

Making a stop in the bathroom, she combed her hair and

splashed her face with water, for the first time in a long time not giving two shits about makeup. She wasn't wearing any, which in itself would've been a shock to anyone who knew her. She never went out without her war paint.

Then she did something else she'd never done in public. She pulled her hair back in a tail, which reached all the way down her back, the ends brushing just above her waist. Stick-straight and natural blonde. She wondered what her dad would say if she just cut off the whole damn lot of it.

He'd tell her not to make any rash decisions "after all she'd been through."

Maybe after all she'd been through, a few changes would be good.

Her stomach rumbled, and she realized she was hungry. She wanted a cheesesteak. An authentic Philly cheesesteak. The fact that it was barely lunch didn't matter a bit.

Now, she just needed to find her phone to have someone deliver it to her because she was pretty sure she wasn't going to be allowed to leave the house alone.

And right now, she was okay with that.

Halfway down the stairs, she heard voices and followed them to the back of the house, where she found Ben camped on the couch, watching a show about Pompeii. At least, she thought it was about Pompeii. He turned it off as soon as he realized she was there.

"Hey, how'd you sleep?"

Ben's smile put her at ease immediately. It was like his superpower. Unlike his cousin, Ian, who did intense almost as well as Tony, Ben made her feel like she could breathe.

"Fine. I actually feel more rested than I have in a while."

"Glad to hear it. Dorrie had something to take care of at the office, Ian's watching her back."

"And you got stuck babysitting me. Sorry."

"Unless you throw a tantrum or start throwing things at my head, I don't consider this babysitting. Toddlers scare me. You don't."

"I'll have you know there are several men in the city who think I'm the antichrist and run in the opposite direction when they see me."

And two men who wanted nothing at all to do with her, apparently. And how much did that suck?

Ben's smile widened. "Yeah, well, I know you better than they do. Besides, your sister loves you and that makes you okay in my book."

And Ben loved Dorrie. Risa saw it in his smile and his eyes. It made her so damn happy for Dorrie. And so damn sad for herself.

"So," Ben continued, "you hungry? Not sure when everyone else will be home so we should probably go ahead and feed ourselves. I was waiting for you to wake up to figure that out."

Walking around the couch to sit beside Ben, she curled her legs under and put her arms on the back cushion so she could rest her chin on her forearms.

"I'm starving for a cheesesteak. I don't care where it's from as long as it's good. And I want onion rings. And a chocolate shake."

Laughing, Ben patted her arm. "I can do that. Just let me check with Gens."

She blinked. "What?"

"He's putting his stuff away next door." Ben watched her

carefully. "It's not ideal, but Ian and I can't be here twenty-four-seven. Gens can. You need him. You need to get beyond whatever personal stuff is going on and realize this is in your best interest."

"But...next door? I don't—"

She cut off before she could finish the thought, which would've revealed more than she wanted. While her life had never been entirely her own—and she'd never fooled herself into believing it ever would be—she had been able to at least control the people she allowed into it.

She wanted nothing to do with Gens or Tony, not now. She needed them to disappear.

"Because we can't be here every second." Ben's rational, steady tone cut through her anger faster than anything else could have. "Gens can. We're pretty sure no one knows you're here. But it won't be too long before someone finds out. We don't know if whoever took you the first time will make another play for you. They may decide you're not worth the trouble. Especially after your father gets done with them."

She didn't want to think about what her dad had planned. She hadn't talked to him about it. Which was how she'd lived most of her life. She and her dad didn't discuss his business.

When she'd been about ten, one of her best friends at the private school she'd attended had told Risa she wasn't allowed to "associate" with her anymore. By the next day, Risa had been ostracized by most of the class.

For a week, she'd been in shock, hurting and trying to cover it up. She'd tried to figure out what she'd done to make her an outcast. When her dad had realized something was wrong and asked what was going on, she'd told him everything. And she'd caught a glimpse of an emotion she'd never seen on her dad's face before. Despair. He'd wiped it away quickly, but she'd never forgotten that look.

He'd switched her school the next day, to an even smaller, even more exclusive girls' school outside the city, where she'd been registered as Risa Tennison.

Many of the students had been foreign. She'd made a few friends, actually kept in touch with two of her classmates who'd graduated with her from that same school. Those girls, she'd later learned, were the daughters of men who ran similar operations to her father's in Czechoslovakia and Boston.

"I'm sorry you got stuck with me. This situation should—"

"You're Dorrie's sister. This is Dorrie's home. You'll always have a place here. And I don't feel 'stuck' with you."

Tears pricked her eyes, but she quickly blinked them away. She was sick of feeling weak and weepy. She wanted her fucking life back.

Nodding, she managed what she thought was a normal expression for her. "Thank you, Ben. I appreciate that."

His eyes narrowed a little as his mouth curved in a slight grin. "But you don't believe me." A shrug. "I can live with that. For now."

Her sister had once told her that Ben had a sneaky charm that got under your defenses. Risa saw that side of him now. But she didn't want to be charmed, didn't want to be cheered up or placated or coddled. She just wanted to be left alone to work through her issues.

Of which she had many, apparently.

"So I'm gonna order lunch. For all of us."

Fine. She wasn't considered an ice queen for nothing. She could put up with Gens in the same room for as long as she needed to eat. By that time, maybe Dorrie would be home.

Maybe she could convince her sister to sit with her for an hour or so to watch a movie. Something girly and silly and stupid that she could cry over and pretend the tears were because of the movie.

She shrugged. "No problem."

Ben grinned at her. "You and Dorrie are definitely related. Hang tight, Ris. Let me give Gens a heads-up."

"I gave it up when they killed Glen," Gens said. "Wasn't fun anymore, you know?"

"I still watch." Ben shrugged. "I spent all this time on it, might as well finish it. But when they kill Rick, I'm out."

Half an hour later, she sat at the dining table across from Gens, alternately pissed off and frustrated as hell.

Apparently, Gens and Ben shared a mutual love of *The Walking Dead*, forging a bromance bond for the ages. They hadn't ignored her, but they hadn't made an effort to draw her into the conversation, either.

Since she didn't watch the show, she wouldn't have much to contribute. Instead, she spent way too much time trying not to watch Gens. She'd perfected the art of it as a teenager, when he'd lived with her and her dad. He was only a year and a half older than her, but it'd seemed like a decade when she was fourteen and he was sixteen and he'd just moved in with them after his parents' deaths.

He'd been quietly angry for months afterward and she'd grown quietly fascinated with him. With his light brown hair that looked so touchable and his warm blue eyes that made her think of silky ocean water, Gens had been her secret crush. The one who'd kissed her in her dreams. She'd wanted him to be her first lover.

"Risa? Hey, Ris. You finished?"

With a start, she glanced at her plate and realized she'd finished her sandwich and onion rings. She had no idea when or how long she'd been staring at Gens like a lovesick idiot.

Damn it.

Pushing away from the table, she stood and reached for their plates. "Thank you for dinner, Ben. I appreciate you indulging my craving for cheesesteaks."

"No problem. Hey, you don't have to clean up. Why don't you—"

"I've been sitting all day. I think I can do a few dishes."

Ben smiled as she gathered the dirty plates. "No one in this house does dishes. Just stick 'em in the dishwasher. It's probably ready to run anyway."

Without looking at Gens, she headed for the kitchen, her hands full. She was about to set the dishes down when she realized someone had followed her.

She turned to look over her shoulder and froze when Gens came up next to her.

"Let me help."

Without waiting for her to answer, he opened the dishwasher and began taking dishes out of her hands. She gritted her teeth against the urge to tell him to go away. He'd been careful during dinner not to push her for conversation. He'd let Ben guide the conversation, let her sit silently.

Apparently, he was done letting her ignore him. That didn't mean she had to respond. She handed the dishes to him to load then turned to walk out. She didn't get two steps away when his hand landed on her arm, stopping her in her tracks.

"Come watch a movie with me."

Damn him. Her back teeth ground together as she tried not to answer. But she couldn't help herself.

"No."

"What are you going to do? Hide in your room?"

Her gaze shot to his, anger rising.

"What are you doing here? I thought I made it clear I don't want you here."

"Well, that's too bad because your dad wants me here." He paused. "And I want to be here."

"I don't need your pity—"

"I don't fucking pity you. I'm fucking pissed that I hurt you."

Her eyes widened as his closed.

"Damn it. Goddammit. I'm sorry." He took a breath and took a step away, as if he thought she might be afraid of him. "Jesus, Risa—"

"Stop apologizing. Please. Just...stop. I'm already tired of having everyone tiptoe around me. I'm not broken. I'm just..."

A little damaged? Maybe a lot damaged. Maybe she'd been damaged for a long time and was only just now noticing. Maybe none of that mattered.

"Just what?"

Gens didn't move closer, but he didn't move any farther away. And she didn't want him to go. Even with all the unresolved shit between them, she wanted him to wrap his arms around her and pull her against him. She wanted to feel his body against her. Solid, strong. Warm.

Wanted to feel safe, like he would never let anything hurt her ever again. She wanted to know he cared. And not just as a longtime friend.

Staring into his eyes, she felt her expression slip a little, the mask she'd been using to keep her emotions from spilling out begin to slide away.

"I'm tired of hiding everything. Hiding my feelings. Hiding what I want."

She thought he might run then. Or at least pull back, step away. He didn't. In fact, he took a step closer.

"Tell me what you want."

She lifted her chin. "You didn't want to hear what I had to say earlier."

"I've had some time to think."

"And?"

"And I think I'm done talking."

Shock held her in place as he wrapped his hand around her neck and held her steady. Then he lowered his head and kissed her.

For one long second, she couldn't move, her brain buzzing with white noise.

Then he turned his head just enough to make their lips mesh together more completely and she got her first taste of him.

He took her breath away.

Heat, dark and drugging, washed over her like a wave.

Her eyes closed against the onslaught of emotion that threatened to drown her, but his image was imprinted on her brain.

Gens was kissing her. Finally. After all these years.

As his lips melded with hers, she reached for his arms to hold herself upright. Because if she wasn't careful, she might just melt into a puddle at his feet.

His rock-hard biceps flexed beneath her palms, the heat of his body searing her through the thin cotton of his shirt. Her fingers curled around his arm as he coaxed her closer, kissing her with a determination that stole her breath.

She hadn't known what to expect when he put his mouth on hers. She'd wanted him to kiss her for so long that she couldn't even imagine what it'd be like. Couldn't imagine how wonderful it would be. How amazing.

Now, she wanted him to continue to kiss her until she literally couldn't breathe. She didn't want to give up his lips for longer than a second, for fear he'd rethink his decision and pull away. Her hands tightened on him reflexively.

At first, she could only concentrate on the sensation of his lips against hers, the way her lips molded to his. Everything else was a blur.

Until finally, other details began to slip through. The sense of restraint in his tight muscles, the leashed power behind his kiss. The way his hand tightened around her neck then released.

She realized he'd placed his other hand on her hip and, as if she'd given him permission, he began to pull her closer. Her lungs caught and held, and now he released her mouth.

"Breathe."

His voice held a command she couldn't deny. Her lips

parted as she sucked in air, filling her lungs and sending her brain into overdrive. His gaze fell to her lips for several long seconds before he looked into her eyes again. What she saw there threatened to steal every oxygen molecule from her lungs.

A lust so hot, it seared her to her bones, shocking in its intensity if only because she'd never seen Gens look at her the way he was now. That look threatened to make her knees buckle.

Damn him.

Damn him for waiting until after she'd been kidnapped to show her how much he wanted her. Damn him for making her doubt herself and her feelings.

Anger started to creep in, frustration fast on its heels. Combined with her desire, it had the potential to be a toxic mix.

Gens must have seen her emotions bleeding into her expression because his gaze narrowed just before he dropped his mouth on hers again and tried to kiss her back into oblivion.

She wished he could. Wished she could get her brain to disengage completely to the point that she couldn't think about anything but Gens and his lips and how they felt against hers.

Closing her eyes, she let his taste flood her senses, let her body absorb the feel of him pressed against her. Now, he had his hands wrapped around her upper arms and brought her closer, her breasts pressed against the hard plane of his chest. Every move he made brought her closer to losing herself in him.

And when he tilted his head to the right and slanted his

mouth over hers, she finally let go and kissed him back. Because she'd be damned if she just let him take what he wanted without demanding something in return.

Lifting her hands from his shoulders, she sank her fingers into the hair at his nape. He always let it grow just a little too long. She couldn't help sighing a little at the silky feel of it against her skin then gripping it tighter until she knew it had to sting. Maybe she wanted to punish him, just a little. Just enough to let him know she wasn't going to just give in and let him skate on his past transgressions. On making her wait this damn long for his kiss.

No, he was going to pay. And he was going to give her everything she wanted.

Opening her mouth a little wider, she felt his tongue slip between her lips, bringing his taste with it. Like some forbidden treat, she savored it, sucking on him until finally he kissed her even harder. That leash he had on himself started to slip. She felt it in the way his mouth pressed harder against hers, in the way his hands released her arms and slid around to her back. His fingers spread wide, his palms warm through the thin cotton of her shirt.

Kissing him harder, she let her fingers tug one last time at his hair then she let them slide down his neck to his shoulders and finally to his biceps.

The muscles of his arms were rock-hard below her palms, the tension radiating out and into her. Her fingers curled around his biceps, tightened, and tried to bring him even closer.

Her hips tilted forward, searching, and found the thick ridge of his erection.

A moan built in her chest, born from the rush of heat

filtering through her body. The heat that he stoked when he pressed his erection more fully against her.

Clutching him even tighter, she fit their bodies together like a jigsaw puzzle. Every one of her curves had a corresponding niche on his body where she fit perfectly. Every one of his hard angles had a soft spot on hers that took him in.

She wanted him to be even closer, wanted there to be nothing between them, no clothes, no barriers. No history. She wanted them to simply be two people who wanted each other and had nothing between them but heat.

But that ship had sailed a long time ago. The kiss became a duel for dominance, one she was determined to win, if only because she needed to have that control.

When he pulled away again, she gasped at the abruptness and tried not to growl with frustration.

Before she remembered that they were standing in her sister's kitchen. Where Ben could walk in on them at any time.

"We need to take this conversation somewhere more private."

Gens stared at her, watching her with those blue eyes she adored. And couldn't read. She had no idea what he was thinking. She knew he wanted her, could tell that from the erection tenting the front of his jeans. But otherwise, she didn't have a clue.

"I don't—"

"Let's go next door so we can talk about this."

"I don't need to talk about anything."

His gaze narrowed. "Then what do you need?"

"I need you to fuck me."

His gaze narrowed even farther at her blunt statement.

"Is that all you want? Just to be fucked?"

No, of course not. And he should know that. He should know she wanted so much more.

Her frustration rose at the thought that he was either deliberately misunderstanding her or he honestly didn't have a clue. Either one was unacceptable. And depressing.

She took a deep breath before answering. "And if I do want more? Are you going to do something about it?"

He didn't answer right away, his gaze locked on hers until she began to believe he was simply going to walk away.

After several long seconds, he took a step back. Biting her tongue against the need to protest, she clenched her hands into fists at her sides and refused to reach for him. If he walked out now, she was done. Just...done.

His gaze dropped to her hands for a quick second before flashing back up to her eyes.

"Do you really think spending the night in bed with me is what you need after what happened?"

His inability or his outright refusal to talk about what had happened to her made her furious. "Do you mean after being kidnapped and threatened with being sold into slavery and wondering if I'd spend the rest of my life being drugged and forced to have sex?"

His mouth tightened, and she so wanted to lift her hand and run her fingers over those lips, to smooth out the lines surrounding them.

But they were fighting a war and she needed to win this battle. And that meant being strong and going after what she wanted.

"Yeah, I guess that's exactly what I mean." His gaze hardened. "Do you think fucking me will make what happened disappear? Will it make you forget?"

Her chin lifted. "Do you think you're good enough to make that happen?"

He didn't take the bait she threw out so blithely. He just continued to stand there staring at her, like he knew something she didn't.

"I think you should come over with me and we'll find out."

Her lips parted in shock. She hadn't expected him to call her bluff.

"I don't want to talk. I want action. I want you to give me what I need."

She could tell he wanted to say something, but he must have bitten his tongue almost all the way through holding back whatever it was. After a few long seconds, he nodded.

"Fine. Come over later tonight and I'll give you whatever you want."

Heat poured through her, making her shake, and trying to hide it was almost more than she could bear.

She didn't want to hide it. She wanted him to see what he did to her. Wanted him to be happy that he made her hot for him.

Wanted him to be turned on by her.

"I don't want a pity fuck."

His jaw flexed, and he straightened, rising another inch or so above her. She'd never been afraid of him, had never once thought he would hurt her. She didn't now.

But as soon as he realized what he'd done, he took a step away. As if she couldn't handle him.

Anger rose up lightning quick, stinging her nerve endings raw. But before she could say anything, he spoke again.

"Damn it, Ris. It wouldn't be a pity fuck. Hell, I'm not even sure there'd be any fucking at all."

"Why? Because you think I can't handle it?"

"Because I'm not fucking sure I can!"

Her mouth hung open for several seconds before she snapped it closed. What the hell was she supposed to say to that?

"What are you supposed to handle? Me?"

"No. Not you." He ran a hand through his hair and let his head fall back to look at the ceiling. "Jesus, I don't know what the fuck I'm supposed to do here."

"You're supposed to want *me*. That's all I've ever wanted."

"Or am I just the safe choice? Think about that, Risa. Before you decide to cross that line, really think about it."

He turned and walked away before she could respond, leaving her staring after him with her mouth hanging open.

13

Tony sat in his car on the opposite side of the street from Ian's home in Fairmount Park.

Technically, there were two homes, attached at the center but separate from the other buildings around them. The neighborhood was definitely on the way up the social ladder but still not completely gentrified.

A few of the houses needed repairs, some paint, some woodwork. Looked like a nice place to start a family or start a life with your new partner. Or partners.

He wondered what the neighbors thought about the two men living with one woman. Hell, maybe no one blinked an eye at them.

And why the hell was he so hung up about it, anyway? How other people lived their lives shouldn't matter one damn bit to him.

Maybe because he'd been giving some serious thought to living his life the same way.

He'd been honest with Gens earlier. He wasn't sure he wanted to share Risa.

But the more he thought about his life without her, the more he realized how much he wanted her in it. He didn't want to give her up. And if he had to share her, at least he wouldn't hate the man he was sharing her with.

Still...

Could he actually do it? That was the real question. Could he sleep with her one night knowing Gens would be sharing her bed the next night?

Would he be able to be in the same room while Gens made love to her? Could he actually be in the same bed at the same time? Could he and Gens take her together?

He knew it was possible. Dorrie, Ben, and Ian were proof positive that it could work and work well. Dorrie was happier than he'd ever seen her.

Tristan and Adam. Max and Jesse. They shared—

No, not shared. That wasn't the right word.

Hell, Risa would cut out his tongue if she heard him spout that bullshit. Sharing implied that the woman was a lesser partner, an object to be passed between the two men. She'd be an equal partner, or she wouldn't be involved at all.

More likely, she'd be the one dictating terms. The thought brought an actual smile to his lips. At least, she'd try.

His smile slipped away as fast as it'd formed.

He'd circled back to the fact that he wasn't sure he could do this. And yet, here he was, staring at the house where she was staying, acting like a goddamn coward.

His gaze skipped to Gens's car, parked a few spaces in front of him. Apparently, he'd had enough balls to get out of his car.

Fuck.

He opened the door to the rental Beemer from the dealership. The repair guys weren't sure they could save his or if they'd have to total it because of the frame damage.

Karel had already offered to buy him a new car. The thought made his teeth clench.

Fuck.

Not giving himself any more time to second-guess, he crossed the street and headed for the front door. It took at least thirty seconds after he rang, but finally he heard someone approach from inside the house.

When the door opened, he was surprised to see Risa open it herself.

It was on the tip of his tongue to ask why she was opening the door but he bit back the words before he made a really stupid mistake.

"Tony. What are you doing here?"

Her tone sounded so much like her normal self, his lips twitched seconds before he controlled the urge to grin.

"I was invited."

He wanted to ask her how she was doing, wanted her to talk to him. But he didn't want to upset her again.

Stepping to the side, she waved her hand, silently inviting him inside.

He took the hint and stepped over the threshold. Besides, he didn't want her standing there, exposed in the doorway.

She closed the door behind him then went to walk by him without a word. And he realized that wasn't how he wanted this to go.

Laying his hand on her shoulder, he stopped her.

"How are you, Risa?"

She didn't answer him right away, didn't look up at him either. Just stared somewhere to the left of his chest.

"I'm fine. Thank you. Better than I was earlier, if that's what you mean."

Reaching for calm, because he knew she was trying to bait him, he left his hand where it was and waited until she finally looked up at him.

He searched her expression and found the stress he knew he'd find. But he also saw something behind it. Something that made him want to press her to talk.

"I'm glad to hear it. I'm sorry if I—if *we* upset you earlier. I don't want to add to your stress."

She rolled her eyes, another normal expression for her, but let her gaze drop.

"I'm sure you don't." Her tone practically oozed disinterest. "I appreciate your concern but I'm fine."

No, she wasn't. And he realized he wouldn't be happy until she was fine. He wouldn't be happy until he saw her smile and knew he'd played some part in making that happen. Which meant he might need to be here for a while because he wasn't sure Risa was anywhere near happy and might not be for months.

Surprisingly, that didn't seem like a problem at the moment.

They stood there, silent for another few seconds, his hand on her shoulder. The urge to pull her close and wrap his arms around her continued to build until he knew he had to release her or do what he wanted.

And risk upsetting her even more.

Fuck.

With an effort, he let her go, withdrawing his hand and

letting it fall to his side, where he had to make a conscious effort not to let it curl into a fist.

Frustration seeped in. His inability to know what she needed or wanted made him grind his teeth. After what seemed like forever, she turned and began walking farther into the house.

"If you just came to check on me, you can go now. I'm fine."

His gaze narrowed as he remained where he was. "Are you purposely trying to piss me off, Risa?"

She stopped at the archway that led into what appeared to be another sitting room and looked over her shoulder. Her mouth set in a straight line, her gaze practically scalded him.

"Since I don't know why you're here to begin with, I just assumed you'd be leaving now that I answered your question."

Damn, she was good at this. At keeping people at arms' length. He'd seen her treat other people like this but never him. He wondered if this was how she felt when he treated her like this.

Because, yeah, he'd been building a wall between them for the past several months. It'd been unconscious on his part but now he realized just how hard he must have made it for her to talk to him.

Or maybe not so unconscious, because he'd known just how much he wanted her. He also knew he couldn't have her.

And now...

Gens wanted him to have her. Wanted *them* to have her.

And he'd been thinking more and more that that's exactly what he wanted.

Watching her watch him, he saw the moment she blinked, the instant she realized he wasn't going anywhere. Saw the uncertainty that entered her ice-blue eyes and the unsteady rise and fall of her chest as she thought about what that meant.

Crossing his arms over his chest, he held his ground.

"I'm not leaving."

Her eyebrows rose slowly, haughty disbelief settling over her expression. Anyone who wasn't watching her as closely as he was would miss the longing in her eyes, the emotion that made him grit his teeth.

"If you think you're going to have any say in my plans just because you've decided to stick around, you're going to be majorly disappointed. I don't want you here, Tony. I don't need anyone watching over my every move, thinking they can make decisions for me."

"No, but you do need someone to watch your back, someone to make sure you're safe."

And that someone was going to be him. And Gens.

"I'm sure my dad will—"

"Your dad's already given that job to Gens and me."

Her eyes widened with shock before she managed to control her response.

"And I'm sure when I tell him that won't work for me, he'll find more suitable—"

"No, he won't, princess. You're stuck with us."

Now she turned to fully face him again and her arms crossed over her chest. Actually, they crossed under her breasts, forcing them up and making him hyperaware of how perfect they were. And how much he wanted to put his hands on her.

He'd been dreaming about her for more than a year, practically since the first moment he'd laid eyes on her.

"Not if I don't want to be. My dad won't force me to have —to accept you as my guards."

"Your father wants what's best for you. He knows Gens and I won't let anything happen to you."

Her eyes widened. "Really? And what's changed your mind in the past few hours to make you think you belong here?"

He could hear the anger seeping into her voice now, see the fury in the color in her cheeks.

Risa was usually a perfect ice queen, from her white-blonde hair to those pale blue eyes that could cut a man clean through to his guts. Standing as she was, with her back ramrod straight, you would think she was at least six feet. But he knew the top of her head would fit under his chin if he had her pressed against him.

His cock liked that idea immensely, thickening and pulsing behind the zipper of his jeans. Unconsciously, he must have classified this as a social call because he hadn't even considered wearing a suit. Suits were for work.

Risa wasn't work. Yeah, she was going to take some work to get her softened up to him again, mainly because he'd been so fucking stupid before. But now that he'd made up his mind to go after what he wanted, he wasn't going to back down.

"I realized a few truths. I can't deny that I want you. I never should've tried to deny it to begin with. I don't like to think of myself as stupid. You make me feel like an idiot."

If possible, her body stiffened even more, and her mouth

opened, probably to rip him a new hole he didn't need. But he pressed on before she could say a word.

"I'm not saying that's your fault. It's not. It's mine. I'm the one with the issues. But I'm working through them. But I know I can't let you out of my sight while there's a threat out there against you. I'm gonna be attached to your hip while your dad hunts down this asshole."

She didn't answer right away, seemed to be considering her words very carefully.

"And if I truly don't want you here?"

He took a few steps closer, watched her track his every step. She couldn't hide the fact that she sucked in a huge breath as he closed the space between them.

Good. She wasn't unaffected by him. He stifled a smile, not wanting to rile her any more than she already was.

"Then I'll walk out the door and I won't come back. If that's what you really want."

Risa wasn't sure what she wanted anymore.

Not one damn bit.

After Gens had kissed her this afternoon, she'd spent the following hours alternately cursing him and telling herself he had no idea what he was talking about.

Of course, she didn't just want him because he was safe.

"Risa?"

She'd wanted Gens for years, had never stopped wanting him. Not since the moment her dad had brought him home and told her Gens was going to live with them. She'd been fourteen and home from school for the weekend. Gens had just turned sixteen and was still grieving his parents.

And when Gens had introduced her to Tony, her desire for him had somehow morphed into an all-consuming desire for both of them. She'd never seen Tony as a bonus, a second to Gens's first. No, he'd become an equal object of her fascination. And just as unattainable as Gens.

Had that been part of the appeal? The fact that she couldn't have them?

Or had the fact that she couldn't have them molded her into the ice queen she'd become?

Would she still want them so desperately if they'd given her what she wanted from the start?

Maybe it'd be better if she told herself the answer to that question would be yes.

But she didn't want to lie to herself.

Or to Tony.

"No. I don't want you to leave."

Forcing herself to hold his gaze, she saw something pass across his expression, something she very much wanted him to acknowledge.

But she'd started so she might as well continue. "What I want is for you to spell out exactly what you're saying. I don't want any more misunderstandings. I want to know what you're thinking."

His gaze narrowed slightly, head tilted back. "Is that a two-way street? Are you baring your soul here, too?"

Could she do it? Could she bring herself to say everything she'd kept hidden for so long?

Her lips parted to speak but she honestly had no idea what she should say. Or what she honestly thought. What she did know was this.

"Are you honestly telling me you never realized I wanted you?"

His jaw clenched briefly. "No. I'm not going to lie to you."

"Then tell me why you never acted on it."

"Besides the fact that your father was paying me to guard Dorrie?"

Okay, yeah, she could concede that point. But... "You haven't been her guard for months."

"Have you been waiting for me to ask you, Risa? You know you could've asked me yourself. I can't imagine you not asking for whatever you want."

Except she'd never been able to bring herself to ask the two men she really wanted.

"I guess I have my own reasons."

"And now?" His gaze intensified even more. "Do you still have those same excuses?"

She paused, not knowing how to answer that question. Because she didn't have excuses. She had reasons, valid reasons that hadn't changed since her kidnapping. In fact, maybe they'd been exaggerated by her kidnapping.

A weight lodged on her chest, compressing her lungs and making it hard for her to breathe. That weight wouldn't shift, no matter how much she tried to will it away.

Damn it. She didn't want to let his moment slip away because she was afraid it might never come again. She was determined to grab hold with both hands.

"The reasons haven't changed, but..." she continued on when Tony's expression began to harden, "I'm willing to try to see if we can make this work."

He didn't speak right away, but he watched her even

more closely. And now he took a step closer. She sucked in air but had no desire to move away. In fact, she wanted him to come closer, wanted him close enough that she could touch him.

What did it say about her that the only two men in her life she'd ever truly wanted to touch had only now come close?

"Make what work? You and me? You and Gens? You and me and you and Gens? Or you, me and Gens?"

She knew what he was asking, knew exactly how he was working the math in his head.

Did she want to date Gens? Did she want to date Tony? Did she want to date both of them separately?

Or did she want them together?

What answer did he want? What answer would keep him here?

Unfortunately, the answer was simple. She only had to swallow her pride to admit it. "I'm willing to try whatever will keep you here."

Shock registered in the slight widening of his eyes and the way his lips parted for several seconds before he realized and snapped them shut. Then he blinked and wiped the shock away, replacing it with the poker face he was known for.

He hid everything so well. Maybe better than she did, and she'd been called Ice Queen for so long, she practically answered to it.

It was second nature now, and the words she'd just spoken had taken more courage for her to say than she may have ever needed before. And now that she'd spoken them, and continued to wait for his response, she knew exactly why she needed that stone-cold exterior. Because it fucking hurt when you opened yourself up to someone else, when you made yourself vulnerable to them...and they didn't respond.

Just as she was drawing in much-needed air to tell him to forget she'd said anything, he took a step closer.

She had to tilt her head back to maintain eye contact. In another man, that would put her at a disadvantage and she really hated feeling that way.

With Tony, she felt safe and anxious, all at the same time. It infuriated her and turned her on.

And if he didn't want to be with her, then she needed to make sure he stayed far, far—

"You better be damn sure that's what you want." His voice had an edge that made her shiver. "Because this isn't just sex, Risa. This is lifelong friendships and our livelihoods. There's a lot more at stake here than just scratching an itch."

The urge to snipe back immediately rose up but she tamped it down. Because he wasn't wrong. If they attempted this, it would affect more than just their relationship. Hell, it would affect everything and everyone in their entire, small universe.

And yes, this was probably the absolute wrong time to attempt this. But she didn't fucking care. Not one damn bit.

"If I want to scratch an itch, I can go back to that bar and pick up any man I want."

The thought made her physically ill, but she wasn't wrong. She knew what she looked like. She knew men considered her beautiful, desirable, and she wasn't above using her looks to get what she wanted from men who would otherwise dismiss her.

What Tony might not know was that she wouldn't do it. She didn't want some random guy in her bed simply because he was hot and might be able to get her off.

She wanted Tony and Gens.

And if she couldn't have them, it was time to cut and run. A complete break. Maybe she'd move to the west coast or overseas for a while, somewhere no one knew her.

She'd be lonely, but it wasn't like she couldn't find someone to make her come occasionally.

"And it wouldn't do a damn thing for that itch, would it? You'd just get more and more unsatisfied until sex didn't hold any pleasure."

Tony's voice had lowered to a level she would almost call a growl. And the look in his eyes… She swallowed reflexively, though not out of fear. No, his look made her shiver with an emotion that definitely was not fear.

Her lips parted but he beat her to it.

"You don't need to answer, Risa. Because I already know what you're going to say. I know because it's the same damn thing I would say."

"And what's that?"

He took another step closer and now he was close enough that she could breathe in his scent, masculine and clean. She wanted to lick him from his shirt collar to his ear, then she wanted to bite the lobe hard enough to make him groan.

She needed a response from him that wasn't so tightly controlled. She needed him to loosen up, just a little bit, and show her that he wasn't always so controlled.

"No. It wouldn't. It will never be good because it's not you."

It was exactly what she'd wanted to hear, what she'd needed to hear, and it made her shiver with pent-up lust.

"Then why did you never make a move?"

"Because this doesn't just involve the two of us."

"Well, maybe I am damn sick and tired of waiting."

"Risa—"

"Gens kissed me." The words blurted out before she could stop to them, but she needed him to know that whatever was going on between the three of them, Gens had already made the first move. "Earlier today. He thinks I'm making the safe choice to want you, both of you. He thinks I can't decide what I want for myself."

"Maybe he's right."

She rolled her eyes, shaking her head at the same time. "And maybe he's spouting bullshit to give you an out."

He frowned, staring at her from narrowed eyes. "And how the hell did you come to that conclusion?"

"Because he's worried that if you don't say yes, he's the consolation prize. Maybe you're thinking the same thing."

He didn't answer right away, and she could tell he was mulling that over, giving it some real thought without dismissing it out of hand.

Fear began to creep in, shoving out the hunger and frustration. If they both decided not to do this, she was finished.

She'd have to leave because she couldn't be anywhere near them knowing she'd lost the only two men she'd ever truly wanted. Yes, it might sound juvenile, might sound like the temper tantrum of a teenager who was dumped on prom night.

She hadn't gone to her prom. She'd been home with her dad, hosting a dinner party for a group of Chinese investors looking to get a foothold in the states. She'd enjoyed it more than she would have enjoyed the prom.

"Do you honestly think we can make a relationship like this work?"

It was totally not what she'd been expecting him to say, and she took a few seconds to really think about what she should say.

"My sister is. Mally is. Why can't I?"

He stared down at her, gaze burning.

"I'll move in next door with Gens for the next few days. We'll have dinner tonight and we'll talk some more."

She bit her tongue hard, because she really wanted to say she was done talking. She nodded instead.

And when he turned and walked away, she let out a sigh of relief only when he'd disappeared out the front door.

"Are you pissed? I can't tell. Please don't be pissed. I'm worried about your safety and this seemed like the best possible solution. I mean without them actually staying in this house with you. I figured this way, if you don't want to see them, you don't have to. But they'll be next door if you need them. But you'll be here. A wall between you. Shit, you're pissed, aren't you?"

By the time Dorrie finished, Risa was having a hard time controlling her smile.

Her sister had the most pitiful look on her face, which

would be funny if the situation weren't so goddamn confounding.

But it wasn't funny enough to let Dorrie off the hook right away.

Her sister had walked through the door a minute ago, taken one look at Risa's face, and winced.

Now, she continued to wait with a grimace on her face for Risa to respond.

"I'm not pissed."

Okay, maybe she was a little pissed. But not enough to torture her sister. At least, not for long.

She sighed. "I'm just not sure it will help my mental health to have them so close."

Dorrie's gaze narrowed. "Did something happen?"

With a sigh, Risa nodded her head toward the kitchen. "That's going to require a bottle of wine to explain."

Dorrie followed her back to the kitchen without comment. But when they finally had seats at the small table at the back of the kitchen overlooking the small backyard, full wineglasses in hand, Dorrie had apparently restrained herself as long as humanly possible.

"All right, Risa. Spill it. What happened?"

"Gens kissed me and then he accused me of using him to get over what had happened. And Tony still doesn't believe a three-way relationship can work. At least, not for him."

Dorrie's eyes had widened farther with every word until they wouldn't open any wider. Then she started to shake his head.

"I don't... I'm not even sure where to begin."

Risa took a healthy swallow of her wine before shaking her head and raising her glass in a sarcastic salute. "Welcome to the club. I want to smack them and then I want to tell them to go jump off a very high cliff. Somewhere far away from here. And you…" She pointed her glass at Dorrie. "You are definitely not off the hook. How could you think having them next door would be good for me? If you wanted me to run screaming back to Dad's house, well done, because I am this close," she squeezed her left thumb and forefinger together, "to doing it."

Dorrie sighed then took a drink. "Damn, I'm sorry, Ris. I honestly thought being here would be better for you. Dad wanted to send you away, like, west coast or Europe. I told him you wouldn't be happy that far away. Maybe I was wrong." Then wrinkled her nose. "And when you say Gens kissed you, you mean…"

"I mean he kissed me, tongue and all."

"Okay." Dorrie drew the word out to about five syllables. "And what did you do?"

"I kissed him back. And then he told me he didn't want to be with me simply because I thought he was safe."

Dorrie blinked, then tilted her head to the side, mulling that over. "Do you think that's true?"

"What? That I think he's safe and that's why I want to tear off his clothes and let him throw me on a bed and fuck me senseless?"

A shrug. "Well, when you put it that way, I guess I can see where you might be confused. But, Ris, is there some part of you that considers Gens safe? You've known him for years. You've lusted after him for years, but you've never had him. Same with Tony. Maybe, subconsciously, you do think they're safe. And I only mean that in the context that you know they would never physically hurt you."

"I told you I wasn't hurt."

And even though she hadn't been, just talking about being kidnapped made every muscle in her body tense.

Kissing Gens hadn't made her tense. Pushing Tony to be with her hadn't triggered any feelings that reminded her of what had happened.

What those incidents had triggered was a wave of frustration so intense, she wanted to kick and scream, not run and hide.

"I heard what you said, Ris. I also know not all wounds are visible. Or even recognizable to those who have them."

Risa clamped her lips closed on the words that wanted to escape, and she wanted to shriek in frustration.

"Look, I get that what I went through was traumatic. I understand I'm going to have issues. I've dealt with issues all my life. I know I'm fucked up and that's not going to change overnight."

"Wait, I never said—"

"But I've wanted those men for years, and being kidnapped didn't change that. It only made me realize that I'm sick of waiting around for them to make a move. Because tomorrow may be the day I get hit by a bus. Or kidnapped by some asshole who wants to sell me as a pawn to be used against my father."

Dorrie had her teeth lodged in her bottom lip by the time Risa had to stop to take a breath, heart pounding against her ribs like a trapped bird.

Okay, maybe she had a little suppressed anger. Maybe she really wasn't ready to jump into a relationship with two men, even if they were two men she'd been lusting after for years.

Maybe...

Tears welled, pissing her off until she seriously wanted to scream and throw things. Not the wine, though. Couldn't waste the wine. It might be the only thing keeping her sane at the moment.

"Maybe they're right."

"Maybe who's right?" Dorrie asked.

"Gens. Tony. You. Maybe you're all right. Maybe I'm not ready. Maybe I'll never be ready."

"No, Ris." Dorrie reached across the table and wrapped her hand around Risa's, which she hadn't realized was clenched into a fist. "That's not true and you know it. You're one of the strongest people I know. Any other person would've been a broken mess crying in a ball on the floor after what you went through."

"And maybe I just haven't processed it all yet."

"Probably not. It's going to take some time. Okay, so maybe you don't leap into bed with Gens and Tony right away. But don't shut them down before you test the waters. And maybe it doesn't work. But if you don't try, you'll never know. And after everything you've been through, I think you at least owe it to yourself to try."

Dorrie sounded so rational. Risa had always envied her sister's ability to be kind and compassionate, even when faced with unrelenting assholery. Maybe it went with the job. More likely, it was just Dorrie. It was why her men loved her unconditionally.

Maybe Risa was just too much of a bitch to be loved.

"Hey. What are you thinking?" Dorrie tightened her grip on her fist, which she consciously tried to loosen. And couldn't. "Whatever it is, I don't think it's good."

No, probably not. It probably revealed things about her Risa didn't want anyone else to know. But she couldn't keep it locked inside either.

"What if I'm just not loveable?"

"Bullshit," Dorrie said immediately. "That's total bullshit and you should know that. I love you. Dad loves you. Those stupid-ass men love you, even if they don't realize it yet."

She really wished she could believe that. "Two people, Dorrie." She wasn't counting those men. She couldn't. "You could only come up with two people. How cold am I that there are only two people in the world who love me?"

And oh my god. Could she be any more pitiful? Why the hell had she said that.

Dorrie's expression firmed, her mouth setting in a straight line. "That doesn't say anything about you, Ris. It says more about your life. And Dad bears a lot of that blame, not you. The life he chose hamstrung you from the beginning. I had it easier. I know that."

"It doesn't change the facts. And I am never *not* going to be Karel Antonoff's daughter."

"Then you need to take what you want when you get the opportunity. You want Tony and Gens, then take them. Figure out the rest of the shit later."

"And if it doesn't work?"

"If it doesn't work, you cry. And then you go out and find someone who will love you. And there *is* someone out there for you. Don't let anyone make you believe there isn't. Especially not two men who absolutely should know better than to believe you don't know what you want."

Dorrie started to smile. "And, Ris. Don't let them off the hook. Yeah, you've taken a hit. But you're not down and you're not out. And I will never bet against you. Go to dinner tonight and show them you're dinged but not broken. Go after what you want and don't let them try to manage you."

Risa nodded. But that little voice of doubt kept chirping in the back of her head.

Taunting her.

14

"Just get the hell out of the kitchen, for fuck's sake. You're not helping."

"You don't have to do everything yourself. I'm capable of chopping fucking onions."

"Well, you're doing it wrong. Just grab a beer and take a seat. You're in the way."

Gens did what he was told, but not before giving Tony the finger.

Tony left the meat browning in the pan to finish the onion. Gens had to admit, compared to what Tony was doing, he'd been butchering the damn thing.

Seconds later, Gens had poured himself a glass of wine from the bottle Tony had added into the meat and was leaning against the counter on the other side of the stove.

Tony had something on his mind and Gens had been trying to figure out the best way to get him to talk because he was pretty sure whatever Tony was keeping inside had something to do with Risa.

And if it had something to do with Risa, then it affected all of them.

Of course, he hadn't told Tony about what he'd said to Risa earlier, and he figured they needed to talk about that, too.

Shit. He wouldn't be surprised if she didn't show up.

"You're thinking so hard, you're giving me a fucking headache. Just spit it out, for chrissake."

Tony's words came out as a growl, surprising the shit out of Gens. He couldn't believe Tony was inviting him to question him. Especially tonight.

"Fine. What happened between you and Risa earlier?"

It took Tony a few seconds to answer and Gens could tell he didn't want to say anything. So he got a second shock when Tony actually answered.

"I invited her to dinner and told her I wasn't sure this was going to happen."

Since he knew what Tony meant, he didn't bother to ask. "Does this dinner mean you're at least willing to think about it?"

Another pause. "I'm not willing to walk away. At least not yet."

"Then you should probably know I kissed her earlier today."

A muscle in Tony's jaw twitched but he kept his mouth stubbornly closed. So Gens took his life in his hands and poked the bear.

"Nothing to say about that?"

Tony grabbed the cans of tomatoes off the counter and dumped them into the pan.

"Okay, fine. You don't want to talk. You can fucking

listen. We need to figure this out between us before she gets here."

Tony set the empty cans on the counter and reached for the wooden spoon again, deliberately stirring the pot. And sending Gens's blood pressure even higher.

"I'm willing to give her what she wants. Hell, I'm willing to try to give her everything she wants. But she wants both of us. You've got to figure out whether you can handle that. Because if you can't, we have to tell her tonight."

Reaching for the spice jars, Tony measured out oregano and basil and a few other herbs into his hands then dumped them into the pot.

Waiting him out this time took every ounce of his patience, but Gens controlled the urge to take a swing at his best friend. Finally, Tony brushed his hands over the pot, stirred it a few more times, then leaned against the counter to face Gens.

"What do you want me to say? That I'm gonna be okay watching you fuck her? That I'm gonna be okay being in the same bed with you while I fuck her? I don't have a fucking clue. Is that what you want to hear?"

Gens swallowed a sigh of relief and tried not to punch Tony for being an asshole and trying to rile up the situation.

"No. What I want to hear is you're either gonna commit or you're gonna take yourself out. You can't fuck with her and then tell her you can't take it. You're either in or you're out, and you have to be fucking sure."

"So you get to tell me how I have to feel? Is that how'd it be with Risa too? You'd control everything?"

It took an effort, but Gens managed not to snarl back. He

knew it wouldn't help, even though he wanted to tell Tony to fuck off.

"No, that's not how it would work. And if you'd calm the fuck down, you'd realize that."

Okay, maybe he wasn't doing such a good job toning down his own anger. But damn it, this wouldn't work if they weren't both on board.

Tony took a deep breath and Gens braced for another verbal attack. Tony could cut with his tongue just as well as he could with a blade. Just because he didn't say much most of the time didn't mean he couldn't cut you to the bone with a few words.

But Tony didn't lash out. Instead, he set his hands on the counter, bowed his head, and just breathed. Gens could hear him sucking in air until, finally, he shook his head.

After another few seconds, he lifted his head and turned to face Gens, mirroring his position, down to the arms crossed over his chest.

Gens had no idea what Tony was going to say. He couldn't read Tony's expression, another of his strengths. The guy was a fucking vault when he wanted to be.

"Do you love her?" Tony asked.

Gens's eyebrows shot up his forehead. He certainly hadn't expected that. And he wasn't sure how to answer.

"It's an easy question," Tony pushed, something he was good at. "Do you love her?"

No, it wasn't an easy question because, yeah, he did. From the moment he'd met her, he'd known she was important to him. The façade she presented to the rest of the world wasn't the real Risa and he loved that he got to see her true nature. The vulnerable side, the sweet side. The daughter who worried and fretted over her father and the sister who loved Dorrie with no reservation.

He also saw how much it cost her to hold all of that inside her when she was out in the world.

But he couldn't explain that to Tony without him walking out the door and never looking back. Tony was looking for any excuse to bail.

Gens wasn't going to give him one.

"I don't know. I only know I want to explore what we could have. And this is what she wants. Do you?"

To his credit, Tony responded. "I know I'm not ready to step back. So I guess we're going to have to work through this shit while we figure it out."

Relief hit Gens like a shot of good whiskey, making his lungs relax enough to breathe deeply. He tried not to be obvious about it, but Tony knew him too well. He shook his head and went back to stirring his sauce.

"Make yourself useful. Fill the pot with water and get it started."

Now, this felt more like normal. They'd been friends since grade school, had grown up in the same Philly neighborhood, and Gens had spent a lot of time at Tony's house, where Tony's Italian grandmother had fed them like she thought they would starve when they left the house.

Tony's parents had never once made him uncomfortable about what Gens's dad did for a living. Not that he'd known until he was about twelve. Yeah, he'd suspected but his parents hadn't talked about that shit. It just was what it was and you either got the hell over it or you moved the fuck out.

Same with Tony's parents, though Gens had always

suspected that Tony's dad had a few connections they didn't discuss in polite company, as Gens's mom used to say.

Then there was Tony's grandmother, whose husband had definitely been involved in organized crime. He'd had a heart attack when Tony had been in sixth grade. It was the first and only funeral Gens had attended until his parents'.

"Hey. Gens. The pot's overflowing."

Shit. Snapping out of his thoughts, Gens shut off the water and lugged the huge pot to the stove.

"You sure you're as okay with this as you say you are?"

Gens nodded at Tony's question before he leaned back against the counter. "Just thinking about your grandmother."

Tony grinned openly. "Nonna was the best. She had a soft spot for you. You almost never got whacked with the wooden spoon. I used to think she loved you more."

"Yeah, you know that's not true. You ever think about opening a restaurant? You cook just as good as she did."

Tony huffed out a laugh, still stirring. "Just because the food I make is edible compared to what you can do doesn't mean I should open a restaurant."

"True, but you'd be your own boss."

"Yeah, and that would mean I'd have all the headaches that came along with it." Tony slid him a glance. "You trying to tell me you want to go into business and open a restaurant?"

Gens shrugged. "Not sure what I'd contribute. I can't cook, I can't do the books. Guess I could be the bouncer."

Grabbing the dishrag from the counter, Tony grabbed his wineglass then mirrored Gens's position on the other side of the kitchen.

"Why do you do that?"

Tony looked seriously curious and Gens had no idea what the hell he was asking.

"What are you talking about?"

"Why do you make yourself out to be clueless muscle? You're one of the smartest people I know. I don't have a fucking degree. You do. So it's a freaking biology degree. I'd trust you to run a business over some snot-ass kid with a business degree from Temple."

"Then why—"

A noise from the next room caught Gens's ear and he turned to see Risa standing in the next room.

She didn't look at all guilty for eavesdropping. She looked curious, which was unusual for Risa. He'd seen her at her most unguarded, seen her vulnerable, seen her pissed off. But he could honestly say he'd never seen her this interested in anything.

Even when he'd watched her working on something for her foundation, he saw determination, not this open interest.

As if she realized he'd seen something she didn't want him to, the expression was gone in the blink of an eye, replaced by her typical aloof reserve.

But he knew what he'd seen.

She came forward, a bottle of wine in her hands. Because he was looking so closely, Gens could tell how uncertain she felt. And that was so unlike her, he wanted to punch the fucking wall.

"Sorry. I knocked but no one answered so I let myself in. Dorrie said the doorbell didn't work. I didn't mean to interrupt."

Before Gens could answer, Tony walked over to her and took the bottle.

"You're not interrupting. You want a glass of this?"

"I'll have whatever you're having. We don't need to open this one right away."

"Gens and I nearly kicked the bottle we were working on so you can get started on this and we'll join you, probably sooner rather than later."

"I really didn't mean to interrupt." She waved a hand toward the door. "If you want to finish your conversation—"

"The conversation was about you," Tony said, "but now that you're here, we can clear up a few things before we eat."

Okay, Gens wasn't going to punch the wall. He was going to punch Tony. Why the fuck—

"Good. I'm all ears."

Gens heard the relief in Risa's voice. Maybe he wouldn't punch Tony.

Damn it, he should've realized Risa would respond much better to straightforward honesty than pampered coddling.

"I'm willing to try to figure this out, whatever this is." Tony flicked a glance at Gens to include him. "But I'm still not convinced you're ready to jump into a relationship, especially one this...unconventional."

Fuck. Just...fuck. If Tony wanted to take this relationship down before it got started, he was doing a damn job of it.

"I didn't know you were an expert in my mental state."

Gens grinned as Risa shot back a response that made Tony's jaw set. Good. She needed Tony to see she wasn't going to let him dictate all the terms.

But Gens wasn't stupid enough to think Tony didn't have valid concerns.

"I'm not." Tony sounded like he was speaking through gritted teeth. Probably was. "I'm only trying to keep you from doing something you're going to regret later."

Risa took a deep breath. Gens could see her trying to shove down her response. He was almost upset that she finally managed to.

"The only thing I'm going to regret is coming to dinner if all you're going to do is worry you're somehow going to upset me. I'm not that fragile."

They stared each other down for several seconds, until Gens thought he might have to get between them and send them each to their respective corners. But that wouldn't get them anywhere.

"So, do you still want that drink or are you two going to snipe at each other some more?"

Tony and Risa turned their attention on Gens and he fought back a smile at the matching frustration he saw on their faces. Not anger, which was good. But a little frustration never hurt anyone.

In fact, it could stoke your desire hotter.

Risa was the first to recover.

"I'll take that drink. And whatever's cooking smells great. Since I know you can't cook to save your life," Risa smiled at Gens, "it must be Tony's handiwork. I didn't know you could cook."

Gens practically held his breath waiting for Tony to answer, and when he did, Gens covered his relief by turning to get Risa a glass from the cabinet.

"It never came up in conversation. My grandmother owned a restaurant when I was a kid. I spent a lot of time with her in the kitchen."

Out of the corner of his eye, Gens saw Tony turn back to the stove.

Then he took a deep breath and prepared for a bumpy night.

Stop being an asshole.

Tony must have repeated this to himself at least a hundred times since Risa had walked through the door tonight.

After that first, tense exchange when he'd nearly derailed the entire night—and pissed off Gens—he'd managed to get his mood swings under control by focusing on things other than what had happened to her.

When she'd asked Tony about his grandmother, he'd practically sighed with relief. Finally, a subject with no pitfalls. For the most part.

They'd talked about his grandparents, how his Italian immigrant grandmother had fallen for a Russian immigrant who also happened to be a Jew, shocking her parents and their families, who'd tried their damnedest to break them up. Hadn't worked because his grandmother had been a force of nature who, once she decided on something, wasn't going to be turned from her course.

Risa reminded him of his nonna, in some ways. She had the same fierce determination, but where you never had any doubt where his grandmother had stood on any subject, Risa could be a goddamn brick wall.

He wanted to be allowed behind that wall, but he'd realized he had a damn long road to go if he was going to get there.

Gens had the advantage of knowing her for years. Like, right now.

"Barbie still blames me for you never asking her out." Risa pointed at Gens with her empty fork. "She says I cock-blocked her."

Gens laughed, seemingly so at ease. "She was always a bitch. There was no way in hell I was ever going out with her to begin with, I don't care who her father was."

"Well, she thought I had to have something to do with your rejection because otherwise you would have been worshipping at her feet. I told her she was delusional because you weren't the kind of guy who worshipped anyone."

Gens went silent for a second, and Tony could practically see Gens's gears working. Risa had turned her attention back to her food, but Gens continued to watch her.

"Do you still think that?"

Because he was watching her so closely, Tony saw the way her lips pursed for a second before she let them curve up in a slight grin that he could tell held little amusement.

"Honestly, I don't know. Our relationship hasn't been as close as it was back then."

"Do you ever wonder why that is?"

If she was taken back by Gens's question, she didn't show it. She was rebuilding her wall, brick by brick. And that made him want to tear it down with his bare hands. Which he couldn't do if he kept himself on the sidelines.

She set her fork by her plate, maintaining eye contact

with Gens. "I sometimes think you just don't want the hassle of being friends with me."

Gens's mouth dropped open. "What the hell does that mean?"

"It means I know I can be…difficult." She flashed a look at Tony that made him narrow his gaze. "My…friendship," she said the word almost like she was testing it, "with Mally has highlighted my deficiencies in that department."

"What do you mean, deficiencies?"

Even though Tony felt he knew exactly what she meant, he needed her to say it out loud.

He'd sat on the sidelines for most of this conversation between her and Gens, mainly because he didn't know the people they were talking about. But now, he was pretty sure he wasn't going to like her answer.

"I know I can be cold and difficult to get to know. I don't trust people easily and that makes me come off as a bitch."

Yep, that's exactly what he thought she was going to say. And yeah, it pissed him off to hear her talk about herself like that.

"You're not a bitch, Risa."

She and Gens turned to look at him. He kept his attention squarely on Risa, who he could tell wanted to say something to him.

The Risa from before the kidnapping would have demanded he continue, would've forced him to give her an explanation of his statement. Now, she shrugged him off.

"The fact remains. People believe I am. It's a hard perception to change, especially when you don't know that you want to change it."

"And why is that?" Tony leaned back in his chair and kept his gaze squarely on hers.

"You know why that is." She didn't back down this time or shrug him off. "For the same reason you act like a hard-ass. To keep people away. We do a damn good job of it."

Well, shit. She was absolutely right. He couldn't deny it.

"So what exactly are we doing here tonight?"

"We," Gens broke in, "are having dinner and trying to see if we have a chance in hell of giving you what you want. Don't make me put you over my knee and spank you for being a brat."

The look on Risa's face was priceless. Stunned amazement followed by total shock. Her lips parted as if she was going to say something. After a few seconds, she must have realized that her mouth was hanging open and snapped it shut. That's when Tony realized her cheeks were turning pink.

Damn, he'd never seen her blush. Her skin was so pale, she couldn't hide her response. It made her look young, especially when she blinked and dropped her gaze.

Interesting.

After a few more seconds of silence, her mouth firmed, and she lifted her head. Staring straight at Gens, she said, "How do you know I wouldn't like that?"

Lust hit Tony like a punch in the gut, stealing his breath and forcing him to suck in air. Neither Risa nor Gens seemed to notice, their attention focused fully on each other.

With a flash of insight, he realized he was getting a glimpse of what it would feel like to watch Risa and Gens in bed.

He didn't hate it.

That was the second punch to the gut, but he didn't manage to hide his reaction this time because Risa slid her attention his way and the heat he saw there made his heart pound double-time.

Out of the corner of his eye, Tony saw Gens's gaze narrow, but Tony kept his attention squarely on Risa.

Leaning back in his seat, he crossed his arms over his chest. "Would you like that?"

She blinked but didn't drop his gaze. "I don't know. I've never allowed anyone that close. I'm not sure I ever will."

Well, fuck. His chest felt like an elephant had sat on him and his cock hardened until he swore he could bat with it. His lungs contracted, forcing him to part his lips so he could breathe deeply.

"But you want to, don't you?"

When she didn't answer, he pushed a little more.

"Would you allow Gens to? Would you allow me to watch?"

The pink in her cheeks deepened and he had a mental flash of her bare ass cheek turning the same bright color as Gens brought his hand down.

"I don't think," she paused to take a breath, "I want to answer that question."

"Why is that?"

"Because I'm not sure I want to know the answer."

"If you don't know the answer, what are we doing here tonight? Maybe I'm right and you're just not ready for any of this."

He wanted her to get pissed off, wanted to get a rise out of her. He figured it was better than this quiet, diminished version of the woman he'd known before her kidnapping.

He didn't expect her to just sit there, quietly staring back at him.

God damn it, he was going to find the bastard who had taken her and rip his fucking head off—

She rose from her chair slowly, barely making a sound.

Sonuvabitch. He'd pushed her just far enough to make her walk away.

But she didn't. She stood there staring at him, as if contemplating her next move.

His breath caught in his throat, and he swallowed down the urge to stand as well and walk around the table to get to her.

He also knew he needed her to make the first move, so he knew whatever happened next was what she wanted.

Tony could tell Gens thought the same as he sat with his hands braced on the table. Maybe he was holding himself in place. Tony didn't know, didn't care. As long as Gens didn't interfere.

After what seemed like forever, she moved. And now he did catch his breath...because she started toward him.

She kept her eyes on him as she made her way around the table to stand by his side. The chairs had no arms and he swung one leg over so he could face her more directly.

He wasn't expecting her to do anything more than talk to him and then leave.

So when she leaned down and put her mouth against his, he went still.

Don't scare her.

The first touch of her lips set off a spark deep inside, an ache that crept slowly through his body as she let her lips linger on his. She kissed him softly, at first, her lips pressed against his without moving. She seemed to be taking it slowly, feeling him out.

He didn't want to startle her or do anything to make her step back. He wanted to part his lips and draw her even closer, taste her deeper. But he kept telling himself not to rush her. To let her go at her own pace.

That didn't mean he didn't enjoy it.

Just having her this close made his muscles tighten with the urge to grab her and pull her onto his lap and kiss her how he wanted. Nothing held back. No restrictions. And no fear.

Instead, he sat there and let her lead.

Keeping his eyes closed, he breathed her in through his nose, her perfume causing his fingers to flex on his thighs. He almost reached for her then, but she moved, changing the angle of her lips, and he felt the first touch of her tongue against his lips.

His lips parted with a barely suppressed groan. How the fuck was he supposed to keep his damn hands to himself when he'd wanted to kiss her for years?

Every part of his body hardened as he forced himself to stay still in his chair, trying to give her the freedom—

With a growl of frustration, Risa pulled away and huffed out a sigh. Her hands left his shoulders and resettled on her hips as she glared down at him.

His gaze narrowed as he realized she wasn't going to continue.

"Are you really that uninterested in me? Do you want me to—"

With one hand on her hip, he pulled her down onto his lap, wrapped his hand around her chin, and held her steady.

He watched her draw in a deep breath as he moved his head toward hers, his lips hovering centimeters away from hers.

"What I want you to do is say yes."

Her eyes went as wide as they could go a second before she nodded.

"I want to hear you say it."

Her expression didn't change as her lips parted and she said, "Yes."

"Good answer."

15

Tony didn't give her time to say anything more. He swooped in and kissed her. Hard. Probably too hard. He thought about letting up a little, but she wriggled her ass on his thighs as she turned, her hip brushing against his throbbing cock.

Goddamn. Heat ripped through him and the hand he had on her hip tightened, wanting her even closer. He had to make a conscious effort to keep the hand on her chin loose. Didn't want anything to remind her of the few days she'd been captive.

But going by her response, that wasn't on her mind at all.

Her hands came up to frame his face as she faced him fully, tilted her head to the side, and let him kiss her. She gave herself over to him completely, let him consume her as his hunger became a raging beast.

The softness of her body pressed against his made his blood thunder through his veins. He wanted to move his hands, currently splayed across her back, to her ass to bring her even closer, to pet the sleek muscle that taunted him whenever he watched her walk away.

Nothing had prepared him for the actual feel of her in his arms.

His every instinct wanted more, faster.

He wanted to strip off her clothes like he'd imagined doing every fucking day since the moment he'd met her. Wanted to spread her out on the damn dining room table and put his mouth between her legs and lick her until she screamed his name.

Wanted Gens to hold her down while he did it.

The thought made his brain stutter and his fingers tightened reflexively. Risa moaned into his mouth, her arms tightening even more around his neck as she squirmed closer.

Now her hip pressed hard against his cock and her mouth and tongue were fully engaged with his. He wasn't sure he could stop, even if he wanted to. And there was no way in hell he wanted to right now.

Releasing her chin, he let that hand trace the curve of her jaw to her neck then down to her shoulder. Her shirt had a v-neck and the tips of his fingers brushed against her collarbone. He felt her shiver, felt her shift on his lap, making every muscle in his body ache with restraint.

He wanted to lift her and rearrange her on his lap until her legs straddled his, wanted to feel her breasts crushed against his chest, feel the softness between her legs pressed against his aching cock.

As if she'd read his mind, she moved again, putting her hands on his shoulders and attempting to swing her right leg over his lap.

Grabbing her around the waist, he lifted her just enough

that she could get where she wanted to be, which was exactly where he wanted her to be.

Then he took a second to pull back and make sure she was really with him.

Her eyes opened at the same time and looked straight into his. He saw nothing but desire.

Thank Christ.

As soon as her ass hit his thighs, he spread his hands across her back and pressed her close again. This time, she came flush against him. Her breasts hit his chest as she tilted her head and meshed their lips together again.

The sense of relief that swept through him when she came back into his arms willingly would've been embarrassing if anyone other than Gens had been there to witness it.

A second later, he honestly couldn't have cared less because his entire focus was her. The weight of her body on his thighs made him crave more of her. That craving should've tempered his response. Instead, it made his desire for her explode.

His arms tightened around her as his head tilted to the side and he kissed her so deeply, he felt like he could consume her. He wanted to lose himself in her, have her lose herself in his arms.

But they had an audience.

He tried not to think about Gens sitting across the table, watching them. Tried to completely put it out of his mind. Instead, the knowledge festered.

No, not festered. It simmered.

Was Gens pissed because he wanted the same from her? How would he feel watching Gens put his hands all over her?

Desire ate like acid at his gut as his hands ran down her back to cup her ass. The sleek muscles warmed under his hands, sending that heat into his blood until he could think of nothing but making her want exactly what he did.

Slow and easy seemed to have been replaced by fast and hard. He still wasn't sure that was a good thing. But when her hand slid from his neck to his shoulders then down his back, he lost that train of thought and chased the next one.

That train wanted to shoot out of the station and head straight for the nearest bed.

Slow down.

He couldn't seem to find the brake. His hands gripped her ass and brought her closer, his cock hard and aching for relief. Relief he was only going to find in her body.

Pulling away, he moved back far enough that she had to look at him.

"I need to know you're going to stop me if we cross a line you're not ready to cross."

She blinked, as if trying to process his words. Then her brows arched.

"And I need to know if you're going to be able to cross your lines." She deliberately looked behind her at Gens before turning back.

On the other side of the table, Gens sat with his arms crossed over his chest, no smile on his lips, but a heat in his eyes that was hard to miss.

"Don't mind me." Gens flicked his gaze to Tony. "I'm perfectly content to sit and watch the show. For now."

The deliberate taunt in Gens's voice forced Tony to acknowledge it or ignore it.

"Then let's move this show somewhere more comfortable."

Tony caught a glimpse of Gens's smile before he refocused his attention on Risa. Her expression held hope tinged with a slight hint of hesitation.

His gaze narrowed. "You okay with that?"

Her immediate nod made him breathe easier. But he still wanted to know what that hesitation was about.

"Then what—"

"I'm worried you won't follow through." Her low-pitched voice hit a chord deep inside him. "I'm worried this will be too much for you and you'll walk away and won't look back."

Hell no. "I'm still here. I'm not going anywhere. If this is really what you want, I'm ready to give it to you."

Her eyes seemed to brighten but she shook her head. "I need you to spell it out. I need you to tell me you're not going to walk out on me when this gets more...personal."

Her gaze didn't falter and neither did his.

"When you say more personal, you mean when you're naked and I have my mouth between your legs and Gens has his cock in your mouth?"

Her mouth dropped open at his bluntness and her eyes widened in shock. Then that pink blush washed across her cheeks again. Her breath audibly caught in her throat and she swallowed hard. His gaze dropped to watch her lips part as she sucked in air.

He leaned forward to kiss that surprise off her lips. She froze for a moment before she melted into him, her arms tightened around his neck and dragging him even closer.

He sucked her scent into his lungs and licked his way into

her mouth, tasting her desire and letting her pull him under even farther.

Was she messing with his head? Maybe.

Was he going to regret this? No. Absolutely not. He'd never regret one damn minute spent with her.

And if he had to share her...he'd come to terms with it because it's what she wanted.

Standing, one arm around her waist, the other around her shoulders, he released her mouth and looked at Gens, who rose more slowly.

When Gens nodded, Tony set Risa on her feet. She wasn't expecting it and she wobbled for a second. Tony kept his hands on her waist, making sure she was steady before he turned her toward the living room...and smacked her ass to get her going.

The look she gave him over her shoulder made him grin. Her look promised retribution. That look was from the Risa he'd known before the kidnapping.

Raising his brows, he crossed his arms over his chest. Out of the corner of his eye, he saw Gens smiling. Luckily for him, Risa didn't, or he would've been on the receiving end of that look of hers, too.

Selfishly, Tony wanted that look for himself. Probably not a good start but something he'd work on getting over.

Then he put it out of his head and focused on the woman still glaring at him. She made him hard and hot and so fucking horny he knew he wouldn't fucking care if he had an audience, just so long as he had her.

"Move, Risa. Or I'm going to think you want out."

He saw her lips firm then part, as if she wanted to say something. And she did. He could see it in her eyes.

Instead, she looked at Gens for several long seconds before she headed for the front room.

Tony watched her take the first steps toward the living room before he turned to Gens. Who stared back with his brows raised. Waiting. Daring him.

Tony had come too far to back down now. Hell, he didn't want to back down. He'd made up his damn mind and now he was ready to take this step and not look back.

"What?"

Gens grinned openly. "Not a damn thing." He waved a hand in front of him but didn't say another word.

It was on the tip of Tony's tongue to ask Gens how they should handle this. Until he realized Gens had already told him.

Tony followed her into the front room, where she stood in front of the couch, staring at him with her chin in the air and her arms crossed over her chest.

The heat in her gaze hadn't abated, and now he saw how fast her breasts rose and fell with her breathing. She wasn't as calm as she tried to appear.

Good. He wanted to keep her off-kilter. It would help keep her from dwelling on the past.

He walked straight to her, stopping only inches away. She had to lift her head to look him in the eyes and he realized she wasn't as tall as he'd always imagined her to be. She'd always seemed larger than life to him, her personality so forceful, that he was always shocked when he stood this close and realized the top of her head only came to his chin.

Dressed in a plain pale purple t-shirt, washed-pale jeans, and a pair of loose sandals, she looked younger than he'd ever seen her. She wore little if any makeup and her hair hung loose around her shoulders and down her back.

She'd never looked younger. Or sexier.

"You're beautiful."

The color in her cheeks deepened and he couldn't stop himself from reaching for a long, loose curl that lay against one perfect breast. His fingertips brushed against the upper mound, but he wasn't trying to cop a feel. No, he wanted to rub the strands between his fingers, to see if it was as silky as it looked.

Her breasts quivered with each breath, drawing his gaze and making his own breath catch in his throat. Wrapping that curl around his fingers, he watched her as he released it slowly.

Her lids lowered but she didn't drop his gaze as her arms released and fell to her side.

"I want to strip you naked and put my hands all over your body." His voice sounded rough, brutal. He needed to temper it, but he wasn't sure he could. And he needed to know. "But you have to be sure. I don't want to do anything to make you uncomfortable."

"If I wasn't sure, I wouldn't be here."

She sounded so damn confident, he wanted to take her at her word.

Hell, maybe he was the one who wasn't sure. Which sucked. Because he finally had her exactly where he'd wanted her for so fucking long.

"You only have to say stop and—"

"Stop talking," she said. "How about that for—"

Wrapping one hand around her neck, he yanked her forward and covered her mouth with his, kissing her hard and releasing the pent-up desire searing him from the inside out.

She came without hesitation, her arms winding around his waist as she tucked her body against his. Her breasts nestled against his chest and his erection pressed against her stomach. Not exactly how he wanted everything to line up, but his brain was having trouble keeping up with all the sensory input.

Her lips moved under his, opening to allow her tongue to slip into his mouth, teasing him until he groaned into her mouth as heat continued to build in his lower body. When her hands spread across his back then moved lower, he had to consciously loosen the hand around her neck. She petted him and every muscle in his body tightened to the point of pain.

He realized he'd allowed her to set the pace but that was fast becoming a problem. Because he knew she needed more from him. His hand on her hip slid around to her ass, palming one firm cheek and moving her even closer, while the hand on her neck slid down her arm until he could cup one perfect breast in his palm.

The sound she made as he squeezed confirmed his suspicion that Risa liked pressure. She liked it a little harder. Maybe a little rougher. The problem was going to be reining in his baser instincts before they became too much for her.

Because he liked sex rough. Hard. Forceful. He liked to be dominant in bed and the women he usually took were submissive.

Risa was not submissive.

But she also wasn't saying no.

He kissed her harder, chased her tongue back and practically fucked her mouth with his. When her body went even softer against his, he squeezed her ass a little tighter and ground his erection against her belly. Blood throbbed through his cock, making him ache. Making him want to ram inside her and come until he passed out. Or she did.

And then he'd watch Gens take her. He'd be able to watch how she opened her mouth to let him in even farther. How she pressed her breasts even harder against his chest, as if she needed more than he was giving her.

Maybe she did.

With another smack to her ass, he moved that hand to her other breast and now he squeezed, just a little harder than before. Her breasts overflowed his hands and now he wanted to see them, taste them.

She moaned into his mouth, her hips grinding against his with more urgency now. Breaking away from the temptation of her mouth, he sucked in air as he stared down. She looked dazed, blinking up at him.

Lifting one hand to cup her chin, he brushed his thumb over the swollen curves of her lips.

"Take your shirt off, sweetheart. I need to see you." He paused. "And I'm pretty damn sure Gens will enjoy the show, too."

Tony saw her turn to the left, where Gens was sprawled on the chaise lounge across from the couch.

"Don't mind me." Gens's voice sounded low and raspy. "I'm content to wait my turn."

And then Tony would be watching. He got hotter thinking about it.

For now, he pushed that thought out of his head and concentrated only on Risa.

She turned back to face him, her expression still a little dazed. She didn't move right away, simply continued to stare into his eyes. But then she drew in a deep breath…and gripped the hem of her shirt. She stripped it over her head without hesitation and let it drop to the floor. The lace bra she wore left absolutely nothing to the imagination. The pattern enticed him to run his tongue along it. The straps barely seemed wide enough to hold her weight.

Her nipples poked through, and his chest hollowed at the idea of putting his mouth on them.

What the hell are you waiting for?

Cupping her breasts in his hands again, he leaned forward and sealed his mouth on one nipple. The lace felt rough but as he wet it with his tongue, it became softer. Risa shivered, her hands gripping his shoulders, fingers pinching deep.

He swore he heard her moan, a low, deep sound in her chest, as she arched her back and pushed more of her breast into his mouth. Sucking at the tight tip, he laved it with his tongue until he felt her take a breath then he switched tactics and nipped at her until she squirmed.

Switching to the other side, Tony gave that breast the same treatment, letting her every move guide him. When she arched, he sucked her deeper. When she twisted, as if to get away, he nibbled the flesh between his teeth.

All the while, her pelvis rubbed against his cock, inciting his lust to grow even hotter. He could only take so much before he clapped one hand on her waist, yanking her forward so he could grind himself against her.

Her arms slid around his neck now and she went onto her toes, trying to get closer.

"Tony."

He'd never heard anyone say his name with such deep yearning before. The fact that it was Risa made him hungry to hear her say it again.

Wrapping her hair around one fist, he tugged her head back as he laid a string of kisses up her chest to her shoulder. From there, he nuzzled his nose into the curve of her neck then rubbed the tip up her soft skin to right below her left ear.

She shivered but bent her head back even farther, giving him more access.

Back at her mouth now, he kissed her like he'd been starved for her for decades and she kissed him back just as hard. He had his tongue deep in her mouth when he released the clasp on her bra with a twist of his fingers.

Her moan was followed by her hands gripping his t-shirt and shoving it up to his chest.

He obliged her unspoken request and reached behind him to rip the shirt over his head, stepping back only for as long as it took him to shed the shirt and drop it to the floor. Stepping back into her, he took another second to pull her bra down her shoulders and let it drop to the floor, as well.

Damn, she made him want to lay her out on the sofa, spread her legs and pound into her.

Slow down. Savor. Don't rush.

But holy hell, it was impossible to go slow when she practically threw herself at him, her arms wrapping around his shoulders as she went on tiptoe and rubbed her breasts against his pecs.

One arm went under her ass as he lifted her off the floor. Her legs wrapped around his waist without any urging on his part and he wished to hell he'd taken off her jeans. Because the feel of her soft flesh against him made his blood heat and pound through his veins.

Her kisses turned a little desperate now, as if he wasn't giving her what she needed. And that wasn't fair, was it?

"What do you need, Ris?" Tony kept his voice low as he moved his mouth to her ear, but he still spoke loud enough for Gens to hear. "What do you want?"

"I want you to make me come. I need it."

Just the sound of that word coming from her mouth made his cock pulse against the zipper of his jeans. When he finally did get his pants off, his dick would bear the impression.

"How do you want me to get you off first? With my fingers? Or with my mouth?"

She shuddered, sucking in an audible breath as her forehead landed on his shoulder.

"I want both. Everything. Anything. I just need you to make me come."

"Do you want Gens to put his hands on you, too?"

Her head lifted, her gaze connecting with his. She didn't say anything right away, just stared, until finally, she took a deep breath. "Yes. Can you han—"

He kissed the question off her lips, taking his time and making sure she understood what he was saying before he spoke.

"If that's what you want, that's what you'll get."

Worry created little furrows on her brow. He didn't want her to worry about anything.

"I think she needs to be convinced." He turned to look at

Gens, still sprawled in the chair across the room. "Are you going to help me show her I can handle this?"

The subtle grin on Gens's lips was for her. The question in his raised eyebrows was for Tony.

"If that's what you want."

Tony would deal with Gens's attitude later. Right now, he was focused on Risa.

"It's what she wants. And tonight, she gets to call the shots."

Gens sat forward. "But only to a certain extent. Because I'm pretty sure she was enjoying the whole dominance thing. Weren't you, Ris?"

So Gens had noticed that, too? When her lids lowered to hide her gaze for a few brief seconds, Tony knew they were right.

Good.

"I'm going to set you down and I want you to strip off the rest of your clothes."

He saw the first hint of hesitation now as her gaze skipped to the windows, all of them covered with heavy drapes.

"Don't you want to go upstairs?"

"No."

Honestly, he didn't want to take the time to walk up the stairs. All the doors were closed and locked. All the windows secured and covered. No one could see inside.

And he had to admit he liked the idea of her naked and spread out on that couch.

She swallowed hard and nodded fast. Then he lowered her back to the ground and let her get her feet before he took a step back and hooked his thumbs in his pockets.

Her gaze swept from him to Gens, who stood and started to make his way to them.

When Gens stood at her side with only a foot or so between them, she took a breath, unbuttoned her jeans and toed off her sandals.

Every muscle in Tony's body went taut. His immediate reaction was to strip the damn jeans off himself. But that would've defeated the purpose.

Apparently, he and Gens were in agreement on this because Gens held his ground, even when she pushed the denim down her legs then had to bend to get them off her feet. His gaze devoured the naked line of her back and the curve of her ass.

His jaw tightened enough to crack, Tony managed to hold himself steady as she straightened and stood before him naked. His fingers actually fucking ached to touch her.

Risa watched him with defiance in the lift of her chin, but her eyes held a hint of worry.

Was she going to back out now? What the hell was she worried about? He was about to ask when he realized what she was thinking.

"Are you seriously worried that I *don't* think you're the sexiest fucking woman I've ever seen?"

Holy shit. That's exactly what she'd been thinking because her cheeks flushed bright red.

"Risa—"

"How would I know otherwise?" Now her expression was pure pissed-off female. "You avoid me most of the time and ignore me if you can't. What was I supposed to think?"

Christ, were they really going to have this conversation now? With her naked and him so fucking aroused, he hurt?

No, they weren't. But he needed to make sure she knew exactly how wrong she was.

"You're absolutely right. And we'll talk about that later. But first, I'm going to make it up to you. Sit on the couch and spread your legs."

She froze, and he thought he might've finally pushed her too far. Then she blinked and sucked in air like she'd been suffocating. But she still didn't move.

Fuck.

No, if they were going to do this, he couldn't second-guess everything.

This was him. She either took him as he was, or she walked out. He wasn't going to sugarcoat anything for her. If she wanted him to be okay with this situation, she had to be okay with who he was. How he was.

After several silent seconds, she moved. And he released the breath he'd been holding.

She turned her head to look at the couch, staring for a couple of heartbeats. Then she turned back to look at him, then at Gens, then back to him.

The color remained in her cheeks, but her lips had softened enough to hint at a grin.

"Am I going to be the only one naked?"

Relief shot through him, singeing his nerve endings and forcing even more blood into his cock. The pressure continued to build until desire gnawed at his lower body and threatened to spread everywhere.

He needed to rein it in or he'd come in his jeans. And that wasn't an option.

"No. But if I take off my clothes now, you'll be spread out

under me in a split second and I have other plans before that happens."

He heard her drag in a deep breath before she closed the short distance between her and the couch. He watched her perfect ass the entire way and, when she turned back to face him, he had a hard time dragging his gaze up her body. Because now he was staring at the slightly darker blond hair on her mound.

She'd trimmed it into a neat little inverted triangle that pointed exactly where he wanted to go. Where he wanted to put his mouth and his hands and, eventually, his cock.

When she didn't sit right away, he looked up into her eyes.

Holding his gaze, she lowered herself onto the couch as if she were seating herself on a throne. Thighs still pressed together, she situated herself with her back against the cushions and her hands on the cushions on either side.

The oversize couch looked like it'd been chosen for exactly how he planned to use it tonight. Wide and deep enough to accommodate all three of them in whatever position they wanted to try.

He wanted to try them all.

So why the hell didn't you go upstairs?

He shoved the question to the back of his mind, where it couldn't fuck with him. Because if he let it, it would.

Instead, he walked to the couch and stood in front of her. Gens remained behind.

Amazingly, that didn't bother Tony.

"I told you to spread your legs."

Holding his gaze, she moved her legs apart.

His gaze dropped and so did he, to his knees. He went down slow and ended exactly where he planned to spend the next hour, at least. Between her legs.

She sucked in a breath as he gripped her thighs and spread her legs apart even farther. He felt her tremble beneath his hands, her muscles quivering, but her gaze steady as his thumbs caressed her soft skin.

The strength in her gaze made his lips curve in a slight smile.

Finally, he let his gaze fall.

Christ. So fucking pretty.

Bare except for the hair on her mound. She made his mouth water for a taste.

"Are you going to let me have everything I want?"

A breath. Two. "Yes."

"Then lean back and keep your eyes on me. I want you to watch."

As she complied, he moved in. Slowly. He was no longer worried about scaring her. Now, he wanted to please her. Wanted to take his time with her.

And then he'd sit back and watch Gens take her. The thought made him even hungrier.

Close enough now to touch her, he dragged his hands up her thighs until his thumbs reached her labia. Gently, he spread her lips until he could see her clit.

Then he put his mouth on her.

As she groaned above him, he used his tongue and lips to make her squirm. The taste of her hit him hard, practically stealing his breath. The hunger he thought couldn't get any hotter seared him to the core. The urge to hear her scream out his name built deep in his gut, his tongue working her clit with a sure, steady pressure.

He learned what made her sigh, what made her squirm, and what made her pant.

And when she opened her legs even farther, he slid his hands under her ass and pulled her forward, thrusting his tongue into her slit and fucking her with it.

With a groan, she gripped his shoulders, fingers digging into the muscle, making him work her that much harder. She proved, with every sound she made, that she wanted him, wanted this. Wanted to come. It made him want to give her that and so much more.

Looking up at her, he pulled away until only the tip of his tongue remained on her clit. Then he pulled that away, too.

Risa rolled her hips, trying to follow him, her fingers clutching him tighter.

"Tony. Please."

Giving her another lick for saying his name, he felt his cock throb as her breasts swayed.

He needed to taste her nipples, feel them harden against his tongue. But first...

He licked through her slit, tasting the honey seeping from her. Tilting her even closer to his mouth, he now had a singular purpose. To make her scream as she came.

Ravaging her with his mouth and tongue and teeth, he let himself go, let himself forget where they were. Let himself only have one goal.

Nipping at her clit, he heard her breath catch, his teeth catching at her swollen flesh, maybe a little harder than he should have. But when he made a move to pull back, she put one hand on his head and held him in place.

So he did it again. This time, she moaned even louder. She liked that hint of pain. He gave her a little more. And when her back arched, he shoved his tongue inside her channel and felt her convulse around him.

For those long, long seconds that she came on his tongue, he let his own hunger burn even hotter, let it consume him until he could barely contain it.

And when she finally eased back into the cushions again, he pulled away and watched her gasp for air.

Then his hand went to the button on his jeans. She didn't notice him undo that but when he cranked the zipper, her eyes blinked open and she met his gaze, hers bleary with lust.

"You're on the pill, yes? Because I don't have condoms. I'm clean and I don't want anything between us. I'd never do anything to hurt you, Ris."

For a second, he thought she was going to deny him or, at least, tell him to get a condom.

Instead, she reached for him with one hand then leaned forward so she could touch him. Putting her hands on the waistband of his jeans, she pushed them down, helping him release his cock from its confines. It sprang forward, seemingly with a mind of its own.

Hell, even his little head wasn't stupid. It knew where it wanted to be.

They worked his jeans down far enough to get his cock free and then, finally, she put her hand on him. He almost came right then and there.

Her fingers wrapped around his shaft and squeezed, her index finger and thumb forming a collar under the head. The pressure was almost too much to bear but she'd read him correctly. He liked it rough.

Dragging her hand down his shaft, she didn't stop until she reached the base then ringed him tightly as her fingers swept under his balls to fondle them.

He let her play with him, let his head fall back as she brought herself closer. She kept one hand on his cock and the other on his head, rubbing her hand on the bristles covering his head. As if she liked the feel of them against her skin.

Concentrating on the hand between her legs, he clamped down on his urge to thrust into her hand.

Her fingers teased along his balls before moving back to his cock, sliding along the taut skin and sliding all the way up to the tip. Rubbing her thumb over the slit, she spread his precum over the sensitive skin.

After several long moments, he couldn't take any more. Grabbing her by the hips, he slid her into his arms as he took her seat on the couch and settled her knees on either side of his.

She rearranged herself easily, eagerly, scooting forward until the tip of his cock almost touched the lower lips he'd made slick and puffy.

"Come on, Ris. Come closer. Sit on my cock."

Her gaze blinked up to his and he wondered if the language was too much for her. Not that it mattered. This was him. She'd said she wanted every part of him. She'd either deal or she'd walk. He'd walk funny for a week, but he wouldn't try to stop her if she left. This was all for her.

She moved even closer with a hitched breath and burning excitement in her eyes.

Taking his cock in her hand again, she pulled him away

from his stomach. He was so hard, she had to hold him there as she maneuvered into position.

His cock poised at her entrance, she held steady long enough for him to look up at her. And then she started to take him in.

She went slow as the head split her lips then lodged at her slit. He wasn't long but he was wide, so he understood her caution.

Until he saw her lips curve and realized it wasn't caution. No, it was pure, sensual tease. Every centimeter he gained made her smile widen as his jaw set.

Holy fuck. She scalded him. He couldn't remember the last time he'd had sex without a condom. Didn't care to because he'd only remember this first time. With her.

So hot and wet. And tight. Her pussy gripped him like a fist, her flesh barely ceding to him. She didn't stop, though, didn't adjust, didn't wriggle.

She...just...slid...down. A centimeter at a time, until finally she'd taken him in as far as she could. And then she wrapped her hands around his neck, leaned in to rub her nose against his then spoke against his lips.

"Fuck me. Hard. Please."

That word on her lips struck something deep inside, made him burn even hotter.

Taking her at her word, he gripped her hips and lifted her. Her sex gripped him tight, but she was so wet, he wasn't worried about hurting her when he took her as hard as he wanted.

He started slow, savoring the friction that seared him to his core. The glacier pace taxed his control, but he'd be damned if he rushed. He wanted everything she had to give and then he wanted more.

Her eyelids fluttered shut as he let gravity bring her down, pushing him high inside. Her fingers dug grooves into his shoulders, her lips parted as he spread her, his cock thickening even more as she moaned.

His lungs tightened until they fucking hurt, until he had to do something to ease the tension. Tilting his head, he kissed her. He took her mouth, locking their lips together. Slipped his tongue between her lips and tangled them together, tasting her.

Risa bucked in his hold and tried to increase their pace, but he wasn't ready. He wanted to savor every second.

Every throb of his cock as he pushed his way back inside her. Every drag of flesh on flesh as he pulled out. His heart thundered against his ribs and he heard the blood rush in his ears. It nearly drowned out the sound of her moans that rumbled in her throat and into his mouth.

His next thrust was a little harder, making her moan a little louder. Releasing her lips, he strung kisses along her jaw to just below her ear and, as he seated himself deep once again, he bit her.

Squirming on his lap, she managed to take him even deeper, her sex tightening around his cock like a fist, pumping him, eliciting a response he tried to stave off.

With his forehead resting on her shoulder, he rolled his hips and began to fuck her a little faster now. His hands settled on her waist, but with every passing second, she took over the pace. Leaning closer, she forced him to retreat until his back hit the cushion behind him.

Then she rolled her hips on his and made his blood surge.

Holy fuck. Every move she made caused his body to respond in ways he didn't expect. Yeah, his cock hardened every second, but he'd never expected his heart to pound as hard as it was. Never expected to be so overwhelmed by her that he couldn't think straight.

So he shut off his brain and gave her what she wanted. He gave it to her hard and fast.

And somewhere in his brain, he remembered how turned on she'd been when they'd mentioned control. He gripped her tight as he fucked her, controlled the speed and force of his thrusts, which controlled her every breath.

Her arms tightened around his shoulders, and her head fell back as he bit her neck, making her shudder against him.

Heat exploded in his gut, his balls drew up tight, and he tried desperately to hold out just a few more minutes. She felt so damn good, he didn't want to stop. And he didn't want to come before her.

Sliding one hand from her waist to her mound, he found her clit with his thumb and brushed it. Every time he connected, she shuddered. And when he stopped and pressed hard, she came apart.

Her sex rippled around his cock, tightening and releasing until he couldn't take it anymore. Wrapping one free hand in her hair, he tugged her head back and ground his mouth down on hers as his other hand gripped her hip and brought her down on his cock. Her ass hit his thighs and he groaned into her mouth as she rocked to get even closer.

Then he was pumping his release into her, his bare cock throbbing inside her tight channel as he kissed her until he literally couldn't breathe. His cock still hard, his heart thundering, he pulled away and crushed her against his chest.

He couldn't help himself. He needed to have her right here, right where he wanted her.

His.

Except...she wasn't just his.

His eyes opened slowly and saw Gens. Watching them. The lust in his eyes burning as hot as Tony's had.

16

Gens had never been more turned on than he was right now.

He never would've admitted it to Tony but watching him with Risa flipped a switch he hadn't known he possessed. And it wasn't because Gens lusted after Tony. He loved the guy, but he didn't want to fuck him. But he sure as hell got off watching Tony fuck Risa. Or maybe he got off watching Risa being fucked by Tony.

Didn't matter because he was so fucking hard from watching, he had to clamp his fingers around the base of his cock to keep from coming as Risa went limp and collapsed against Tony's chest.

He waited as patiently as he could, as Tony and Risa slowly began to catch their breath. It took a couple of minutes but, finally, Tony opened his eyes and looked at Gens.

Gens saw no embarrassment, no regret...and no hesitation as Tony shifted Risa around to face him.

She looked like a completely different woman from the

one he thought he knew. Her hair in messy waves around her face, it cascaded over her shoulders and down her chest to cover her breasts. Because he could, he let his gaze fall and noted that the hair on her mound was only a shade or so darker.

He took his time on the way up her body, letting his gaze linger on her hips, her breasts, her mouth and, finally, back to her eyes. The heat blazing there nearly scorched him.

Maybe he'd been a little worried that she'd be sated. Maybe she'd gotten what she needed from Tony.

But if he was reading the look in her eyes correctly, she wasn't finished.

He was about to lift his hand and crook a finger at her when she shifted forward and rose to her feet.

His breath caught in his chest as she began to walk toward him. Her eyes burned with desire, crushing his lungs in a vise as she sank to her knees in front of him.

Her expression made blood surge through his body, pumping even more to his already throbbing cock. And when she put her hands on the button of his jeans, his cock pressed against the zipper like it had a mind of its own. And wanted every ounce of her attention.

She held his gaze as she worked the button through the hole, her fingers tugging and pulling. The pressure on his cock eased then increased, fueling the lust bubbling in his gut. His fingers dug into the arms of the chair. He wanted to reach for her but didn't want her to stop. He wanted her to do whatever she wanted and not because she thought he wanted her to do it.

Apparently, what she wanted was to drive him crazy.

It took her forever to open the button, or at least it

seemed like it did. When it finally released, he breathed easier for all of second before she began to tug on the zipper. His cock actively impeded her, pushing against the zipper and making it harder for her to tug it down.

After a few seconds of torture, she dropped her gaze to stare and brought her other hand into the game. She grabbed the other side of the zipper so she could be sure she didn't catch anything important in the teeth. Yeah, that would've hurt like hell but the time she took was almost as bad.

He could barely breathe by the time she'd pulled the tab to the bottom. Now, his cock had more room, pushing out and toward her.

"Lift up."

He followed her husky command without thought, lifting his hips so she could tug his jeans down far enough to release his cock completely. She took his underwear down as well and now both rested just below his ass. It might've been awkward if he'd been thinking about it at all.

But he wasn't because every ounce of his attention remained on her.

And she was staring at his cock. Eight inches of thick, swollen flesh that ached for her to touch him. With her hands, with her mouth, he didn't care. He just needed her to give him *more*.

As if she'd read his mind...and decided to torment him... she looked back up into his eyes. Then she put her hands on his thighs and pressed them out as far as they could go given the constraints of his jeans, making a space for her between his legs.

She came closer, close enough that he could feel her breath brush along his shaft. Holy fuck, he needed her to touch him. He dug his fingers into the chair arms a little harder, when what he really wanted was to thread his fingers through her hair and tug her closer.

Her lips curled at the corners, as if she'd read his mind... and had no intention of giving him anything he wanted.

Then her hands moved, sliding up his thighs until they rested at the crease of his hips, her thumbs only inches from his cock. She scooted forward as well, until her breasts rested against the edge of the cushion.

"Ris."

She turned her head to the side and met his gaze. "Yes."

"I want your mouth on me."

Her lips spread into a wider grin, stoking his lust higher. "I'll get there. Eventually."

Her hands slipped closer until, finally, she wrapped her fingers around his erection. He fought back a groan and clamped down on his immediate need to wrap his fingers around hers and make her stroke him hard.

He needed her touch, needed her to squeeze him tight and jack him off until he came. Which would take seconds, at the moment.

Calm the fuck down.

Yeah, that wasn't happening. Maybe after he'd had her a few times.

"Stroke me, Ris. Don't tease me."

She swallowed hard, her fingers tightening around him until he had to groan. When she started to release him, he did wrap his hand around hers.

"Hard, Ris. And then put your mouth on me."

She took him at his word. Her gaze dropped to watch as

her hand squeezed him tight then eased up and down his erection. The friction made his head drop back against the cushion, but he kept his hand on hers. That connection settled something deep inside him, allowed him to fall into the rhythm she set until his heart beat in time with her pumps.

He wasn't sure how much longer he could let her go before he came all over her hand. His lungs struggled for air and he tried not to gasp but it became increasingly harder to breathe.

He felt her jostle between his legs, felt her shoulders brush against the inside of his thighs, her hair drifting along the tops of his thighs. Electricity shot between his nerve endings, making his cock jump in her hands.

Lifting his head, he was just in time to watch her head bow over his lap and her hair fall forward to curtain his thighs.

And then her mouth settled over the tip of his cock.

"Fuck."

His voice came out in a growl as he pulled his hand away and let her take him inside. Her tongue flicked at the slit in his crown before swirling around the head. Her lips tightened around him before she began to sink down, taking more and more of him into her mouth until her lips reached about midshaft.

She paused for a second, then she sucked hard and drew back up to the tip. His stomach hollowed as she licked at him, his breath stuck in his throat as he felt her pause. Then he saw her head tilt back just enough so she could look in his eyes.

Fucking hell. She put every other woman to shame. She

was the only woman he'd ever truly burned for. And now she was going to be his.

Closing her eyes, she sucked him back in and went just a little farther. Every time she came up, she'd swallow just a little more of him on her way back down.

He drowned in the heat of her mouth and the feel of her fingers kneading his thighs like a cat. Every sensation built on the last until his body practically vibrated in her control. And he was definitely under her control. He wouldn't move, not unless she told him he could. She could call every fucking shot.

If she wanted him to come, she only had to tell him. But he wouldn't until she gave him permission. But when he got her under him, she would give him what he wanted. How he wanted. And he'd make sure she enjoyed it.

He opened his eyes—didn't remember closing them—and found her staring up at him, her gaze locked with his as she released his cock with a slight pop.

She didn't speak, but he knew she wanted to say something.

He reached for her, cupping one hand around her jaw.

"What do you want, Ris? You can have anything."

She blinked, her gaze hot and smoky. "I want you to take me."

"How?"

"Hard."

That one word hit him like a kick in the gut.

Reaching for her, he put his hands under her arms and pulled her up onto the couch beside him. His mouth covered hers a second later as he lowered her to the cushion. She wrapped her arms around his shoulders, but he pulled back a second later.

Ripping his shirt over his head, he stood and shoved his jeans down and off, along with his briefs.

Naked, he enjoyed the way her eyes traveled from his thighs to his chest before reconnecting with his gaze. Then she reached out for his hand and tugged him down.

His control shredding, he spread out on top of her, loving the way her arms and legs swept around him and clung.

Slotting his cock between her thighs, he didn't thrust inside immediately. Fitting his mouth over hers, he kissed her. Their mouths locked, the kiss became a wet, hot declaration, their tongues tangling, teeth gnashing. A decade and more of unrequited lust surged out of him, looking for appeasement.

She obviously felt the same because she met his aggression with her own until he had to pull back a little or risk hurting her. He didn't care that she hurt him. Her fingernails dug into his shoulders, the sting sending more sensation though his body.

Her thighs gripping tight around his waist, she tilted her pelvis and rubbed her sex against the tip of his cock. She was slick and soft, and it wouldn't take more than a centimeter's adjustment to slide inside her.

But he waited, wanting to take his time, needing everything she was willing to give him.

He watched her carefully, saw her swallow hard then take a deep breath.

"Are you ever going to move?"

He grinned at the thread of demand in her voice. "Maybe I want to hear you beg."

Her right hand slid from his shoulder into his hair until she could grip the short strands tight between her fingers. Then she tugged, hard. He liked the slight sting of pain.

Leaning forward until her nose practically touched his, she spoke against his lips. He could barely hear her over the pounding of his heart.

"I will if you want me to."

The vulnerability in her voice nearly broke him. Risa never begged for anything. She'd never had to, but he knew it was more than that. She didn't beg because it would show weakness. And she couldn't afford to show any weakness. Not to anyone.

Except here, with them.

Heat flared in his gut and poured into his cock. Threading one hand through her hair, he kept himself upright with the other and dipped his pelvis to ease his cock into her. Her head fell back as he forged forward, stretching her, filling her, until he could go no farther.

Lodged between her legs, he pushed forward again and heard her moan.

He'd listened to each sound she'd made with Tony, had lusted after them. And now she was making them for him… He wouldn't be able to hold out long.

His retreat was slow and steady, torturing them both. Her head fell back onto the cushion, her hand falling from his hair to reach for his hip. Tugging him closer, she tried to get him to move faster.

"Not gonna happen, sweetheart. You're just gonna have to wait. Like I've been doing for fucking years."

Her eyes flashed open and she stared into his. "Not my fault."

Pulling his hips back, he paused with the tip of his cock spreading her lips. "All your fault. You were too perfect. The princess in the tower. Never to be defiled."

Her lips curved in a sweet grin that turned into a gasp as he shoved back inside her, this time a little faster than the last.

"So I'm not a...a princess anymore?"

Her voice had become low and breathy and breathtakingly sexy.

Grinding his hips against hers, he watched her eyelids flutter shut.

"No, you graduated to queen, baby. And I'm going to worship every fucking inch of you."

His next thrust was harder and caught her off guard. Hell, it caught him off guard. But he couldn't stop himself now. She was too much of a temptation. Too fucking hot.

He had to be inside her, had to create friction until his cock burned with it.

With his hands punched into the cushions by her head, he held his body above hers just enough to be able to see her face as he took her. Every thrust made her gasp, made him groan. Every retreat made him frantic to get back inside. He restrained the urge to just fuck her hard because, if he gave in to it, he'd come in seconds.

Instead, he caught and held her gaze as he maintained a pace that punished them both. Her fingers gripped and released his hips in perfect unison with his thrusts, her thighs tightening around his waist.

He held out as long as he could, reveling in the feel of her gripping him and the heat of her gaze on his and the thought that kept cycling through his head.

Finally. She was his. Finally.

It only took one word from her to break him.

"Gens."

He heard her plea in his name, heard her ask him to give her what she needed.

Sliding one hand between their bodies, he teased her clit and watched her eyes close as she broke around him.

Her pussy clamped around his cock on his next inward thrust, squeezed him tight until he pumped his release into her and collapsed over her with a huge sigh.

Mine.

Except not completely

17

Risa lay against Gens's chest, heart pounding against her ribs so hard, she was sure he could feel it.

That was okay. They'd just had mind-blowing sex. Of course, she was going to be affected. Hell, she'd had mind-blowing sex with Tony not that long ago. It shouldn't surprise anyone that she was having a hard time controlling herself.

The problem was the panic.

She felt it building low in her chest, like a balloon that kept filling, except it wasn't filling with air. It was filling with lead. She tried to talk herself down from the edge. Tried to reason with herself as Gens tightened his arms, drawing her even closer.

Opening her eyes, she tried to focus on something, anything, other than her rising anxiety.

What the hell is wrong with you?

She'd just lived her most intimate dream. Tony and Gens. She'd had them both. Why the hell was she freaking out?

"Risa. Breathe."

She sucked in air at Gens's command.

Shit. Was she being that obvious? No. She couldn't—

"Hey." Gens cupped the back of her head, the gesture so tender, she hitched in a breath. "Are you okay?'

"I'm fine."

"No, you're not." Tony's voice made that balloon fill a little faster. "You want a drink? Hell, I guess we could all use one. Hang tight."

God, yes. Maybe alcohol would help.

Nodding, she turned her head in time to see Tony pull his pants up his legs.

Her body reacted to the sight of Tony's naked chest with a surge of heat and she mentally shook her head. She needed help. Like, serious help.

What the hell is your problem?

Tony disappeared from her sightline, and she closed her eyes, focusing on calming the anxiety...and she still didn't know where it was coming from.

Before she knew what she was doing, she'd pulled away and shifted off Gens to the cushion next to him. If he'd tried to stop her, she was afraid she might've pushed him away. And that would've been mortifying.

Forcing herself to meet his gaze, she fought the urge to wrap her arms over her chest. After what they'd just done, was she really going to turn prude?

Where the hell was this coming from?

Gens looked straight into her eyes for several long seconds. Then he moved. It took every ounce of her control to not flinch as he rose to his feet, pulled up his pants then reached for her clothing.

Through sheer force of will, she took them with hands

that didn't shake and stifled the urge to cover herself and run out the door. Running wouldn't do any of them any good.

But it might keep you from having a panic attack.

The fact that she hadn't had one in years made it that much harder for her to control the one that wanted to break out now.

She'd never told anyone about them. Not her dad, not her sister. She'd only ever confided in the therapist her father had taken her to after her mom had died. Dr. Feingold had taught her how to deal with them, given her tips to control them. And for years, they'd worked.

The fact that she wasn't sure they'd work now was adding to her anxiety.

Slipping on her panties and jeans, she didn't bother with her bra, just pulled her shirt over her head and stuffed her bra in her jeans pocket.

Gens had moved across the room, standing in front of the door, hands in his pockets. Almost as if he wanted to be able to catch her if she made a run for it.

The idea appealed at the moment. She was just about to tell him she was leaving when a glass half-filled with what smelled like whiskey appeared in front of her face.

"Drink it."

The command in Tony's voice didn't grate, which was just another indicator of how far gone she was. She took a healthy sip, enjoyed the burn down her throat then the warmth that spread through her stomach.

A deep breath and another sip and she felt marginally better.

But when she looked up, Gens and Tony stared at her from across the room.

And she couldn't take it.

She swallowed the rest of the glass in one gulp, then stood and shook her head.

"I need to go. I'm sorry. I just...can't."

She rose on shaky legs, shoved her feet into her sandals then forced herself to walk to the door.

Neither man said anything and they didn't stop her.

She couldn't decide if she wanted them to or if she was glad they let her go without a fight.

She had her hand on the doorknob when she realized Tony stood behind her.

"Let me check first."

Damn, she'd almost forgotten. She couldn't go anywhere alone. She wasn't safe. She might never be safe.

Without a word, she withdrew her hand and let Tony open the door. He stepped out and down the stairs, looking up and down the street before motioning her forward. Gens at her back, she went down the four stairs from their door and up the four stairs to Dorrie's door.

She had the door open to her sister's home when she heard Gens call to her.

Forcing herself to turn, she held his gaze through sheer force of will.

"We'll still be here tomorrow, Ris. We're not going anywhere."

Over her shoulder, she saw Tony nod. And the anxiety eased a fraction.

Nodding, she stepped into the house and shut the door behind her.

Leaning back against the door, she took a deep shaky breath and closed her eyes.

Oh my god. What the hell had she done?

The shakes hit her a second later and she wasn't sure she wasn't going to fall into a quivering heap on the foyer. The stairs to the second floor, where she was staying, were directly in front of her. She should go hide herself away before anyone found her like this. Then everyone would be freaked out. Her sister would want to coddle her. Her dad would think this was all his fault or, worse, would blame Tony and Gens.

It wasn't their fault. Not at all. She'd practically forced them to have sex with her, had thrown herself at them. And they'd given her exactly what she wanted. And she'd enjoyed the hell out of it.

So why the hell was she freaking out now?

She took another breath and shook her head.

You're being ridiculous. Snap out of it.

After another few breaths, she finally felt a little bit more in control.

Opening her eyes, she looked toward the back of the house, where her sister probably was hanging with her men.

Did she want to talk to Dorrie? Or would that make it worse?

Out of the corner of her eye, she saw movement in the sitting room to the left.

"Hey, sorry. Didn't mean to scare you." Ian took a few steps forward then stopped, as if he didn't want to get too close.

Damn it. Was she really this transparent right now?

"If you ask me if I'm okay right now, I think I might scream."

It took Ian a few seconds but finally his mouth quirked in a grin.

Unlike Ben, who smiled quick and often, Ian very rarely did. He and Ben balanced each other, she realized. It's why they made a good trio with Dorrie. But as much as Risa liked Ben, she and Ian had a more problematic relationship. Maybe because they were a lot more alike.

"Okay. I won't ask. But maybe you want to head upstairs before Dorrie takes one look at you and decides you need to be back in the hospital."

"You're probably right." But her feet, for some reason, seemed to be glued to the floor. "But I'm not sure…"

What? That she could make it without help? How fucking embarrassing would that be? To get halfway up the stairs and collapse?

Jesus, she was a nutcase.

"You want to talk about it?" Ian took a step closer.

"About what?"

"The fact that you're about to freak out. You're not covering as well as you normally do. Come on." He held out his hand. "Come sit down. I know I'm not your first choice for confidant but I'm not gonna go soft on you and want to know all your problems. You want to talk, you're welcome to spill your guts. I'll never say a word to anyone. You just want to sit and have a drink, I'll get you a glass and—"

"I'll take a drink. Whiskey." She paused. "And the company."

Without hesitation, Ian nodded and disappeared. Risa stepped through the doorway he'd vacated and into the sitting room. This room Risa had deemed the quiet room. No screen, no speakers. Just books. Both Dorrie and Ben loved to read and the bookshelves that lined the walls were over-flowing.

Risa wasn't much of a reader—she preferred movies—but this room had an undeniable calming effect. It even smelled different than the rest of the house. Not bad, just... peaceful.

Maybe she needed to read. Maybe that would take her head out of whatever hole it happened to be in now.

While she waited for Ian to return, she walked across the room and looked at the shelf in front of her. She only recognized a few of the authors but one stuck out from the rest. Stephen King. She loved horror films and had seen many adaptations of his work. But she'd never read one of his books. Pulling *The Stand* off the shelf, she opened the cover and read the blurb on the inside.

The book had to weigh at least five pounds and had more than a thousand pages. If she wasn't going to bed with a man tonight, this looked interesting enough to keep her mind off the other issues in her life.

The jangle of ice in a glass caught her ear and she turned to see Ian walking toward her, two glasses in his hand.

"Jack Daniels." He handed her a glass then clinked his against hers before he took a step back. "Not fancy but it'll do the job."

She took a healthy swallow before she stared back at Ian.

"You don't like me much, do you?"

Her question didn't seem to knock Ian back at all. Probably because it was no secret that he thought she was a spoiled princess with a chip on her shoulder.

The fact that she hadn't decided if he was good enough for her baby sister probably had something to do with it.

A slight grin curved his mouth. "What gave you that idea?"

"Let's just say I've gotten pretty good at reading people."

He took another sip before he tipped his head to the side. "Yeah, well, you're wrong."

Her eyebrows rose. "Really? I find that hard to believe."

"Why? Because I don't smile and make you laugh?" He shrugged. "That's not me. I'm not warm and fuzzy."

"And still my sister loves you, so you must have some redeeming qualities."

"See, this is why I like you, Risa. You're not afraid to speak your mind."

Oh, if you only knew.

His gaze narrowed as if she'd spoken out loud. "But you have something else on your mind tonight and it's not me. Wanna unload some of it? I'm a good listener. I know how to keep my mouth shut."

Surprisingly, she did want to talk. She just didn't know how to start.

"I hate this."

The words came out with more force than she'd intended, and Ian's brows rose. She regretted her outburst immediately and began to shake her head.

"Sorry. That's not—"

"Hey, you'll get no judgment from me. And whatever you say here, stays here. Just consider me Vegas for the night. Besides, Dorrie's worried about you so this is my way of helping her. You look like you could use a sounding board."

She wanted to take him up on the offer. Wanted to believe she could trust him but she'd only known him for six months. It usually took her years to warm up to someone.

Benji was a special case. He was easy, and he so blatantly loved Dorrie.

Ian...was just like her.

Turning, she headed for the nearest chair and dropped into it with a sigh. Ian followed, sitting in the matching chair beside it. He didn't say anything, just waited for her.

After at least a minute, she finally blew out a frustrated breath.

"I had a panic attack. With...Gens and Tony." She figured Ian didn't need to know the nitty-gritty details. Maybe he suspected they'd had sex. Hell, she hadn't looked in a mirror so for all she knew, she looked like she'd just come from their bed.

"Do you get them a lot?"

"Not anymore, no. I haven't had one in years. I used to get them frequently in high school, then again in college. They faded as I got older."

"Do you wanna talk about what brought this one on? Or you wanna just talk around it? I'm okay with either. Just thought I'd ask so I know whether to avoid the obvious."

A blush burned her cheeks. Yes, he knew or suspected she'd just had sex with Gens and Tony. She didn't know whether to walk out or throw the book she still held at him.

And damn it, he made her feel more like herself. Her backbone had started to stiffen already.

"You don't need to avoid anything. I'm not going to break." At least, not now. "I just...jumped into a situation when I probably should have waited."

"Are you hurt?"

She saw an expression cross Ian's handsome face that startled her. Until she realized that, like Tony and Gens, Ian was hardwired to protect. He wouldn't hesitate to kick some-one's ass if he thought they'd hurt her, no matter who it was. Or that she wasn't a friend.

But maybe they would be someday.

She smiled at him, probably the first true smile she'd ever given him.

"No. I'm not, but... Thank you. It's not like that."

"Then what is it like?"

She fell silent, and to his credit, Ian didn't push her to talk. He sat back in the chair and waited for her to work through what she wanted to say. Like he had all night to just sit here and wait for her to speak. Or not.

Finally, she shook her head and said what was in her head.

"I finally got what I've wanted for years and it was every-thing I dreamed it would be. And I'm not sure I deserve them."

Ian's brows lowered hard and fast. "Deserve?"

She pulled a face. "Maybe deserve isn't the right word."

"Then what is?"

"Maybe I just wasn't meant to be happy. Maybe I'm not wired for it."

Ian went quiet for a few seconds. "So, what makes you happy?"

It wasn't the question she'd been expecting, and it threw her for a moment.

"Seeing my sister happy. That's been a load off my mind. And the credit for that is partially yours."

His lips quirked, and she saw exactly why Dorrie had fallen for Ian. The man's sex appeal simmered below the surface, just waiting for the right moment to emerge.

"Damned by faint praise. I'm honored."

"Nothing faint about it." She smiled, amazed she could. "And you should be honored. I don't give out praise often."

"No. You don't give much of yourself to anyone. Your sister and your dad. And those two," he lifted his glass and tilted it in the direction of the wall separating the two homes, "over there. So yeah, I can understand your freak-out. It's a lot to process."

She nodded. "It is. Maybe too much. Maybe I'm more screwed up than I thought."

"And maybe you should give yourself a fucking break. At least for a few days. Jesus, Risa, you were kidnapped, for fuck's sake. You're not gonna get over that in a few days. So yeah, maybe you pushed yourself a little faster than you should have. But tomorrow will be better. And if it's not, then the next day will. And I'm pretty sure those guys over there aren't gonna throw up their hands in defeat after tonight. I'm pretty sure they're gonna still be there tomorrow."

Had she actually been worried that they might turn their backs on her?

She grimaced at Ian. "I don't give you enough credit, do I?"

She couldn't help herself, couldn't help needling him. He was like the brother she'd never had, the older, annoying brother who mercilessly teased his sister but would beat down anyone else who even attempted it.

Ian actually laughed out loud, the sound ringing through the room and probably down the hall, where Dorrie was sure to hear it.

"No, you probably don't. That's okay. I never expected you to have a heart. I know how wrong I am now."

That organ was taking a beating tonight.

"Hey, Ris."

She looked up at Ian, a surprising tenderness in his eyes.

"Sleep on it. Sometimes, it helps. And I can't believe I'm about to say this but... Things *will* look different in the morning."

"I'm not sure I'll be able to sleep."

"Well, lucky for you, I have the rest of a bottle of Jack and I'm willing to share."

Tossing back the rest of her drink, she held out her glass. "I guess you're my guardian angel tonight, Ian."

"Just don't come at me with that sharp tongue tomorrow when you wake up with a hangover."

Her own lips curved in a smile. "Don't count on an overnight transformation. Just fill me up."

18

Risa did wake with a slight headache, but she didn't think it was from the alcohol. At least, not entirely from the alcohol.

She'd only slept a few hours when her phone rang.

She was going to ignore it until she saw the caller ID.

"Bree. Hi. What's up?"

Bree Walters was her right hand at the Madelaine Foundation. She'd been with the foundation since the beginning, had been a friend of her mother's, maybe her mother's only true friend in this country. As such, Bree was her unofficial aunt.

"We have a problem with the venue for the fundraiser."

It took Risa a few seconds to process what Bree had said and then another few seconds to actually remember what fundraiser she was talking about.

"You mean the one in two weeks?"

"Of course, that's the one I mean. I know you took a few days off, sweetheart, but have you really forgotten the fundraiser is in fifteen days?" Bree's voice began to show cracks. "And now it looks like we're going to have to find a new place to hold it."

Risa's brain slowly came up to speed. The foundation she'd started in her mother's name held an annual event to raise funds. That event drew not only from Philadelphia's elite society but from international society as well.

Tickets were $30,000 a pair and they capped it at five hundred. They could sell more if they wanted but Bree was a brilliant strategist. She knew that if you made something exclusive, you built buzz.

When you built buzz, you built excitement. And with excitement came money. Money they used to help at-risk youth and young adults. They funded several shelters around the city, gave millions in scholarship money every year, and provided help for everything from mental-health counseling to medical care to employment.

Since the beginning, Bree, who was European royalty five times removed, had been the face of the foundation, which meant all those rich people who would've turned up their noses at anything associated with Risa because of who her father was were much more inclined to give generously.

Of course, they knew she was involved, but they thought she was only involved as a curiosity, an oddity to stare at and whisper about.

"What happened with the Ritz?" They'd booked the hotel three years in advance for this date.

"Electrical fire. And they don't have another room to accommodate us. They're more than willing to take the hit through the insurance and pay us back, but that still leaves us with no venue."

Risa heard the frustration in Bree's voice and knew the older woman was barely reining it in.

"Okay, let's not panic yet. Give me a couple of hours to make a few calls and I'll get back to you. Are you at home?"

"Yes. Are you? You sound a little off, sweetheart. Did I wake you? I didn't think you were going out of the country."

"I'm not. I'm, ah, staying with a friend for a few days but I'm in the city."

"Oh, really?" Bree's tone immediately changed to teasingly curious. "Is this friend possibly male?"

All at once, memories from last night shoved into her brain, taunting her. She tried to shake them out and took a breath to make sure her rising panic didn't come through her voice.

"Sorry to disappoint. My friend is female. We're just... hanging out."

"Well, good for you. You need to get out more, Risa."

This was an argument they'd been having for the past couple of years, one Risa wouldn't win until Bree had her way and Risa moved out on her own, away from her father.

It wasn't that Bree didn't like her dad. It was that she hated him with a fiery passion, blamed him for her mom's death, blamed him for every one of Risa's tears, and probably blamed him for every bad thing that happened in Philadelphia, if not the world.

Not that Bree ever said one bad word to Risa about her father. She didn't. She never had. But if Bree found out Risa had been kidnapped... Risa wasn't sure Bree would be able to hold her tongue. And then they'd have to have a talk they'd so far avoided.

Her dad knew Bree hated him, but Risa loved her, and

he'd never said a bad word about her in Risa's presence. Maybe he never had ever.

"We have bigger problems than my social life at the moment."

"What social life?" Bree muttered under her breath but immediately continued. "You're right. We need to find a venue and we need to do it in the next few days or we're not going to be able to salvage this. I'll start calling around to other venues, see if anyone has an opening."

Then Bree sighed, and Risa heard the disappointment in that sound. She wasn't holding out hope.

"I'll see if I have any favors I can call in."

Risa's name might not be anywhere on the formal paperwork of the foundation, but people in the community knew she gave it preferential treatment. And just maybe her father's name would come in handy. But that was a last resort.

"Okay. I'm really sorry to interrupt your holiday—"

"You haven't." Totally true. This would actually give her mind something to focus on that wasn't the two men next door. "We'll figure this out."

"Okay. Okay." Bree took a deep breath Risa could hear through the phone. "Sorry, I should've taken a breath before I called you. I'm sorry, sweetheart. We'll get this worked out."

They hung up after they'd agreed they would split the list of hotels and venues in the city large enough to accommodate them. And if they couldn't find one in the city, they would have to start working their way out.

With a purpose in mind, she got out of bed, took a quick shower to wash away the cobwebs, and took her laptop downstairs to the kitchen.

It was Thursday. At least, she was pretty sure it was Thursday. At 9:30 a.m., Dorrie and her guys should already be at work. She remembered Ian saying something about him and Ben needing to go to a meeting this morning.

But of course, they wouldn't leave her alone.

So when she walked down to the first floor, she wasn't completely surprised to hear voices coming from Ian's office.

Instead of heading there, she went toward the kitchen.

And came face to face with Tony. He'd been on his way out and she very nearly walked right into him as she entered the kitchen.

Luckily, she didn't scream or flinch or do anything else that would've embarrassed her.

"Damn." Tony wrapped a hand around her waist to steady her. "Sorry. Didn't hear you coming. You must be in stealth mode."

The sound of his voice struck a chord inside her that immediately sent all her senses into an uproar. Her body remembered how he'd made her feel last night. Her brain wanted her to panic.

And her heart skipped a beat.

Fuck this shit. I've got work to do.

Sucking in a breath, she looked up into his eyes. Tony looked uncertain and unsure, as if he'd been the one who'd had the panic attack last night. And she realized two things. They needed to get beyond this. She still wanted him. Well, both of them.

And she wasn't going to give them up that easily.

But convincing Tony could be the biggest hurdle to that. "You okay?"

His rough voice made her muscles tense, and that,

surprisingly, made her feel more confident. Yeah, maybe they'd gone a little fast last night, but that didn't mean they just threw up their hands in defeat.

It was on the tip of her tongue to say just that when she remembered she had work to do.

"I am." Then she tilted her head to the side and took a better look at him. "Are you?"

Surprise surfaced in those dark eyes before he blinked and covered it.

"I'm fine." He paused before he sighed. "Are we going to talk about last night?"

He actually looked pained as he said the words and she considered taking it easy on him. Hell, just the fact that he was unsure about talking about last night made her feel better.

"Yes, we are."

He nodded and straightened, as if he was getting ready to take a beating.

"But not now. There's a problem with the foundation's fundraiser. We lost our venue."

It took him a couple of beats to come up to speed but when he did, his gaze narrowed.

"What do you mean, you lost your venue?"

"I mean the hotel we'd booked had an electrical fire in the ballroom and we have to find a new place to hold it."

"When did this happen?"

"Last night." Sidestepping him, she laid her phone and laptop on the counter before heading for the coffee machine. Thank God there was fresh coffee. She was going to need it.

As she poured a cup, Tony turned and leaned against the doorframe, watching her.

"You want me to check and make sure that's what really happened?"

She froze with the mug at her lips. "Why would anyone try to sabotage the hotel where a foundation with no ties to me personally is having their annual dinner and dance? No, I think it's just a rotten coincidence." She took a sip. "Do you always automatically assume the worst?"

His lips quirked at the corners, as if he were going to smile. And then he did.

Damn him. He looked edible when he did that.

Encouraged to think that she wasn't permanently damaged and that last night's panic attack might have had nothing to do with the men and more to do with leftover stress from her kidnapping, she smiled back.

And the heat she'd seen in his eyes last night made a reappearance. So did the butterflies in her stomach.

No. No, no, no. I don't have time for this now.

"Yeah, I do. Hazards of being a cop."

She sometimes forgot that about him. That he'd been a cop before he'd become Dorrie's bodyguard.

"Do you miss it?"

"Miss what?"

He hadn't taken his eyes off her but now they narrowed slightly.

"Miss being a cop."

"Yeah. Some days."

She wanted to ask about what had happened in San Antonio. Wanted him to talk to her about it. She also didn't want him to turn her down.

"Have you seen a pad and a pen around here?"

He didn't answer right away but that smile returned. As if he could read her mind.

"Yeah, I'm sure I can find you one. Be right back."

An hour later, Risa closed her laptop with a frustrated sigh. She thought about throwing the pen in her hand across the room but didn't want to mess up anything in her sister's kitchen.

"No luck?"

Tony had been sitting across the table from her, listening to her bitch for most of the past hour. He'd made himself scarce a few times, disappearing for ten minutes once, but always returning.

"We can't find one damn place in the city that has availability that night to hold the number of guests we have. I really hope Bree's having more luck than I am. Otherwise, I'm afraid we're going to have to cancel."

"I didn't want to say anything before I checked, but I think I may have a solution for you."

Her eyes widened at the totally unexpected comment. "Really? Where?"

She'd called every person she knew who might've been able to help her. Not one had been able to.

"I know the owner at Haven."

Haven. Small, boutique hotel in Center City. Emphasis on small. "I don't think the ballroom's big enough, is it?"

"Not the main ballroom alone. But they're willing to reconfigure the first floor so you can use the atrium and ballroom as well as the space between."

She pulled up a mental image of Haven's atrium but had trouble picturing the area outside and around it.

"I need to see it. Let me get dressed and we can run over there."

Tony sighed and rubbed his hand over the back of his head. "I had a feeling you were going to say that."

Her brows rose at his tone and she gave him a look that would have people who knew her backing away slowly. Tony just stood there.

"Excuse me? Is that a problem?"

His head cocked to the side and he gave her a look she could only interpret as, "Yeah, and you're it."

But his only audible answer was a short, "No."

She'd had a shitty night's sleep, after she'd had the best sex of her life with the two men she'd been lusting after for years and after she'd had an epic panic attack after the best sex of her life. She wasn't in the best of moods, and this situation with the fundraiser wasn't helping.

And the fact that she still wanted to undress him and rub herself against him every time she looked at him made her crazy.

So when she took a deep breath and straightened, hands planted firmly on the counter, Tony very wisely started to look concerned.

"Risa—"

She lifted one finger and held it up in front of her, making his mouth snap closed. Nice to know she still had the ability to shut him up. Which made her want to laugh because all she'd wanted for the past two years had been for him to talk to her.

Right now, she needed to do the talking.

"I am not here as a prisoner. I was one for three days. That's never going to happen again. I am also not stupid. I know I could be in danger the second I step out the front door. That's why I'm not suggesting I leave the house without you."

She paused for a second, just to make sure he was listening. The damn man raised one eyebrow, daring her to continue.

Holy fuck, that was sexy.

She swallowed to make sure her voice wouldn't break when she spoke again. That would totally ruin the image she was trying to project.

And with the counter separating them, she felt somewhat…safe. No, safe wasn't the right word. Which didn't matter at the moment; she had more to say.

"I'm going upstairs to change and then we can drive over to Haven. Or you can stay here, and I will call Ian or Ben and ask them to take me."

Crossing his arms over his broad chest, Tony watched her for several silent seconds until her teeth began to grind.

"You haven't asked where Gens is."

His question came out of left field and drew a frown out of her.

"What does that have to do with—"

"What made you freak out last night?"

She blinked, frankly shocked that he'd asked the question. She would've thought both he and Gens would've avoided the hell out of that. She wasn't sure she wanted to answer it now. But then, if she wanted a relationship with these men, they were all going to have to make concessions.

"Honestly?" She took a breath and prepared to bare

herself to this man who could do so much damage to her heart. "I think it was the fact that I'd finally gotten exactly what I wanted, but I wasn't sure it was going to be enough."

"And why's that?"

Her chin lifted. "Because I'm not sure you or Gens will ever be able to give me what I need."

She'd shocked him. She saw it in the lift of his eyebrows and the slightly widening of his eyes.

"And what do you want, Risa? Spell it out."

She took a second to think about her answer. "I want you to tell me you're going to be here for me. And I want you to kiss me like you want me and that you don't care who my father is."

She must've hit a nerve on that last one because he shifted from one foot to the other. She'd gotten really good at reading body language, and she'd just made him uncomfortable.

"I want to kiss you right now because you are who you are. Not because of whose daughter you happen to be."

Her heart gave an extra thump. "But that's always going to be a problem for you, isn't it? The fact that my dad is who he is?"

"Your dad's not you."

"No, he's not. But I'm not sure you can overlook that. It's always going to be there, like an ache you can't get rid of."

His lips curved into another one of those smiles that made her blood heat.

"You're a little dramatic this morning."

"And you're avoiding the question."

"Right now, I only see you."

Shoving away from the door frame, Tony closed the

space between them. Startled but not frightened, she held her ground as he stopped inches away. Staring up at him, she saw the turmoil raging in his gaze.

"And what do you see when you look at me?"

"The woman I've wanted from the first moment I saw her."

"Then why did it take me being kidnapped to do anything about it?"

He didn't answer right away. One hand rose to cup her jaw, thumb caressing her skin with a whisper-soft touch that made her shiver in response. How the hell did he manage to make her hot with only the slightest touch?

But it wasn't just his touch. It was the way he stared into her eyes, the intensity and the heat.

She wanted to melt at the ache that started between her legs. She wanted to glance down to see if he was similarly affected but couldn't look away.

"Because I was an asshole."

She couldn't help herself. She was who she was. She arched her brows. "And you've been reformed?"

"No. But I'm willing to try if you're willing to give me the chance. I can't say that you're going to get everything you want. I can only say I'm willing to try. Last night..."

He paused, and she watched him as he tried to find the right words. She didn't want the right words. She wanted to know what he thought without a filter.

"You were uncomfortable?"

"No. Not in the moment."

"But afterward?"

Another pause. "I wasn't uncomfortable. I was jealous. Sharing you..."

Ice crept through her veins. She'd pushed for what she wanted, pushed too hard, and now she was going to pay for it. She'd lose them both—

"...watching you with Gens, that wasn't the problem."

She blinked, unsure now where he was going with this. "Then what was?"

"It's not knowing how to handle this."

Shaking her head, she tried to follow his reasoning but failed. "I don't—"

He grabbed her hip and pulled her flush against him, pressed the hard ridge in his cargo pants against the softness of her belly and made her hormones dance in delight.

"Am I allowed to have you while he's not around? Am I allowed to kiss you and strip you naked and make you come if he's not here to share? I don't understand the rules to this game."

She swallowed hard around the lump in her throat. "This isn't a game." It was the first thing that came to mind, but it was the most important. "And there are no rules."

Resting her hands on his hips, she gripped him tight as she rose onto her bare toes, dragging her pelvis against his and watching the heat in his eyes burn hotter.

"Do you want me?"

His jaw flexed as she moved her hands around to his back then down, cupping his ass. Damn, he had an ass she wanted to bite. Tight, perfect.

"Of course, I do."

"Then you don't have to ask permission from anyone but me."

"So if I say I want to pull your pants off and fuck you against the wall, you're gonna be okay with that?"

She swallowed hard, her lungs tight from lack of oxygen. "I think you already know the answer to that question."

"I want to hear you say it, Risa."

Moving her hands up his back, she pressed him even closer.

"Yes."

No hesitation. His mouth covered hers as a fierce rush of heat snapped through her, weakening her knees and dampening her panties.

He kissed her hard, smashed their lips together and slid his tongue against hers, licking at her with a demand that she kiss him back just as hard.

She gave him what he wanted and demanded more. She wanted him to run his hands all over her body. To mold her breasts in his big palms and put his mouth on the tips that ached.

Arching her back, she pressed forward, breasts rubbing against him as her head tipped back even farther.

Apparently, Tony was a mind reader because his hand slid from her chin to her shoulder and down to her breast. He cupped her, squeezed her, made her moan into his mouth. She wanted to wrap herself around him and force him to go fast.

She didn't need to use force. She only needed to slide one hand around to his groin and cup his cock to make him kick into another gear.

The hand on her hip tightened for several seconds before he shoved her yoga pants and underwear down her hips, baring her pussy. The cool air in the kitchen made her sex clench. She needed him to fill her. Hard and fast.

He did, with his fingers.

He slid a couple through her slick lower lips, being sure to pass over her swollen clit several times, sending shocks through her entire body.

The hand on his cock tightened before she forced herself to release him so she could work his zipper down.

She needed him now. Desperately.

As his zipper released, he slid two fingers into her sex and began to fuck her with them. She clenched around him, her own fingers momentarily frozen as he pushed her closer to orgasm. On his next thrust, he held deep and stroked her with the tips of his fingers, making her shudder.

Oh my god.

She was so close.

He withdrew, leaving her gasping and cursing him silently because he continued to kiss her. But in the next second, he rubbed two fingers over her clit then caught it between them and squeezed. Not to hurt. God, no, it didn't hurt. It felt amazing.

With a moan, she shoved his pants down and released his cock. Wrapping her fingers around the hard shaft, she stroked him from root to tip. A second later, he released her mouth, wrapping one hand around her neck while he continued to slide his other hand between her legs.

Lust seared from between her legs, through her gut then lit through her entire body.

And when he put his hands around her waist and lifted her off her feet, she kicked off her slides and let her pants and underwear fall. As soon as they hit the floor, she wrapped her legs around his waist and ground her pelvis against his cock.

It was his turn to groan, his fingers digging into her hips for several long seconds as he held her tantalizingly close but not close enough. She tried to lift herself higher, to slot his cock into position and slide down on him.

He wouldn't let her, just held her tight and continued to kiss her hard and deep. The ache between her legs intensified, causing a fierce fever to spread through her lower body.

She needed him inside her, needed him to fill her, to stretch her. Needed him to pound into her and make her come so that ache receded just a little.

She wasn't sure it would ever completely go away.

A sliver of fear wanted to lodge in her gut. Then he began to rub his cock against her clit, setting off a firestorm of need that exploded through her body. Tearing her mouth away from his, she sucked in air and tightened her arms around his shoulders.

She turned and nuzzled her nose into his neck, then pressed a kiss just below his ear.

"Tony, please."

His hands tightened even more before he shifted her an inch higher and lodged his cock at the entrance to her body.

She was so wet, he slipped in and she wriggled until she'd taken at least an inch. Finally, he allowed gravity to take control. She took him in completely, the thickness of his cock easing one ache but creating a whole different one.

This new ache caused her to lift her hips and slide back down, riding him, taking him deeper each time. She couldn't get enough of him, needed him to move, to do something to help her.

He seemed content to let her control their movement, at least for the moment, and she fucked him as best she could.

Until it just wasn't enough.

"Tony. Help me."

He lowered his head, rubbing his rough cheek against hers before pressing his lips to her temple. Then he moved his hands to her ass and pulled her down until she could go no farther.

"Oh my god."

He felt amazing, stretching her so wide, she throbbed around him. The slight bite she felt as her flesh stretched to accommodate him made her moan. Her arms and legs trembled with the effort she expended to wrap herself around him.

He stood, solid as a rock, his erection stiff and deep inside her.

"You don't need my help. Ride me, sweetheart."

His voice held a deep need that touched something inside her, made her almost frantic.

She took what she wanted, riding his shaft, stoking that fire burning in her gut into a blaze. She lost any sense of where she was, and the world narrowed down to her and him and the satisfaction he could give her.

Time no longer mattered, only that she continued to have him stretch her, the tightening of her muscles around him as lifted off him and the stretching as she sank back down.

Her orgasm built until she couldn't hold it back if she tried.

Crying out, she broke, her pussy clenching around him, ecstasy coursing through her. And when he followed her seconds later, pumping his seed into her, she sagged against him and clutched him tight.

19

ell, shit.

He'd totally fucked up that decision.

With his arms tight around Risa's waist and his cock still throbbing inside her, he remembered how he'd vowed to stay on task this morning. Keep her safe. Not fuck her in the fucking kitchen like a teenager who couldn't keep his dick in his pants.

Christ. Now what?

First things first. Get her feet on the ground.

But he couldn't lie—she felt pretty damn good wrapped around him like this. Like she was meant to be right here. In his arms.

And what the hell are you going to tell Gens?

Nope. Not dealing with that now.

Right now, he had his arms full of a woman he didn't want to release.

And again, not dealing with that now.

"Risa, I'm going to put you down, okay?"

As she hitched in a breath, he felt her lips move against

his neck, where she'd buried her face. It made his fucking knees weak. How fucked up was that?

"Okay. Sorry. I must be heavy."

What the hell?

"You're not heavy, Ris. But if you stay where you are any longer, I'm gonna get hard again and I'm going to want to fuck you again and apparently you've got work to do."

She shivered against him, felt her pussy tighten around him, before she nodded. "Bet you say that to all the girls you have sex with in kitchens."

Amazingly, he laughed, unable to help himself. "You're the only woman I've ever had sex with in a kitchen. Or watched have sex with another man."

Maybe he should've let that last part out because she sighed heavily and lifted her head away from his neck.

Obviously, she wanted to be put down now.

Lifting her away, his cock already half-hard, he set her down and grabbed for the drawer with the dishtowels. Grabbing two, he handed one to her and used the other to clean himself off before he pulled up his pants.

Then he watched her. He had the almost overwhelming urge to help her, to get down on his knees, use that towel between her legs, then he'd put his mouth there and make her come again.

She didn't catch his gaze again until she'd pulled up her pants. Then she looked straight at him. And waited for him to say something, her brows slightly raised.

Goddamn, she made every cell in his body burn for her. Even after he'd just come inside her. He bit back the urge to ask her if she was okay. She looked better than okay. She looked fucking amazing.

"So...you want to get dressed and head over to Haven?"

He honestly didn't know what else to say.

Her lips twitched, and he couldn't be sure if she was going to laugh or curse him.

She did neither. She nodded and walked around him, heading for the doorway out of the room.

"Sure. I'm just going to take a quick shower. Give me five minutes."

And she left.

Standing in the middle of the kitchen of her sister's house, he stared at the doorway for several seconds, trying to figure out what the hell to do.

What he wanted to do was talk to Gens. Gens was the only person he trusted to spill his guts to, the only man he felt comfortable enough telling secrets.

But they hadn't discussed last night. Not after she'd left. Not after they'd shared her.

Gens had let him avoid the subject, not because he didn't want to talk about it but because he knew Tony didn't want to talk. Gens knew Tony would need to process and he'd open up when he was ready.

It worked the same in reverse. Tony knew Gens needed to talk, and soon, because not knowing what Tony was thinking would grate on him. So, yeah, Tony should've stopped Gens from leaving this morning to go to Adam's office so they could hash this out.

And now, he was about to take Risa out the front door and drive her downtown without backup.

Which meant he needed to call Gens and tell him where to meet them.

Grabbing his phone with a sigh, he punched in Gens's number and waited.

"Yeah, what's wrong?"

Tony's eyes rolled, though that was probably exactly how he would've answered. "Nothing's wrong. At least, not now. I need to take her downtown. Can you meet us at Haven in about a half hour?"

A couple seconds of silence. "Yeah. Sure. Wanna give me a clue?"

"Her fundraiser venue had a fire. She needs a new one. I called in a favor."

Another pause. "You think it's related? Her kidnapping, this fire?"

"Not sure. Don't think so but we probably should look into it. I think you should be there this morning."

"I will. Wanna tell me what else is wrong?"

His turn to pause. "Nothing to discuss over the phone."

"Okay. Fine. We'll talk later. I'll see you there."

Gens hung up and Tony tapped his phone against his hand, staring at the floor, wondering how the fuck he was going to tell Gens about this morning.

Maybe he'd go wait for her in the living room.

He walked through the house, stopping when he caught sight of a photo on a table by the front door.

Since he hadn't noticed any other photos in the house, he picked it up. It was a collage with five pictures. One was Ben and Ian as children, arms slung over their shoulders. Two were of Ben, Ian, and Dorrie. Amazingly, they were all smiling, even Ian. One was Dorrie and her mom.

The last was Dorrie and Risa as teenagers. If he hadn't

known the women as well as he did, he might not have recognized them. It was a selfie, their faces barely fit in the same screen, and they'd both pulled silly faces. Risa had stuck out her tongue and Dorrie had her eyes crossed. They looked young and carefree and completely at ease with each other.

Since he knew some of the backstory between the sisters, he knew that hadn't always been the case. They hadn't always been so close.

"We both have that picture on our phones. We use it as our contact photos. It was taken at least ten years ago."

He turned toward the stairs and saw Risa at the bottom, watching him.

"Whenever we'd get to spend time together, we would always take photos." She walked over to stand next to him, reaching out to run her finger over the glass. "We'd delete most of them because Dad didn't want anyone to know about Dorrie. When I was younger, I used to think he was ashamed of her. At least, that's what I told myself. It took me a while to understand that he was protecting her."

"And how did that make you feel?"

She huffed out a tiny laugh. "Like a bitch. When I first found out about Dorrie, I was such a bitch. I didn't want to share him with this other perfect little princess who didn't get sent away to school and got to have friends and date boys and had a mom who loved her and wasn't crazy."

He kept his mouth shut, just let her find her words in her own time. He could admit, if only to himself, that he was a little, okay, maybe a lot, jealous of the fact that Gens had known her for years. But now she was giving him a piece of herself and didn't want to interrupt her.

"But you know Dorrie. She gets under your skin. And I don't mean that in a bad way. I love her. And I learned that just because my dad loved her too didn't mean he loved me any less."

Tony couldn't think of a damn thing to say to that. He had to wonder if she was talking about more than her sister. If she was talking about him and Gens. It was on the tip of his tongue to ask but then she withdrew her hand.

"So, are we ready to go?"

He turned and felt his brows rise as his eyes widened.

Holy shit.

She looked...not at all like herself.

She'd pulled her long hair into two braids that fell over her shoulders, making her look like a teenager. The lack of makeup helped the image, as did the loose, plain white t-shirt tucked into weathered jeans and the Chuck Taylor sneakers that looked lived in.

She had a Phillies cap in one hand and sunglasses in the other. She looked ready for a ball game. And he wasn't sure he'd recognize her if he passed her on the street.

Well, damn. Was this the real Risa? The one beneath the designer clothes and haughty attitude? Or was this just another facet of her that he'd never seen before?

This Risa turned him on just as much as the one who wore slinky dresses and tight skirts.

"Tony? Is something wrong?"

He shook his head, trying to get his thoughts together. "No. I've just...never seen you dressed down."

She shrugged, just one shoulder, the movement seemingly offhand, but her gaze issued a challenge.

"Doesn't mean I don't."

He lifted his hands in the air in classic surrender. "Not trying to start a fight. Just making an observation."

Nodding, she took a breath. "I guess there's a lot we don't know about each other."

Yeah, you could say that. And every new piece of information he learned about her, the more he liked her. Not just lusted after her. He genuinely liked her.

"True. But...I'm willing to give this a shot, Risa."

Her chin tilted a little higher in the air. "Give what a shot?"

His jaw clenched. "Don't be a brat. You know what I'm talking about. This. Us. This threesome, whatever you want to call it. I'm here. I'm not going anywhere. And I'm trying my damnedest not to let every freaking little thing get to me. Yeah, I watched Gens fuck you last night and it turned me on. Never thought I'd ever say those words. But they're true. So, give me a little breathing room, okay?"

She sucked in a breath, her teeth lodged in her top lip. And damn, the look in her eyes made him want to forget leaving the house and take her back upstairs so he could lay her out on the bed and fuck her until they both passed out. And then he'd get off watching Gens do the same.

Finally, she dipped her chin. "Okay. I can do that. But now we need to head over to Haven. We don't have much time to get everything in order."

He stared at her for another few seconds, let her see his lust simmering just below the surface. And watched the color rise in her cheeks again.

God damn, how the fuck was he going to keep his hands off her all fucking day?

The more time Gens spent at Haven, the more he appreciated its vibe.

Mellow, almost zen, with an undercurrent of sex and sophistication. Didn't make much sense but he swore he felt his stress levels drop almost as soon as he walked through the front door and into the lobby.

Music played softly, no Muzak here. Jazzy, slinky. Kind of sexy. Not his usual style but he knew it'd be something Tony would know the name of and love.

Speaking of...

He looked around the lobby area but didn't see Tony or Risa. Guess he should grab a chair and wait. He found one in a corner with its back against the wall, facing the front door. Perfect.

Settling in, he let his gaze sweep over the place. There weren't many people lingering in the lobby. One man waiting at the registration desk. A woman rolling her luggage headed for the elevator.

The only other people were employees, including the doorman who nodded as he glanced his way. Probably security. Guess he didn't look like a threat dressed in dark slacks and a white button-down.

He'd had a meeting with one of Karel's legitimate business partners this morning, which meant dressing the part. He'd left the tie and the jacket in the car. His next stop was a construction site.

Two women and a man worked the registration desk, wearing the same uniform of white shirt and dark skirt or pants, all of which looked expensive as hell.

Guess the owners paid pretty damn well. He'd done a little research on the Golden brothers after Tony had told him to meet them there. They seemed like decent guys, smart businessmen. Tony had introduced Gens to the older brother one night. Tyler. Quiet. Gens hadn't been able to tell if Tyler had known who Gens was. Or if he just didn't care that he'd been introduced to a local mob enforcer.

"You're not just muscle, Gens." Karel had told him that more times than he could remember. *"You've got a brain. Use it."*

Karel had been trying to get him more involved in the legitimate side of the business for the past couple of years. And Gens had discovered a love of construction. Building things.

Which was why he appreciated the architecture of this place, especially the atrium.

The doors were open to the glass-enclosed area in the heart of the building and the more he stared at it, the more he wanted to explore it. Glancing at his watch, he figured he had a few minutes before Tony and Risa showed up.

Standing, he made his way through the lobby and into the atrium.

The first thing he noticed was the change in humidity. It wasn't hot in here, but the air certainly held more moisture.

And damn, just seeing it from the outside didn't do it justice.

The gardeners must have been in the middle of switching from summer to fall because the flowers in the beds and planters all appeared to be shades of orange, red, and yellow.

The area was split in quarters around a central circle.

Each area had its own design but it all worked to create a tranquil oasis.

Just standing here made him feel like he could breathe a little easier.

"Can I help you with anything, sir?"

Gens turned to find a pretty young woman smiling up at him. Golden brown hair pulled back into a tail that probably made her look younger than she really was. Dark eyes, bright smile.

He was surprised the desk hadn't sent the male employee to find out what he was doing here. You just couldn't tell anymore. Yeah, he looked legit but...

"Just waiting for friends."

Her smile widened, no sign of tension anywhere in her face.

"Of course. If you need anything, please let me know. I'm Sabrina." She held out her hand, which he shook without thought. "It's beautiful out here, isn't it?"

"It is. I've been here a few times before but never really noticed."

"I find it soothing." She leaned closer and he automatically bent down. Damn, the girl had no self-protection instincts at all. "And don't tell my boss, but I think he's pretty damn brilliant. He designed all of this."

Gens couldn't help himself. He smiled down at her. "No problem. I can keep a secret."

"Would you like anything while you wait? A drink, maybe?"

"I'm good. But thanks, Sabrina."

She nodded, her smile never wavering as she walked away, leaving him alone again.

Shaking his head, he watched her walk away just as the front door opened and Tony and Risa walked through.

And total tunnel vision took over.

He would recognize Risa anywhere but, dressed as she was now, he wasn't sure a casual acquaintance would. Still as beautiful as if she were wearing silk and satin.

She and Tony paused in the middle of the lobby, not far from where he'd been sitting, and Tony leaned down to speak to her. He didn't touch her, but Gens had learned to read body language pretty well. He wanted to touch her. Wanted to do a lot more than simply touch her.

Gens wanted the same. Even more now since last night.

And that was something he really shouldn't be thinking about now. Not unless he wanted everyone around him to know how much he wanted her.

After another few seconds, Tony scanned the room, obviously looking for someone. Probably Gens. Or maybe the contact he had here.

Gens figured he should probably make himself known. Instead, he let himself watch for a few more seconds.

She looked...okay. Not frightened or tense or nervous. She looked a little flushed but that could be due to the heat of the day. More probably, it had to do with the way she watched Tony. Like she wanted to lick him all over like an ice cream cone.

Did she ever look at him like that when he wasn't aware? Christ, he hoped so. He hoped like hell that after all this time and finally getting to have her, he wasn't just an itch she'd finally scratched.

Wouldn't that just suck?

Huh, after that talk he'd had with Tony the other day and

the night they'd spent with her, you'd think he'd be a little more confident.

Yeah.

As he watched, Tony's attention focused on something on the other side of the room and he touched Risa on the shoulder, drawing her attention.

When the tall, dark-haired man reached Risa and Tony and held out his hand, Gens started moving. Yes, he recognized Tyler Golden from having met him before. No, it didn't matter that the guy had absolutely no reason to cause her harm. Gens still wanted to be at her back.

He made it to them in seconds.

"...sure we can accommodate you for that date and the number of guests."

The three of them looked up as he arrived but he only had eyes for Risa. She brightened as he stopped by her side, her lips curving just for him.

Yeah, he liked that a lot. It gave him hope.

"Mr. Marcov, nice to see you again."

He took Golden's hand and shook it before Golden continued his conversation with Risa.

For the next hour, they walked through almost the entire first floor of the hotel, while Risa asked questions, Golden answered them, and he and Tony stayed the hell out of the way.

She obviously knew what she was doing and exactly what she needed. Every question had Golden responding with a lengthy explanation that didn't seem like bullshit.

He loved watching her work. She looked so damn professional, it made him horny. Seriously. Watching her quiz Golden about how much extra catering staff they'd need to hire and where they would put the orchestra and how the removable walls actually worked gave him a hard-on.

Maybe it was the fact that he'd never really seen her in this context. Maybe it was just the fact that he now knew what she looked like naked. None of it mattered, only that, if he wasn't careful, everyone else would be able to see just how much he wanted to fuck her.

He was pretty sure Tony felt the same.

When she and Golden moved into the atrium and he started to point out places where they would add tables, Gens stopped, far enough away that she couldn't hear them.

Tony stopped beside him.

"You hear anything about Turner?" Tony asked.

"No. No one I talked to knows if he's still in town. We'll keep digging. Eventually we'll find him."

"Find out who hired him to begin with?"

Gens gave Tony the side eye. "Don't you think I would've told you?"

Tony's jaw flexed but he didn't speak. And Gens realized Tony was chewing something over.

"What's on your mind?"

Tony shook his head without looking at him. "Not here."

Okay, that didn't sound good, but he was right. They couldn't talk freely here. But that meant he'd have to wait until they got back to Dorrie's to talk. Which sucked because he was sick of having to watch every word out of his mouth.

He felt like he'd been walking on eggshells all fucking day, even though he hadn't been with them—

Gens took another look at Tony. And realized that's what he'd been picking up on between them.

She and Tony had had sex this morning. That was the

undercurrent he'd been feeling between them for the past hour. And Tony felt guilty.

Shit.

Reaction hit him like a punch in the gut. Not anger. Not jealousy. At least, he wasn't jealous that Tony had taken her without him. He wasn't jealous of Tony.

All right, maybe he was a little jealous of Tony, but he wasn't about to kneecap the guy for not waiting for Gens to be there with them.

Christ. Why the fuck couldn't they just skip past all this bullshit and get to the part where nothing mattered but how the three of them felt about each other? Why did everything have to be so fucking hard?

And when the fuck was he going to find Turner so he could rip his fucking head off for putting her through this?

Of course, if he wanted to be fair, he should thank Turner before he decapitated him. He'd brought Risa to them. Not the way he'd wanted their relationship to start but...

"Gens?" Risa's voice drew him out of his thoughts. "I'm finished here. Are you ready to go?"

Glancing at Tony, who stared at him with narrowed eyes, Gens nodded. "Whenever you are."

Her head tilted to the side, as if she'd heard something in his voice that intrigued her. And when Risa got that look on her face, the people in her life had learned to be wary. Hell, he'd even seen her dad tread lightly when Risa had that expression.

For good reason. The woman had the sharpest fucking tongue.

And he wanted her to use it on his cock when she sucked him into her mouth.

Her brows lifted slightly but she turned and headed for the door. He'd been planning to go back to the construction site after this and let Tony take her home. Now, he couldn't wait to get them both alone and work through this.

At least, he hoped they could work through this.

Risa's heart picked up speed the closer they got to Dorrie's place.

She'd managed to keep her emotions under control at Haven, which had turned out to be a better match for the fundraiser than she could've hoped.

The owner, Tyler, had been amazingly generous with his time and, even after he'd realized who she was, hadn't treated her any differently.

It happened sometimes, when people realized who her father was. It was like a wall came down over their face. Not fast enough to hide their disgust, of course. She'd seen none of that from Tyler, although he could have been just a really good actor. And she'd been just a little preoccupied.

Tony and Gens had stayed quietly in the background, let her ask her questions without interruption. But she couldn't forget that they were both there. Or that she and Tony had had sex in her sister's kitchen before coming to Haven.

What the hell was she going to say to Gens? It didn't feel right not to tell him what had happened. It would be lying by omission and she didn't want to lie. Hell, she'd gotten exactly what she wanted last night but now it seemed like that had just continued to mess up everything around her.

She needed to sit down with both of them and talk, but

every time she tried to think about what she should say, her brain shut down and her heart started to race and she got so fucking upset with herself she found herself fighting back tears.

And that was *so* not going to happen. There was nothing to cry about, damn it.

Beside her, Tony's entire concentration was on driving. Downtown Philadelphia traffic sucked on a good day. Today was not a good day. Asshole drivers were everywhere, and Tony had a few choice words to say several times.

They were alone in the car and hadn't said more than a few words to each other. Gens followed behind.

By the time they'd reached Dorrie's, she still had no idea what the hell to say or even how to bring up the subject.

Did she just blurt out the fact that she and Tony had had sex and if Gens wanted to even the score, she'd be more than happy to oblige?

Ugh. Why did this suck so much?

"I'm going to open the front door. Don't get out until Gens opens your door."

With a sigh, she realized that Tony had parked down the street from Dorrie's house.

"Risa? Did you hear me?"

"I did."

She turned to see Tony staring at her with a narrow gaze, one hand on the steering wheel, one on the door handle.

"You okay?"

"We need to tell Gens."

He didn't pretend to not understand her. "We will. Let's get inside first."

He didn't wait for her to continue. He got out and walked around the front of the car as Gens appeared at her door.

Opening the door, he reached for her hand to help her out. She took it automatically, but her body responded with a leap of her pulse and shortness of breath.

Gens didn't notice as he swept her to the front door of the house next to Dorrie's. The one he and Tony were sharing.

Seconds later, she stood in the living room where they'd had sex last night. Staring at those couches, she couldn't stop thinking about it. She couldn't get enough air. Heat gathered low in her body and spread outward.

For so long, she'd been on a sex diet, only indulging herself when she absolutely couldn't take the loneliness, or her vibrator just wasn't doing it for her.

She'd had more sex last night than she'd had in the past six months and she wanted more. She'd woken up this morning wanting them. She'd taken Tony in the kitchen this morning and the ache in her gut and between her legs had only been satisfied for a little while.

"Risa? Everything okay?"

She turned toward Gens, staring at her with a narrowed gaze.

The man wasn't stupid. Gens might like to make himself appear less than smart. But she knew better. Anyone who knew him knew better.

"We need to talk. All of us. About what happened last night. What happened this morning."

His brows rose at that last bit. "You left last night. We didn't have a chance to talk then. I assume what happened this morning has something to do with why you and Tony have been avoiding each other."

Her back stiffened at his tone. "We haven't been avoiding each other."

Gens curved his mouth in a slight grin. "Uh-huh."

"Gens—"

"We had sex in Dorrie's kitchen." Tony's voice cut off her reply and she looked over her shoulder to find him standing with his hands braced on the back of the couch, his gaze shifting back and forth between them. "Don't blame her."

Her turn for eyebrows to rise. "Don't blame me? Like you forced me to fuck you?"

Tony's eyes rolled before his head dropped. "Jesus, Risa. That's not—"

"Are you seriously trying to take the blame—"

"Oh for fuck's sake." Gens slashed his hand through the air, cutting them off. "Enough. Both of you. Christ, just stop. Look, I know we're in uncharted territory here. Okay? I get it. But jealousy will tear us apart faster than anything. So, let's just stop now and talk this through."

She fell silent, trying to catch her breath, which seemed to have left her again.

"You're right." Tony nodded. "Let's do that. Let's talk."

Tony came back around the sectional sofa separating him from them and dropped onto the cushion, almost exactly where he'd been last night.

Memories flashed through her head, making all the air in her lungs disappear before she could blink the images away.

Movement caught her eye as Gens walked over, put his hands on her shoulders, and eased her down onto the sectional cushion opposite the one Tony sat on.

Gens sat in the middle looking between both of them.

"You two had sex this morning." He paused and looked between them. "I don't see the problem here. I don't expect to be here every time you two wanna scratch an itch. I'm not going to be the sex police. That's not..." He shook his head, as if trying to get his thoughts in order. "That's not how this is going to work. If this is going to work."

Her breath caught in her chest and her gaze went to Tony, whose expression had a hard edge.

Was it all going to end before it even began? Damn it, she wanted more. She felt like she was so close to getting what she wanted for so long but that it might all slip through her hands in seconds.

She sucked in a deep breath. "It *will* work."

Tony looked into her eyes, as if he'd been able to read her mind. Or maybe her thoughts showed so plainly on her face he had no trouble figuring out what she was thinking.

"You're right," Tony continued. "We've got to stop thinking about this in terms of yours, mine, and ours. We're not always going to be together twenty-four-seven."

"No, we're not, are we?"

The question slipped out, almost unexpectedly. She hadn't really planned on saying it out loud, but now that she had, she wanted more than a vague "we'll cross that bridge" discussion.

She wanted more from them.

"We're not always going to be under the same roof. You both have your own places. And I..."

Still lived with her dad. Something she hadn't considered changing recently. And after her kidnapping, did she even want to?

Shit. *Shit.* No, goddammit. None of her decisions would be dependent on what had happened.

"I'll eventually have my own place, as well."

Eyes narrowed, Gens stared at her. "You're planning to move out?"

She stared back, bristling a little at the idea that he thought she shouldn't. Or that she couldn't.

"Eventually, yes. I can't live at home forever. And I refuse to be afraid to live my life on my terms. When I'm ready, I'll leave."

She glanced at Tony, but he just stared back, seemingly unconcerned. Gens looked agitated.

"And go where?"

"Wherever I want."

"Have you talked to your dad about this?"

Her eyebrows rose and she leaned forward, hands on her knees. "Are you suggesting that I ask my dad if I can move out? You do know I'm almost thirty years old. I don't need to ask my father for his permission."

Gens had the good sense to look a little embarrassed, but he still had the nerve to continue. "I didn't say you needed permission. But have you thought through what leaving your dad's house would mean? You're not some girl with money who can buy a condo in a secured apartment and think you can be safe."

"Why not?"

Gens's jaw tensed. "I'm sure you haven't forgotten that someone grabbed you off the street a week ago."

No, she hadn't. And he knew that. "I refuse to live in fear all the time. I'm sick of living with it now. If I let it get to me, I won't do a damn thing for the rest of my life. I'll never leave the house. I refuse to live like that. I hate feeling trapped."

"Do you feel trapped with us?"

Tony's question made her snap her head around to face him. "No. Of course not."

"Then you move in with us."

Her head snapped back to look at Gens as her mouth dropped open. "What? Are you crazy?"

"Why is that crazy?"

"Because I don't need a keeper."

"I'm not saying you need a keeper."

"Then what are you saying? That I can't be trusted to live on my own?"

"Of course that's not what I'm saying." Gens sounded like he was gritting his teeth. "You know that's not what I'm saying. This isn't about you not being able to live on your own."

"Then what? You want to put me in a box and keep me there, safe in a gilded prison?"

"Damn it, Risa. That's not—I don't want to confine you. I want you to be safe and happy."

"And I can't be that on my own?" Rising to her feet, she stood in front of Gens, hands on hips, steam probably coming out of her ears. "So I'm just going to be passed one from one man to the next like a—"

Gens put his hands on her hips and pulled her onto his lap on the couch, cutting her off by putting his mouth over hers.

He stole her breath with a kiss that was an all-out assault on her senses. He didn't wait for her to give her permission or to get up to speed. He just kissed her with an all-consuming passion that dragged her under immediately and completely.

Everything around her disappeared until the only focal point was Gens. The feel of his lips against hers, the way they moved on hers, demanding a response she freely gave. Any thought of resistance fled as her body flooded with heat.

She didn't want to resist. Hell no. She wanted so much more.

With a moan, her hands went from his shoulders to his head, her fingers sinking into his hair. So soft against her palms. So different from the rest of his body.

She felt the coiled tension radiating off him, like a drug she couldn't get enough of.

Sucking on his invading tongue, she tilted her head to get more of him. He responded by putting his hand on her chin and gripping her tight, not allowing her to move.

Her muscles quivered, and she melted at the show of dominance. She wanted more. She felt like she'd had only a taste last night and this morning of what these men could give, and she wanted more.

Apparently, so did Gens.

Moving both hands to her hips, he rearranged her until she had her knees on either side of his. She let him arrange her how he wanted, never breaking that kiss. Rising up onto her knees, she put her hands on his face and returned his kiss with everything she had.

This time, he let her. At least for a few long seconds. She let her tongue slide around his, drowning in his taste.

Hips lowering, she let her mound rub against his erection, pressing at the zipper of his pants. So hard. So tempting. She wanted—

In the next second, she found her ass on the couch next to Gens, until he rose to his feet.

Staring up at him, breathing so hard she felt like she was gasping for air, she searched for words.

"What—"

"That was for doubting us. We'll finish this tonight. You have work to do, don't you? And I've got a meeting I can't miss."

Then he turned and walked out the front door, closing it with a snick behind him.

What the hell?

Turning to Tony, she expected to find the same shock on his face that she felt. He just stared back.

"What the hell just happened?"

Tony sat silently for another few seconds before he got up. She followed him with her gaze, unable to read his expression.

"You're asking the wrong man. You don't need to go anywhere else, do you? I've got a few calls I need to make. You have everything you need here or did you leave your laptop next door?"

Okay, had she stepped into an alternate universe where she'd completely lost control of the situation? Or had Tony and Gens just decided to throw her life into total chaos? Like she needed any more chaos?

"I left my laptop next door. Can you get it for me? Or am I allowed to walk next door without an escort?"

"I'll get it." Tony also headed for the door. "Don't want you to be recognized in the neighborhood."

As the front door closed again, she forced herself to get off the couch and take her phone into the office. It had a desk and a comfy chair and that was pretty much it. Dorrie and the guys hadn't done much to this half of the house yet. They were still debating whether they were going to keep the house as two separate units or combine them into one.

Sitting behind the desk, she set her phone on the top, tapping her fingers beside it.

Then she picked it up again.

I'm going to strangle them with my bare hands.

A few seconds later, Dorrie responded.

LOL. What'd they do?

They're driving me crazy.

That doesn't exactly tell me what they did.

She paused, not wanting to tell her sister about what she and Tony had done in her sister's kitchen over text.

Call me when you can.

Three seconds later, her phone rang.

"Spill."

"Tony and I had sex in your kitchen this morning. Then Aunt Bree called to tell me we need to find a new venue for the fundraiser because the Ritz had a fire in their ballroom and had to cancel so Tony set me up with someone at Haven and we went over there to check it out and when we came back to the house, I told Gens about this morning with Tony and he kissed me and told me we'd finish it tonight and then he walked out."

Silence from the other end.

"Dorrie? You still there?"

"Uh-huh. So what'd you say to piss off Gens?"

"I didn't say anything."

"Yeah, you did, or he wouldn't have walked out. I haven't known him as long as you have, but I think I know him well enough to know you said something that made him need to walk away before he said something you'd both probably regret."

Risa pulled a face, even though she knew her sister couldn't see it.

"Maybe I might have said something about moving out on my own. But then he acted like *I* was acting like a child. Maybe I'm just sick of being treated like one."

"*Are* you thinking about moving out?"

"Not you too, Dorrie. Jesus, I'm almost thirty years old. Someday I'd like to have my own damn space. A place that's just mine. Why is that so hard for everyone to understand?"

A couple beats of silence. "Have you told Dad?"

Now she physically winced. "I brought it up a couple of times before..."

She was kidnapped. And forced to confront the fact that maybe she'd never be able to live on her own.

She sighed. "Maybe I am just fooling myself."

"Don't say that." Dorrie's voice held a sharp rebuke. "And don't believe it either. Sure, you're going to have to take more precautions than other people, but you don't need to live your life in a tower. You don't now. And when Dad catches the asshole who took you, no one will dare come after you again."

Dorrie's growl at the end actually made Risa smile. And then she laughed.

"Are you laughing at me?" Dorrie asked. "Because you know I have ways of making you pay. I can tell your men about the time—"

"They're not my men."

"Oh, please. They are so. Don't delude yourself. And we're going to have to continue this later. My one o'clock is here."

"Convenient excuse," Risa teased, feeling a little better. "Fine. But I want an hour of your time tonight in a male-free zone."

"Yeah, not sure we can arrange the male-free deal, but maybe we can convince them to all hang out in one house while we stay in the other."

"Good idea. Don't worry. I'll take care of the men. You're in charge of arranging dinner. How's that?"

"Sounds like a plan. I really do have to go. Sorry, Ris. We'll talk tonight."

She hung up just as she heard the front door open.

Walking out of the office, she took the laptop from Tony, who had been heading her way.

"Thank you. I'll be in the office if you need me."

Then she closed the door and thought about barricading it behind her.

Which probably would've been too much. But would've felt good.

"So, what'd you assholes do to get us all banished?"

Gens gave Ben the finger before he grabbed another slice of pizza and pretended to watch the Phillies game on the TV in Ben's living room.

He wasn't going to answer that question, mainly because it wasn't any of Ben's business. Also, Gens was fairly certain

Ben already knew the answer to that question. Maybe not the specifics, but Ben had probably been banished by Dorrie a few times in their relationship, so he could probably make a pretty damn good guess.

Gens noticed Tony had totally ignored Ben's questions and was watching the game with the concentration of a loyal Phillies fan. Which he wasn't. Tony was a diehard hockey fan, though not of the Flyers. Smart guy. They'd sucked last season.

"They pissed her off." Ian set his beer back on the table with a clink. "Not that hard to figure out. You get any leads on Turner?"

And this was why Gens liked Ian better than his cousin. "Maybe. Talked to my Romano family contact, the one who gave me the tip about the auction. Said he'd heard the auction was moved but that they still held it."

"So it's unlikely Turner's still in the area." Ian sighed. "Good and bad there."

"I'm not convinced Turner's going to give up that easily," Tony said. "If he was willing to take the risk once, I'm sure he's willing to try for her again."

Which made Gens want to rip Turner's head off when he recalled what Risa had said about moving out on her own.

Did you seriously expect her to live with her father for the rest of her life?

No. Yes? Who the fuck knows. He'd never really thought about it.

Maybe you should have.

Yeah, yeah, well he was thinking about it now. And it gave him heart palpitations.

Karel would have to buy her an entire damned apartment

building so they could be sure she'd be safe. So they could hire the staff and the security and make sure she'd be protected.

Or she could just move in with me.

And what about Tony?

His gaze automatically went to his friend, listening intently to whatever Ian and Ben were discussing. He probably should be, as well. But his brain was too preoccupied to add anything useful.

Would Tony stay? He'd been talking about leaving. Would last night change his mind?

Would tonight bring them closer to the relationship Risa wanted?

And what about what he wanted?

"Gens?"

"Hmm?"

Tony's brows rose when Gens looked his way.

"Did you get any of that?"

"Yeah. You're not sure Turner ran off with his tail between his legs. Me either. So what are we going to do about it?"

Tony's eyebrows lifted. "Then you weren't listening."

Sue him. Gens gave Tony the finger, which made Ben laugh.

"Ian thinks she should resume her normal schedule, see if anyone shows interest."

Gens understood the reasoning, but his immediate response was a hard "Hell no, we're not using her as bait."

He managed, barely, not to make that mistake, but he stared at Tony, trying to figure out if he agreed with Ian.

Tony shook his head, apparently reading Gens's mind.

"You don't even have to ask. My answer's no. But you know Risa. She's not going to agree to put her life on hold so we can feel better."

Put that way, yeah, it sounded pretty damn bad. Then again, Risa couldn't hear them so why not be honest.

"She's talking about moving out of her dad's house."

"Okay."

Ian's lazy drawl put Gens's back up.

"You don't see that as a problem right now?"

Ian shrugged. "She's what? Twenty-eight. I'm surprised she isn't out on her own already. She's not a doll. You can't just put her in a box when you're not around."

That's not what he wanted to do, goddammit.

"I just don't think now's the time for her to be making drastic changes to her life."

"Like starting an affair with two men. 'Cause that's not a big change at all."

Ian rolled his eyes at Ben's sarcastic comment as Tony and Gens glared at him.

Ben held out his hands in surrender, though he didn't look as if he cared that he should be bleeding from holes he didn't need.

"Hey, I'm just saying. You two need to look at the big picture here. If you're going to sustain a relationship with Risa, you're gonna need to learn to bend. Both of you. A relationship like this doesn't work otherwise."

"Or," Ian added, "at least you have to learn to keep your mouth shut and maneuver behind the scenes to get things to go the way you want."

"You know if Dorrie heard you say that, you'd be sleeping on the couch for a week."

Ben's laughing comment made Ian shrug, though a smile played around the corners of his mouth.

"I'm not an idiot. And I've never had to sleep on the couch."

"Only because she hasn't caught you yet. Someday your luck's gonna run out, cousin."

"Gotta pick your fights." Ian directed that comment at Gens. "Some you're gonna win. Some you should win and won't. And sometimes you just need to learn to keep your mouth shut and do it on your own."

"I'm thinking about asking her to move in with me."

Tony barely made a move, but Gens knew his friend well enough to know he'd caught Tony off guard.

But after a few beats, Tony nodded. "I think that's probably the best option. Your apartment's more secure."

"And it's bigger than yours."

"So...what?" Tony's expression clouded over. "You think we're both just going to pick up our shit and move in with you? It's been one fucking night, Gens."

"We're not getting any younger. And I'm fucking sick of dancing around this shit. Look, either we're in this together or it's every man for himself and you know that's not gonna end well. For any of us."

"You really want to do this here? Now?"

"Fuck that. I don't want to do it at all. But we need to be on the same page or this is gonna blow up in our faces and she's gonna kick us both to the curb. And I'm not willing to risk that."

"And you think I am?"

Tony's quiet, calm tone belied the anger and frustration Gens could see in his friend's eyes.

Christ, every fucking conversation lately was a minefield. At least Risa wasn't here to see them going to head-to-head on this.

"Shit." Gens sighed and shook his head. "No."

After several seconds of tense silence, Ian took his life into his hands and spoke.

"You two want a little unsolicited advice from someone who's been here, done this?"

Surprisingly, Tony nodded. "Sure."

"You guys have to get your shit together or you're gonna push her away. And I don't think either of you wants that. But that means you have to work together. It doesn't mean you're always going to agree. It means you need to present a united front about the big things. The things that matter. Like her safety. Like the fact that she's not going to agree with everything you say. You also have to learn not to steamroll her on the things you two agree on."

"Dude." Ben's voice held a note of awe. "You almost sound like you know what you're talking about."

Ian rolled his eyes but didn't look at Ben, just gave him the finger.

"I know exactly what I'm talking about because I'm a lot like both of you. And that's something she's got to come to grips with. Ben's here for comic relief—"

"Hey," Ben said, "you're an asshole."

"—but you two...you've got intense down to an art. And that can get exhausting real fast."

The man wasn't wrong, Gens realized. "So we should take stand-up comedy classes? She's known us for years. If she wanted someone different, she could've found someone else."

"True." Ian shrugged. "But the three of you together was more of a concept than reality until a few days ago. Now, you have to figure out how to make a relationship work between three people. And trust me, sex is easy. It's when you get out of bed that things go to shit."

20

An hour after they'd returned to the other house, Gens got a text from Ian that Risa was on her way back to them.

When Gens raised his head, Tony looked over and Gens nodded.

"We're agreed?" Tony asked.

"Yeah."

"You think she's going to agree?"

"Could go either way."

"You sure you're okay with this?"

"I wouldn't have suggested it if I wasn't. You getting cold feet?"

Tony shook his head. "I'm in. Just not sure she's going to go for this. It's a big step and it's fast."

"You'd rather she move into her own apartment, alone?"

"I'm not convinced she's moving out to begin with."

Gens shrugged. "Doesn't matter if she agrees to move in with us."

"And if she doesn't?"

"We'll just have to convince her."

Tony knew it wasn't going to be that easy. Nothing with Risa was easy. But Gens was convinced this was the first step they needed to take.

Tony didn't disagree. In fact, if he was completely honest with himself, he'd admit he was more than a little excited by the prospect.

He'd been on his own for years. He'd never lived with a woman other than his mother and grandmother. He'd dated, had lovers, none he'd wanted to move in with.

Risa was the first woman he'd ever considered allowing into his personal space. Hell, the fact that he and Gens would be sharing the same space didn't even make him twitchy.

He'd been alone a long time. He'd only recently realized he'd been lonely.

"And how do you expect to do that?"

"By showing her why she should."

Tony nodded, knowing that would be Gens's answer.

"You still onboard?" Gens asked.

"My mind hasn't changed in the past few minutes."

"We need to be on the same page."

"We are. She comes first."

Gens opened his mouth to say something else but stopped when the front door opened. They both turned to watch Risa walk through, turn and wave, then close the door behind her.

She must not have realized they were there at first because she paused for a few seconds, head bent, then took a deep breath and spun around. Only to freeze in place when she saw them.

No one said anything for several seconds. Then her chin tilted and she closed the distance between them.

"You didn't have to wait up for me."

He and Gens exchanged a quick glance. Tony raised his brows, giving Gens the go-ahead.

"Were you expecting us to ignore you? You've been alone with Dorrie all night. We didn't realize you wanted to avoid us completely."

"I wasn't avoiding you. I was spending time with my sister. There's a difference. I'm here now. Is there something you wanted to discuss?"

Tony finally spoke up. "Gens and I have been talking. We want you to move in with us."

Her lips parted in shock and her eyes widened. "Are you kidding?"

"Obviously not or I wouldn't have said anything."

Her lips snapped together as her arms crossed over her chest. Definitely defensive.

Tony had to admit he was turned on. Probably not the exact response he should have right now but what the hell? He was done trying to conceal his feelings from her. Apparently, he'd done that enough.

Now, she was either going to let them act on the heat or they were going to have to give this shit up. No more middle ground.

"I'm not sure I'm up for this toni—"

"Come here, Risa."

Tony didn't raise his voice, but he knew she heard the hard edge in his tone. The command. She'd said she wanted this. Now was the time to put up or shut up.

And no, he wasn't stupid enough to say *that* out loud.

He saw her hesitate, saw her consider every possible angle. Saw the blush on her cheeks deepen. Wondered what the hell she would do if he pulled her over his lap and spanked her bare ass until it blushed a dark red.

Fuck, he'd really love to see.

Finally, she took the few steps she needed to be standing in front of him. Gens watched from the bend in the sectional, looking content for the moment.

Last night, they'd let her be in control, mostly. Tonight, that wasn't going to be the case.

"Say yes."

Tony saw the war she was waging with herself. Did she give him what he wanted? Or did she challenge him? That fight for control was something she had to work out on her own.

He hoped like hell she said yes because if she didn't...

She didn't say anything right away, just stared down at him. Her gaze looked steady, but she nibbled on her bottom lip. There were her nerves.

Damn it. He didn't want her to—

She released her lip. "Yes."

He took a second to breathe then stood. She watched him rise, her head tilting back, until he towered over her.

She looked certain. And excited. That's what he wanted to see.

Looking around her, he glanced at Gens and nodded. Gens rose to his feet behind her and stepped closer, until only inches separated them.

Tony knew she felt Gens behind her because her

breathing came faster and harder. She swallowed hard but didn't drop his gaze.

"Take her up."

In his peripheral vision, he saw Gens having a hard time controlling his grin.

"Strip her."

Her lips parted on a gasp and he saw shock in her widening eyes. But she must not have been able to find the right words until Gens lifted her into his arms and headed for the stairs.

"Hey! What—"

"I have to get something," Tony said. "I'll be right there."

Her eyes went even wider as she stared over Gens's shoulder at him before he disappeared with her up the stairs.

Tony waited several seconds, listening for the sound of Gens's footsteps in the room above. The room with the king bed, where Risa had slept alone last night.

Then he headed for the stairs, planning to make a stop in the bedroom down the hall where he'd stored his stuff two days ago.

She wouldn't be sleeping alone tonight.

Risa's brain raced as Gens carried her up the stairs.

He didn't say anything as they climbed or when they got to the room. She wasn't used to being carried, wasn't used to being told what to do, wasn't used to feeling like she had no control.

She wasn't frightened. Far from it.

She was excited. Her breasts ached and her sex clenched.

Her arms tightened around Gens's neck as she stared up at him.

He seemed intently focused on getting to the bedroom in the shortest amount of time. She could barely catch her breath. And when he walked into the bedroom and set her on her feet, she had to swallow hard before she could even attempt to speak.

"What did Tony need to get?"

Gens had a slight smile. "Scared?"

Her chin went up. "Why should I be?"

Before she knew what he intended, Gens lowered his head and kissed her hard, so hard he stole what little breath she had left.

His hands settled on her shoulders and pulled her closer, her chest against his.

Heat boiled low in her body and spread outward, so fast and hot, she was afraid she might spontaneously combust.

She melted into him, gave herself over him to completely, and shut off the little voice in her head that kept whispering, telling her to run.

Why would she run when they were promising to give her exactly what she wanted? Both of them.

Her hands reached for his hips and held him tight, trying to drag him closer. He wouldn't budge. But his hands slid from her shoulders down her arms until he reached the hem of her shirt.

He broke their kiss long enough for him to pull her t-shirt over her head and to glance down at her half-naked body. She hadn't bothered with a bra tonight and she was bare from her waist up.

"So fucking beautiful." His hands slid up her torso to cup

her breasts, his thumbs and forefingers pinching her nipples hard, making her moan low in her throat. "But I have my orders."

Releasing her breasts, his hands fell to the button on her jeans and, seconds later, he had her stepping out of those, her underwear, and her shoes.

Now she was completely naked. And so turned on her sex ached.

"Now lie on the bed, sweetheart. I have a feeling I know what Tony stopped in his room for."

She didn't move right away, more than a little breathless and on edge.

"And what's that?"

Gens's gaze slid over her shoulder and his slight grin made her turn.

Tony had entered the room, something in his hands. When she realized what he held, a flush swept through her body. Her sex clenched and she swore if a slight breeze brushed her clit, she'd come.

"Are those—"

"We'll get to these a little later." Tony set the straps with their leather cuffs on the chair by the bed. "We'll start a little slower. On your knees on the bed."

Sucking in air, she hesitated, only because she wasn't sure she could get her legs to move.

She only had a second to realize Gens had moved behind her before she felt his hand smack her ass then smooth over it.

Biting her tongue on a moan, she made the decision to give herself over to them.

Without a word, she turned and walked to the bed, climbing up and settling onto her knees, just like Tony had said.

His lips curved in a way that wasn't quite a smile but made her light up inside.

"I'm going to watch while Gens takes you first. I guess you could say we owe him one. But then we're going to put those cuffs on you and we're going to make you come until you pass out. Say yes, sweetheart."

She wasn't completely sure she'd be able to speak but she forced herself to try.

Her "Yes" was barely audible but must have sufficed. Tony nodded, and Gens walked around the bed behind her.

Keeping her gaze locked with Tony's, she felt the bed dip as Gens climbed up behind her.

Gens didn't waste any time. He wrapped his arms around her from behind, spread his hands over her stomach then slid one up to squeeze her breasts and slid the other down between her legs.

She closed her eyes as his fingers slid through the moisture gathering on her labia, sucked in air on a gasp as he slipped two fingers into her body. He didn't force his way in. He didn't have to. Her sex practically sucked him in, she was so hot for him.

Her head fell back against his chest as he fucked her with his fingers, his mouth latching on to her neck and his teeth sinking into the sensitive curve.

Already on the edge, she tried to hold back the orgasm Gens was intent on giving her.

With his fingers tweaking both nipples almost to the

point of pain, he slowed the motion of the hand between her legs until she was arching her back to show him what she wanted.

Her ass brushed against the hard rod of his cock, and she moaned, wanting him to fuck her. She felt like she was losing control, but she was ready to give it over to them. She trusted them.

"You're so slick and hot, sweetheart." Gens breathed against her neck. "And so damn tight."

"Then fuck me."

"Not yet. And this isn't fucking. This is the definition of making love. Because I fucking love making you come."

Moaning as her body shuddered, she ground her ass against him. "Then make me come."

A second later, she found herself on all fours, blinking at the sudden change. And realizing that Tony had stripped and now stood only inches away from the bed.

But her eyes closed again as Gens slid into her from behind. Her head dropped and her back bowed as he began to thrust hard and fast, his hands on her hips the only things holding her up.

She wanted to collapse and let him take her, but she felt the air shift in front of her.

Forcing her eyes open, she saw Tony, or rather, she saw Tony's erection only inches from her mouth.

Without hesitation, she leaned forward and sucked him between her lips, smiling a little as he groaned and put his hands on either side of her head.

"Fuck, Risa."

Yes, exactly.

As Gens took her, she took Tony, the three of them finding a rhythm that worked beautifully.

Her lips and tongue worked Tony's hard shaft with loving devotion as Gens fucked her hard from behind. But when Tony began to go at his own pace, she let him take control.

Caught between them, she thought this was heaven.

Until Gens slowed and Tony pulled away. She must have made a sound of protest as her eyes opened and she looked up.

Tony had his hand on her chin, stroking her cheek with his thumb.

But it was Gens who spoke.

"Hang tight, Ris. We're going to make this better."

She didn't know if her heart could take much better. And when she realized what he meant, the hunger in her gut exploded through her blood.

Gens laid her down on her side on the bed, moving away for a second as Tony kneeled on the bed beside her.

"Come here, hon. Let us make this even better."

He grabbed the strap he'd brought in with him and looped it around the center slat in the headboard, leaving the cuffs on the ends free.

"Hands up."

The fact that he hadn't asked her permission made her blood run even hotter and her lungs tightened to the point that she could barely breathe. And still she followed his direction.

She raised her hands above her head, watching as he tightened the cuffs around her wrists. Her heart beat so fast and hard, it nearly drowned out every other sound.

But she still heard Tony clearly as he stretched out in front of her and said, "Now let us have you completely."

Her eyes closed as Tony's mouth sealed hers and his cock slid between her thighs, the head lodging at the entrance of her body for several long seconds before he arched his hips and slid home.

Moaning into his mouth, she wrapped her hands around the strap and held on as he gave several heavy thrusts before he stopped and held high inside her.

Then she felt Gens against her back. She had to tear her mouth away from Tony's so she could breathe, her forehead resting against his broad chest as Gens cupped her ass in his hands and spread her.

"Relax, Ris. And open for me."

She tried to relax but she was too damn excited. Tony's cock throbbed in her pussy and the tip of Gens's slick cock began to press against the tiny opening of her ass. He went slow. It seemed to take forever until they were both seated inside her. She felt full. Almost too full.

Then they began to move.

And the pent-up excitement in her body released in a wave as they fucked her so slowly she thought she might burst from frustration.

She wanted to move with them, but they held her so tightly between them, Gens's hands on her hips, Tony's on her ribs, just below her breasts.

They took her almost too slowly, as if they thought she might break. But when she opened her mouth over Tony's pec and bit him, he growled and picked up the pace, forcing Gens to, as well.

Yes. This was what she'd wanted. What'd she longed for.

To be taken hard and fast and given exactly what she wanted. What she needed.

She hung on the edge for as long as she could before she couldn't hold back any longer.

Her orgasm snapped through her, her body clenching around them, dragging them into oblivion with her.

21

"We think we found Turner."

Gens sat up in bed, instantly alert. Beside him, Risa stirred but didn't wake. Tony hadn't returned from wherever he'd gone a few minutes ago.

"Say again."

Karel didn't hesitate. "He's still in the states and he's set up another auction, this time in Orlando. I need you and Anton to make sure she's safe. I've already sent men down to take him. As soon as we have him, we'll bring him here. Then we can decide what to do with him."

"I need to be in Florida."

"No, you need to be with Risa."

"I need to make sure that bastard doesn't get anywhere near her ever again."

"You do that by making sure she's protected, not by leaving her unprotected."

"Tony won't leave her side. We'll move her back to the house—"

"No. This isn't the life I wanted for her or you. I'm tired of worrying that someone else will think they can use her against me. No, I'm going to take care of Turner and then I'm getting out."

"Karel, what—"

"You and Risa and Dorrie will be taken care of. I've lived this life long enough to know when it's time to get out. I should've gotten out years ago when the girls were young, but I was greedy and stupid. I like to think I've gotten smarter with age."

Stunned, Gens couldn't think of a thing to say. He hadn't known Karel was even considering getting out. Others had done it. It took a huge amount of prep and a damn lot of luck, but it could be done.

"So you're going to stay with Risa and I'm going to handle Turner. When he and I have come to a mutual understanding, Risa and Dorrie and I will discuss future plans. Understood?"

"Yeah. I understand. Just...be careful."

Karel laughed, a short sound that Gens hadn't heard in months. Maybe years. "I'm not old enough yet to be senile and I like to think I'm not stupid. There are things I still want to do with my life, son. Retirement sounds like a good way to get those things."

Karel hung up a second later and Gens lowered the phone to find Risa staring up at him.

"Did you hear that?"

She nodded. "Most of it, yes. He told you not to go. But you still want to, don't you?"

"Of course. I want that bastard to fry and I want to be there when it happens."

"More than you want to stay with me."

Frustration burned in his chest. "I'd be doing this for you."

"But Dad told you to stay. He had to tell you to stay. Why is staying a problem?"

"It's not a problem, Ris. But I want to make sure this fucker knows not to come after you again."

"And maybe I just want to forget the whole thing ever happened and move on."

"Hey. What's going on?"

Tony stepped into the room, rubbing one hand against the back of his head, eyes narrowed.

"Karel has a lead on Turner."

"And we're leaving when?"

"He doesn't want us to go."

"Neither do I." Risa looked between them. Naked from the waist up, where the sheet swirled around her hips, she looked like sex personified.

Hair mussed and falling over her shoulders, she took his fucking breath away, and if anyone ever tried to take her again, he'd rip their throat out with his bare hands.

Which was why he needed to make this statement with Turner. Anyone who tried to mess with her again needed to know what they were up against.

"Let Dad handle this. I heard him say he wants out. Why can't we do that? Why can't you just let this go and let him handle it?"

"Getting out doesn't mean turning tail." Tony glanced at Gens before refocusing his attention on Risa. "Gens isn't wrong on this. If we don't prove we're strong enough to protect you, someone else might try. And I don't want to be looking over our shoulders for the rest of our lives."

"So this is all about pounding your chests and marking me as yours." Her voice held a sharp edge now. "How do I get to make my voice heard in this so-called arrangement? I'm asking you to put me first."

"We *are* putting you first." Gens shook his head. Why the hell did she not understand what he was saying? "You know this is how it works."

"What about making a clean break? If you do this, you're dragging Tony down into the mud with us."

"This would be my decision, Ris," Tony practically growled, his voice dropped so low. "And I agree with Gens. If we can't protect you, there's going to be someone out there who thinks they'll be able to take you."

Her gaze burned as she looked at each of them. "The benefit is in two days. Are you both going to leave me? Or are you going to play Rock, Paper, Scissors to see who has to stay?"

"Damn it, that's not fair." Gens grabbed his boxers off the bed so he could pace. Frustration made him want to put his hand through the wall. "Why are you fighting this? It's a couple of days and we'll be back—"

"Will you? You don't know that. You can't guarantee me that nothing will happen to you. And then what? What am I supposed to do?"

Her expression somewhere between anger and despair, Risa shook her head.

And sue him, but his gaze dropped to watch her breasts play peekaboo through her hair.

He knew he shouldn't be focused on that, but he fucking loved the fact that she was naked and that he'd spent most of the night with her naked and in bed with him and Tony. Hell, he'd gotten off on the fact that he and Tony had been able to bring her more pleasure together than if they'd been alone with her.

He absolutely hated that they were fighting now. He didn't want to fight. He wanted her to understand.

"Then let us take care of this," Tony beat Gens to the exact words he was thinking. "We'll be back in time for the fundraiser. After that, we'll make plans."

She looked between them with an expression Gens couldn't decipher. After a few quiet seconds, she finally took a deep breath and nodded, her gaze lowering to the bed.

"If you believe this is what you need to do, then go."

The tone of her voice stopped Gens his tracks.

"Risa? What—"

"No, I'm serious." She looked up and looked from Gens to Tony and back again. "If you feel this strongly about it, then you should go."

Gens ran a hand through his hair and tugged on it. "You realize we're doing this for you? So you don't have to worry about this asshole anymore."

She looked like she wanted to say something, something he and Tony probably wouldn't like. Then she took another deep breath and nodded.

"I understand that. When are you leaving?"

Gens exchanged a glance with Tony, who was obviously thinking the same thing.

"In a few hours. And we'll be back in two days." Tony closed the distance between them, sitting on the edge of the bed and cupping her chin in his hand. "We're not going to do anything that'll jeopardize this."

Another pause, another several seconds that left Gens scrambling to interpret what she wasn't saying.

Maybe you just don't want to hear what she's saying.

No, she'd understand. And they'd make it up to her when they got back.

"Everything'll be fine." Gens had to make her see that.

She didn't even bother to fake a smile. She just nodded.

"I'm sure it will be. I guess you'd better pack."

"Are you sure you don't want to come back to my place? I mean...I know you live here but I really enjoyed having you so close. Kind of made up for the years we didn't get to live together."

Risa smiled at Dorrie but continued to pack clothes into her suitcase.

"I enjoyed it, too. But I really need to get away for a little."

"Then let me come with you."

Risa bit her bottom lip, not wanting to get her hopes up. "I would love that. But I don't want to—"

"I've got nothing on my calendar that I can't move." Dorrie frowned. "But what about the fundraiser?"

Shrugging, Risa folded another shirt. "All the hard work's finished. Bree will totally understand when I tell her what happened. I just...need some space. But I would love to spend time with you."

"And I want to spend time with you." Dorrie practically bounced on the bed. "We can do this. Where are we going? London? Paris? Rome?"

"Florence."

Her sister's eyes widened. "Ooh. I've never been. Shopping, right?"

"Yes, shopping. And food. And wine."

"And it's far away from two certain men."

"I'd rather not talk about them."

Dorrie raised an eyebrow. "You sure? You sure you don't want to bitch just a little?"

Of course, she wanted to bitch. She wanted to scream and yell and cry. Yes, she wanted to cry. She wanted to get away from here before she actually broke down and wept.

And she would hate them if that happened.

But the burning pain in her chest hadn't alleviated since Gens and Tony had left yesterday. And she'd decided this morning she wasn't waiting for them to come home.

They'd left her. She understood their reasoning. At least, she understood why they wanted to go. But...they'd left her behind.

She'd wanted them to stay with her. To *want* to stay with her.

Not to run off to avenge her kidnapping.

"No, I don't want to complain. I want to get away. And they should have known that."

"There you go." Dorrie spoke with quiet encouragement. "Come on, Ris. Let it out."

The anger began to boil over, heat spreading through her chest and into her gut, making her hands curl into fists. She had to make a conscious effort to unclench them, breathing through the urge to scream.

"If I let it out, I'm afraid I'll lose part of myself in the process. That's not me. That girl who screams and cries and stomps her feet. I'm not a pretty crier. I don't feel better afterward."

"And how do you know that?"

"Because when I broke down after I was…after they brought me home, I felt like shit."

"Kidnapped, Risa." Dorrie reached out, grabbed her right hand, and squeezed. "You were kidnapped. It's okay to be pissed off, upset, freaked out, traumatized, whatever the hell you want to be about that. It's just not healthy to hold it all in and assume one day it'll go away and disappear."

"I know that. I also know that if I give in and let it out, it won't be pretty. And Daddy's downstairs."

If she'd been a cartoon character, Dorrie would've had a lightbulb appear over her head. Her expression softened as she nodded. "Okay, I get it. But you don't have to fly across an ocean to have a breakdown in peace."

"I need a complete change of scenery."

Dorrie smiled and nodded. "Okay then. I guess I need to tell my guys I'm going on a trip and pack my bag."

Risa jumped off the bed and threw her arms around her sister's shoulders. "Thank you."

Dorrie hugged her back just as tightly. "What are sisters for if not to drop everything and go to Italy when you need them?"

***

"What do you mean she's gone?"

Karel settled back in the chair behind his desk, staring at Tony with an expression that made grown men cringe. Hell, Tony wanted to cringe, but he figured Karel wouldn't want a weak man involved with his daughter, so he forced himself not to react.

"Exactly what I said. She packed a bag, went to the airport, and caught a flight. Two days ago."

"What? Two days?" Gens shook his head, drawing Karel's gaze away from Tony. "She left the day after we did?"

"Yes." Karel held up one hand when Gens opened his mouth again. "She and Dorrie and two personal security guards from DeMarcos went to Europe for a…vacation."

Tony's back teeth began to grind from frustration. He knew exactly what vacation was code for. Space. From them.

Damn it, they'd fucked this up good.

But apparently Gens refused to see the writing on the wall.

"A vacation? Now?"

Karel didn't bat an eyelash. "My daughter is not and never was a prisoner to this house. I made sure she was well guarded and then I drove her and Dorrie to the airport, kissed them good-bye, told them to have a good time, and watched until their plane took off. Now, maybe you want to tell me how your trip went?"

For several seconds, Tony waited to see what Gens would do.

The intel they'd gotten from Karel's contact had led them straight to Turner. He'd been surprised to see them, which was an understatement. Turner had been shocked as shit when they'd walked through the door of the warehouse where he was planning to hold his next auction.

There'd been some bloodshed, mainly from Turner and his men after Gens, Tony, and the three men they'd taken with them to Florida had confronted them. Tony's arm had been grazed by a bullet. Gens probably had a concussion from the hit one of Turner's goons had laid on him. One of their men had cracked ribs and they'd all come away with a few bumps and bruises. Airport security had given them all the side eye, but Gens had grinned at the pretty, blonde TSA agent and cracked a joke about a bachelor party gone wrong, the situation had defused without the need for body searches and delays.

They hadn't said much on the flight home, but Tony couldn't wait to get off the damn plane and back to Risa. He'd had an ache in the pit of his stomach for the past two days. An ache he'd attributed to the threat against her from Turner.

But that ache had only intensified the closer they'd gotten to home.

They'd driven straight to Dorrie's from the airport. That ache had become a gnawing grind when no one had answered the door. Then they'd come straight here.

"We took care of business." Gens' voice was pretty much a growl. "Turner won't come after her or anyone else connected to you again because we told him next time we'd cut off his fingers and toes first and shove them down his throat and then we'd start with other parts that were probably just as small."

"Glad to hear it." Karel continued to stare at Gens. "And now? What are your plans now?"

Gens flashed Tony a quick glance and opened his mouth. Tony beat him to it.

"We're going to make it up to her."

Karel's brows rose again. "Make what up to her?"

"We fucked up." Gens spoke up now. "We left her, and we shouldn't have."

"Yes, you fucked up." Karel's voice held an edge now. "But if you think that's the reason she left, you don't deserve to have her."

With a sigh, Karel shook his head and sat forward in his chair, setting his hands on his desk. "I'm getting out, Gens. I'm tired of my daughters paying for my life choices. Hell, I should've done this a long time ago. What matters is I'm doing it now. For my daughters. And because I'm sick and goddamn tired of not being able to acknowledge the woman I love."

Tony's mouth dropped open at Karel's admission, and a quick look at Gens showed the same expression. Gens got his mouth working faster than Tony would've thought possible.

"You mean you're finally going to ride off into the sunset with Elizabeth?"

Tony knew Karel and Dorrie's mom, Elizabeth, had been seeing each other for decades. He had no idea of the history though because Dorrie had never talked about her parents' relationship with him and he'd never asked.

Going by Gens's tone, he'd never thought it would happen.

"I mean, I'm going to get the hell out of this business and so are you. I'll set you up in whatever business you want. Risa will never have to worry financially. And you," Karel pinned Tony with a look that made Tony feel like a guilty teenager in the principal's office. "I assume you're going to be here for Risa, as well. Whatever you need to take care of my daughter, you'll get. But first, you're going to need to win her back. Because you two managed to fuck up. And you did it amazingly well."

Yeah, Tony couldn't argue with that. Neither could Gens apparently, because he managed to keep his mouth shut this time.

"So." Karel stood, his chair rolling back out of his way. "When she gets back, and not before then, you two are going to need to fix this. Figure it out, gentlemen. But not in my office. I've got a date tonight, which is more than you two can say. You know where the door is."

22

Risa checked her phone for what had to be the thousandth time since she'd gotten off the plane. Still no messages. From either of them.

She sighed, which made Dorrie roll her eyes.

"Oh, just call them already." Dorrie huffed. "Put you and me out of our collective misery."

Risa gave her sister a discreet finger as they sat in the back of Ian's sedan. Ian and Ben had been waiting for them at the airport. Risa didn't begrudge her sister the sweet reunion. But she could admit to herself that she was jealous as hell.

She'd asked Ian to drop her off at her dad's and he'd surprised her by saying that's where they were all going anyway. Her dad wanted to talk to both of them. Right away. Ian had assured them nothing was wrong but he had an announcement he wanted to share.

So, of course, that had added to Risa's anxiety. She'd already been wondering if Tony or Gens, or both of them, would be at the airport to pick her up. She refused to admit it out loud, but she'd been hurt and pissed when neither of them had showed.

She hoped like hell she wouldn't run into Gens at the house. She had no expectation that Tony would be there, which just made her sad. And pissed her off all over again.

Ugh. For the past seven days, she'd shopped, eaten amazing food, consumed copious amounts of really good wine, and basically did nothing except enjoy her sister's company.

It'd been the first time they'd taken a trip together and she'd loved it.

But now that it was over, and she was back in the real world, she needed to put her game face on again.

She was pretty sure she'd managed to will her expression into a pretty good facsimile of her old self. The one who hadn't expected much from anyone and therefore hadn't been disappointed when someone lived down to her expectations.

The fact that she'd expected more from two men and was disappointed was totally on her. She should've known better.

When they finally pulled up to the house, she breathed a sigh of relief. Not because she'd been homesick. She'd simply missed the familiar. Her dad. Her home.

But you can't live at home for the rest of your life.

Forcing the thought out her head, she smiled when the front door opened, and her dad walked through. But her smile turned to shock when Dorrie's mom walked out behind him.

She snapped around to look at Dorrie, who looked just as shocked as Risa felt.

"Don't ask me," Dorrie said. "I don't have a freaking clue."

They practically jumped out of the car, heading for their dad with a purpose.

Risa hugged him first because Dorrie went for her mom and then they switched. Risa liked Elizabeth, though she could probably count on two hands how many times they'd met face-to-face over the years. But Dorrie loved her mom and Risa knew that was all that mattered.

"Dad, what's going on?"

"Mom, what are you doing here?"

Karel actually smiled, something he'd done so rarely lately, Risa's lips parted in shock.

"Welcome home, girls. I hope you had a good time. Come on in and sit down. I realize you have some questions, and we'll answer them. But first come in and get settled."

Half an hour later, the shock over her dad's announcement had faded but a weird sense of unease had settled in the pit of Risa's stomach. She was thrilled for her dad and Elizabeth. Worried, too, of course. Nothing about their life had ever been easy. Getting out of it without more than a few problems was unrealistic.

Being left behind on her own...that was going to suck. But there was no way in hell she was going to ruin her dad's happiness by sulking.

So she smiled, which she didn't have to fake, and asked about what they planned to do. But Elizabeth proved to be much more perceptive than Risa gave her credit for.

When Risa excused herself to go to the bathroom, she found Elizabeth waiting for her alone in her dad's study when she returned.

"Where'd Dad and everyone else go?"

Elizabeth nodded toward the open door that led to the backyard. "Outside. I wanted a few minutes alone with you. I hope you don't mind."

"Of course not. Is something wrong?"

"No, no. Nothing like that. I just..." Elizabeth's smile twisted. "I guess I just wanted to check to make sure you're okay with this. Your dad and I. I know you and he have been a team for years. I'm the interloper—"

"No, Elizabeth." Risa rushed over and sat beside Dorrie's mom. "You're not an interloper. I've never thought that about you."

"I'm glad to hear that." Elizabeth took her hand and squeezed before she pulled Risa in for a hug that Risa returned. "You don't know how relieved I am. I just want you to know that I want us to be close. I want you to feel you can tell me anything. I know this all seems really sudden—"

Risa laughed. "No, it really doesn't. I think you both have waited long enough. You deserve to be happy together."

"Your dad wants the same for you." Elizabeth paused, and Risa had a sneaking suspicion she knew what her future stepmom was about to say. "I hope you don't mind but he told me what happened. That had to be terrifying."

Before she realized what she was doing, Risa nodded. "It was. The worst part was not knowing if I'd see my dad or Dorrie or—well, my family again."

"Does that family include two certain men?"

Risa should've known her dad would've told Elizabeth what was going on in her life. And honestly, she was kind of relieved she didn't have to explain anything herself.

"I thought it might."

"But you're not sure now?"

"They left me."

Oh my god, how pathetic did that sound? She wanted to take the words back as soon as they left her mouth. Elizabeth would think she was—

"I know exactly how you feel." Elizabeth patted her hand. "It's tough to trust someone after they've broken that trust, isn't it?"

Risa nodded, realizing in that moment that Elizabeth had lived with exactly how she was feeling for the past almost twenty years.

"Why did you wait?"

Elizabeth's smile was all the explanation Risa needed but she listened quietly as the other woman spoke.

"Because I love him. That doesn't mean I made it easy on him. It also doesn't mean I caved immediately when he told me what he planned. I think your dad figured I'd fall at his feet and agree to every idea. I made him work for it. And I wasn't a sure thing."

"So you're telling me to give them another chance. I'm not sure they're going to ask for one. They're not here."

"They're not here now. But I can pretty much guarantee they will be soon. Figure out what you want, Risa. But you're not under any obligation to give them an answer right away. Make them work for it."

"And what if I'm not sure I want to...go there again? With them."

Elizabeth's smile was sweet and understanding. "Then tell them flat out and move on. Of course, if I'd taken my own advice, I wouldn't be here now. Sometimes, what you think you want isn't what you need."

Gens had stayed away from the house as long as he could but, three hours after Risa had landed, he couldn't stand it anymore.

Tony had flat-out refused to come with him.

"If she'd wanted to see us, she would've called."

"You're being a dick. We fucked up. We need to fix this."

Tony wiped his hands on the dishrag hanging from his jeans, shaking his head as he turned to face Gens. He had a couple of pots going on the stove. This was how Tony worked through his stress. In the kitchen.

Gens preferred to work his out in the gym or with a hard run, which he'd done earlier today. When he'd come to the conclusion that they needed to go see her.

"I know we fucked up, but I don't think we should overwhelm her. You go in first, make your apologies. I'll go tomorrow."

"You're wrong. This isn't how this should work."

"And maybe it's just not going to work." Tony shook his head. "Did you stop to think of that?"

Since he could tell Tony wasn't going to give on this, Gens had left pissed. He was pretty sure Tony had been just as angry and that the crash he'd heard as he was leaving Tony's house had been the empty pot on the counter hitting the wall across the room.

He and Tony had talked every day she'd been gone but mostly it'd been about what Tony was going to do about the job offer from Tristan and Adam. And if it wasn't that it was about what Gens was going to do now that Karel had decided to retire.

Karel had told Gens he'd be taken care of, no matter what. But Gens didn't want Karel's money. No, Gens wanted his daughter.

He'd thought Tony did, too. He was still pissed at Tony by the time he got to the Main Line mansion he considered home.

He'd called to tell Karel he was coming. Karel had told him he wasn't home, but that Risa was. And she was alone.

So he'd texted her to ask if he could stop by, and a few minutes later she'd replied with "Yes." Only one word but at least it wasn't no.

Since he had a key, he let himself in. Something he did all the time but that he second-guessed the moment he opened the door.

And realized just how much he stood to lose if he fucked this up.

Closing the door behind him, he headed for the family room off the kitchen, figuring he'd start looking for her there.

Turned out he was right.

She was stretched out on the couch, long legs sleek and bare almost to her hips, her shorts barely covering the top of her thighs. The pale pink tank top she wore hugged her breasts and made his mouth water. Her expression, though... That was stone-cold. Apparently Risa had returned with her armor in place.

Well, damn it, he was going to strip it away, piece by piece if he needed to.

He walked across the room and sat on the couch next to her, forcing her to draw her legs up. Yes, he was invading her space but he needed to if he was going to break through that wall of hers.

"Welcome home. How was your trip?"

She stared at him for a moment, her expression calm, cool. But the look in her eyes... Yeah, she was pissed. He didn't blame her. He was pissed at himself. And he was pissed that Tony wasn't here.

One problem at a time.

Finally, she nodded. "Yes. It was nice to get away with Dorrie. We've never been on vacation together."

"I'm sorry we left. I realize it was a dick move on our part. We should've stayed with you. We were thinking with our egos and not with our brains. I want you. I'm not ready to give up on trying to make this work. So my question to you is, are you willing to try?"

She didn't say anything for a few seconds and he had no clue what she was thinking.

Finally, she took a deep breath. "I want to try. I do. But... what about Tony?"

He shook his head. "I don't know. I only know that I want you and I'm not willing to give up."

Another pause. Her head dipped down, hiding her gaze from his.

He wanted to tilt her head back and force her to look at him, but he wanted her to come to him on her own. And when she lifted her head and looked at him, he wanted to pump his fist in the air at the heat in her eyes.

He didn't stop to think. He grabbed her, lifted her onto his lap, and sealed his mouth over hers. She didn't hesitate to kiss him back. Her hands sank into his hair, gripping it tight as she tilted her head and opened her mouth to deepen the kiss.

Yes. This was what he wanted.

His hands slid from her hips to her ribs then up to cup her breasts. No bra. *So damn soft.*

He nearly stripped the tank top over her head but remembered where they were. Karel could come home at any minute.

Not that Risa seemed to mind. She arched her back, making it known that she wanted more. He squeezed her tight, pinched her nipples, and rolled them between his thumb and forefinger. She moaned, low in her throat, and his cock stiffened, rock hard and aching.

And when she rolled her hips forward, pressing her mound against him, he released her breasts so he could grab her hips again and hold her still while he rubbed his erection against her.

She pulled away to draw in air, a rough inhalation that he echoed. Her eyes fluttered open and he saw the same rough need in hers that he felt in every tight muscle.

"My room." She scraped her nails along his scalp, making him groan. "Now."

"Yes, ma'am."

He rose with her wrapped around him, her mouth settling on his neck just below his right ear. She nipped at his skin, bit his earlobe, just hard enough to sting.

Tapping her ass with a broad palm, he had to tighten his hold when she moaned and wriggled in his arms.

"You like that, don't you?' He put his lips against her ear. "That hint of pain."

Her entire body shook but she didn't answer.

He smacked her ass harder this time and the sound of her breath catching in her throat gave him his answer. But he really wanted to hear her say it. He smacked her other cheek as he headed for the stairs.

"Come on, Ris. Say it. I want to hear you."

He was almost halfway up the stairs when she finally said, "Yes."

Her breath against his neck caused goosebumps to rise all over his body.

This is what I wanted. What I've wanted for years.

And if there was a small part of him that said there was something missing, some*one* missing... Well, they'd get beyond it.

Because he would let nothing get in the way of their pleasure.

Seconds later, he nudged open the door to her room with an elbow then kicked it closed with his foot. He stopped for a second because she'd begun to string kisses from just below his ear and along his jaw to his mouth.

Then she cupped his cheek in her hand and kissed him with such complete concentration he wanted to hold her up against the door and get inside her as fast as he could. And the damn bed was only a few feet away.

He stood there and let her kiss him, let her take what she wanted until he couldn't stand not being naked and inside her any longer.

He crossed the last few feet though he didn't remember his feet moving. Suddenly they were sprawled across the bed, kissing. Tongues, teeth, lips enmeshed. Like two teenagers who'd just discovered that sex with someone else was so much better than getting yourself off with your own hand.

And speaking of getting off...

He pulled away and had her flipped over and lying on her front before she could protest.

With her hips trapped between his knees, he knelt over her.

"Grab the headboard, baby, and don't let go."

Her queen bed was white-painted iron, so fucking girly it should hurt any man to look at it. It fit her perfectly. Together, it was gonna be a close fit. If Tony had been here—

She reached for the rails and wrapped her hands around them, her knuckles almost white.

"Good girl. Now don't move."

He moved down until his knees were on either side of hers. It gave him enough room to yank her shorts and underwear down her legs, leaving her ass bare. He pulled them down just far enough that he had access, but she wouldn't be able to open her legs farther than a couple of centimeters.

At his mercy.

Her ass was slightly pink from his earlier slaps and now he took a few seconds to make them blush even harder. A couple smacks to each side had her rubbing her legs together.

"That feel good?" He ran his hands over her ass, massaging her, spreading her cheeks just a little, just until he could see a hint of her pussy. "Good. It's gonna feel even better in a few."

Slipping one hand between her legs and using the other to open his jeans, he rubbed his fingers in the moisture slicking her pussy, then rubbed it up and down his cock, focusing on the tip.

"This first time is gonna be fast and hard."

She nodded her head, hair shimmering along her back. "Good."

"Don't let go. If you do, I'm going to smack that ass again."

"Is that supposed to be a threat?"

He huffed out a laugh. "No, it's a promise."

Shoving his jeans down just a little more, he planted one hand beside her head and guided his cock between her legs with the other. Then he started working his way inside her.

With her legs together like this, she was that much tighter, the friction so fucking good, he groaned. Then he bent down and bit her left shoulder. Marking her. Claiming her.

He took his time getting in, felt her flesh give slowly, not easily. Finally, he couldn't wait any longer and took those last few inches in one hard thrust.

As she moaned, her pussy began to convulse around him, gripping him like a fist as she came.

Holy fuck. How fucking hot was that?

Too hot for him to hold out.

Planting both hands just above her shoulders, he fucked her hard and fast. His balls drew up tight and he teetered on the edge of an orgasm that built like a fast-burning fire. His world narrowed down to his room, this bed, her body.

Making her his.

Every time he thrust inside, he wanted to stay, to let her grip him tight. But he knew that when he drew out and thrust inside again, it would be even better.

After her first orgasm began to wane, she tried to move, to thrust back against him, to get him to move faster, harder.

Pushing back onto his haunches, he put his hands on her

hips and held her down. Which just appeared to turn her own even more.

Gasping for air, she turned her head to the side.

"Gens."

"Ris, don't move. I'll make it feel even better."

"Just fuck me."

"No way. I'm taking my fucking time. You're gonna come again."

But time and her beautiful body were working against him. She squeezed him even tighter, working her internal muscles around him until he had to give in.

One last thrust and he came on a groan. His cock pulsed in her tight sheath as he held high inside her. And she came again, wringing every last ounce of energy from his body until he couldn't hold himself upright any longer and spread out over her.

The next morning, Gens realized getting beyond Risa's walls was going to take more than a few orgasms.

They'd spent last night in her bed. Karel had texted to say he was sleeping at Elisabeth's so Gens had stayed with Risa.

He'd thought she was going to tell him to go back to his room, the one he'd slept in when he'd moved in as a teenager. Surprisingly she hadn't. But this morning, he could tell she'd put him firmly back over that wall.

When he'd asked what she was going to do tonight, she'd said, "Dinner with Bree to talk about the fundraiser. And you?"

Well, he couldn't exactly say he'd been planning to spend it with her, after she'd so firmly put him in his place.

"I'll probably go punch Tony for a couple of hours."

Her eyes had widened but she hadn't taken the bait.

"Have fun with that," she'd said.

He'd left when she'd headed for the stairs, telling him she was going to change and that she'd called for a ride from Orlov, one of her father's men.

He was relieved she'd called for a ride and protection. He was pissed she'd cut him off without blinking.

Tony needed to get on board or Gens really was going to pound him into the mat.

Driving into town, he was pounding on Tony's front door a half hour later.

Tony didn't say anything when he opened the door, just waved Gens in.

Before Tony could open his mouth, Gens lit into him.

"You need to get your fucking head out of your ass before you push her so far away, we don't have a chance in hell of making this work."

"I think she made herself pretty damn clear when she fucking left the country to get away from us. You need to take a fucking hint."

"I spent the night with her. She was pretty damn happy to see me."

Tony looked like he'd been gut-punched before he wiped his expression clear. "Then you've got a clear path. Go for it."

"Jesus, you're an idiot. She wants both of us. What do you not get? Yeah, I will be more than happy to give her whatever she wants. But if you don't figure your shit out, you're going to lose her."

"Do you seriously not have a problem sharing her?"

"No. Not with you. Anyone else touches her, I'd kill them. I trust you with my life and I trust you with hers. More importantly, she trusts you. Or she did. If you want her, you need to make this right. And you need to do it soon."

Tony watched Gens stalk back toward the front door, shaking his head, before he slammed the door behind him as he left.

Anger throbbed in his gut. Confusion rang in his head. And hunger made his cock hard.

He wanted everything Gens had described. He just didn't have the faith that Gens did that everything would work out. And if it didn't...

Was he willing to fail? He'd failed pretty spectacularly in San Antonio. If he failed Gens and Risa...

He didn't even have a goddamn job.

That last one was easy enough to fix. He'd had an offer. But did he want it? And if this relationship failed... What then?

So you make sure it doesn't fail. Where's the problem?

He heard his grandmother's voice in his head. She'd been the dispenser of practical advice and knowledge in his childhood. His parents were always busy trying to make ends meet, so he'd spent a lot of time with his grandmother, either at home or at the restaurant.

It was weird but his fondest memories of his Nonna involved her wooden spoon. She'd either been stirring something with it or spanking his ass with it. Sometimes she'd smack his hand away from the pot with it; sometimes she'd use it to tap the back of his head if he said some stupid.

He wished like hell she was still around to talk to. Coupled with his dad's early-onset Alzheimer's and his parents' move to Florida so they could be closer to his aunts, he felt like he'd been cut loose.

Picking up his phone, he punched in a number.

"Hey, Blank. What can I do for you?"

"You have a few minutes to talk about that job offer?"

"Absolutely," Adam Oleksy answered immediately. "Tristan's here. Why don't you come over to the house instead of doing this on speaker?"

Forty-five minutes later, Adam smiled at him as he shook his hand and pulled him through the doorway and into the house he shared with his business partner and their... girlfriend?

"I'm really glad you called," Adam said as he shut the door behind Tony. "We've been wanting to talk to you again. Adam'll be down in a minute. Tony, this is our partner, Kat. I'm not sure you two have met."

Adam gestured to the woman beside him, whose cool smile reminded him of Risa's.

She held out her hand and he shook it, realizing at that moment that here was another example of a three-way relationship that was working.

Damn, maybe there was something in the water? Or maybe it happened more often than he realized.

"Nice to meet you."

"And you. Sorry I can't stay. I'm meeting my future sister-in-law to discuss wedding plans."

She turned to kiss Adam, ruffling his reddish-brown hair and smiling with so much warmth, Tony felt forgotten.

"Hey, you leaving?" Tristan pounded down the stairs. "Text when you get there, okay? And tell your brother we need to talk about those contracts."

Katrina stepped away from Adam, only to be caught in Tristan's arms and pressed tight against him. She didn't hesitate to kiss Tristan when he bent his head, her expression exasperated when she pulled back.

"I'll let you know when I get there but I'm only going to Berks County. It's not like I'm driving across the country."

"I know that. Humor me. And don't just blame me. You know Adam would've said something, too."

Adam shook his head with a grin that belied the motion as Kat gave them both a look. Katrina reminded him of Risa. And not just physically. Yes, they were both blonde and beautiful, regal and cool, though Kat seemed shy and Risa reserved.

"I'll see you two later tonight." She turned to Tony. "Nice to finally meet you. The guys have been saying great things about you for a few weeks. I hope the next time we meet, we have more time to talk."

"Have a seat." Adam nodded toward the dining room table in the next room. "Let's talk."

Once they were settled at the table, Adam and Tristan on one side, Tony on the other, he realized every question he had about the job had been supplanted by questions he wasn't sure he was comfortable asking.

After a glance at Adam, Tristan took the lead. "I'm gonna be honest. We're hoping you're here to accept our offer. Our business has been growing a little faster than we expected and we're hoping you can jump in immediately."

"Can I ask you a question?"

"Of course." Tristan's open smile invited him to ask whatever he wanted.

"It's probably not what you're expecting."

The other men exchanged a glance

Tristan shrugged. "Not a problem."

"What happens if you can't make it work? If it all blows up in your face, what then?"

Tristin's eyes widened. "Uh..."

Adam chuckled, leaning back in his chair. Then he smacked Tristan on the arm. "You owe me ten bucks."

Tristan rolled his eyes at Adam. "Fuck you. I never should've taken that damn bet. Too damn easy."

Tony didn't let their obvious amusement faze him. He needed answers before he committed to upending his life again. He'd been in limbo for the past couple of years since leaving San Antonio.

"Just to be clear." Tristan cocked his head to the side. "You're talking about how the job impacts my relationships with Adam and Kat, right? Because you're worried about your relationship with Risa and Gens?"

A couple of weeks ago, discussing this with anyone would've shut him down faster than the Schuylkill Turnpike after a fender-bender.

Today, he was willing to cut open his chest and let people dig around in there if it would help him figure out what the fuck to do.

"Yes."

"It works because we make it work." Adam held up one

hand when Tony shook his head. "No, wait. Hear me out. Tris and I have been friends for years. I know how he thinks. Same goes for him. That doesn't mean we don't disagree. It just means we had some shit figured out between us before we added Kat to the mix."

They exchanged a glance and Tony knew they were debating what else to say. Finally, Tristan nodded, and Adam turned back to Tony.

"We have issues. It's not all hearts and flowers."

Tristan chuckled under his breath. "Hell, somedays it's more like rocks and mountains. We don't see eye to eye on everything."

"We're never gonna see eye to eye on everything," Adam added. "The one thing we always agree on is making sure Kat never feels like we're a united force *against* her. We have to be careful not to steamroll her. Sometimes that takes a little more work than normal. But I have a feeling Risa isn't easily steamrolled. Of course, that presents a whole other series of problems. Because then you're going to feel like you need to be united against her. For her own good."

"And that way leads to hell, my friend." Tristan's grin looked pained. "Trust me. You don't want to go there. Of course, eventually you will fuck up. Then you just have to be sure you apologize for being a complete ass because it *will* be your fault."

Adam nodded toward Tristan. "Usually it's his fault."

Tristan rolled his eyes again. "Tell him about the time you slept alone for three days."

"I believe that was after you told her she couldn't go to Washington without one of us and she didn't speak to you for a week."

The banter between the men eased the tight knot in Tony's chest.

The guys went on for another few minutes, seemingly forgetting he was there. He knew they hadn't, knew they were proving a point. And proving it pretty well.

Finally, Tristan sighed and turned back to Tony, cutting off Adam before he could add anything else. "Any other questions? And I mean about the job."

"No, I think I've got a handle on things. I just have one thing I need to do before I give you my answer."

23

The invitation with her name on the plain white envelope had appeared on the desk in her office at the foundation Monday morning.

She'd pulled out the card, the front of which said, "Be Our Guest," written in fancy script. It immediately reminded her of Disney's *Beauty and the Beast*. She loved that movie. Both of them. Then she flipped the card over, expecting to see an ad for a new DVD or something like that.

Instead, she'd seen "Haven Hotel, 8 p.m." and today's date.

Her heart started to pound when she saw the handwritten signature at the bottom.

Tony's. Just Tony's.

Now, an hour before she should leave to get to the hotel on time, she needed to decide if she was actually going to go.

Was he asking to meet her for dinner so he could tell her he was leaving? Was that why only his name was on the invitation?

She and Gens had spent last night together and though

she'd enjoyed every second of it, it had felt like something was missing. She was pretty sure Gens felt the same.

Would the ache go away after a while? She wasn't sure it would.

Be grateful for what you have.

She was. But she wanted it all. The small taste she'd had of the three of them together hadn't been enough.

Her mind occupied, she didn't notice Gens standing in the foyer until she almost walked into him.

She paused, her lips parting as her mind kicked into high gear. Should she tell him she was meeting Tony? Did he know? Why was he here?

Before she could say anything, he gave her a look that made her heart leap into her chest.

"You look beautiful."

"Thank you."

"Are you ready to leave?"

She blinked. "What?"

His mouth quirked in a little smile. "I was invited too. Did he neglect to mention that?"

"He did."

Gens just shrugged. "We should leave if we don't want to be late."

Once they were settled in the car Gens had parked out front, she had to ask.

"Do you know why he invited us to dinner?"

Gens kept his gaze on the road. "Did it say dinner on your invitation?"

She had think about that. "No, it didn't."

"I'm sure there'll be time for food."

"Do you know what he has planned?"

"We haven't talked about it."

"Do you think he's leaving?"

"I think you need to wait to hear what he has to say before you jump to conclusions."

"So you do know what he wants to say."

"Try not to work yourself into a knot, Ris. Just...hear the guy out."

She kept her mouth shut the rest of the way, her brain spinning, her heart pounding. She tried not to freak out, not to think too far ahead. But if Tony left...

By the time Gens parked in front of the hotel, that knot he'd mentioned had settled into her gut. As the parking attendant helped her out of the car, she reached for the icy reserve she'd cultivated over the years. It was harder than she'd expected. And that added another layer of worry to her already frayed nerves.

What if Tony told them he was leaving? That he'd called them here in public to let them know so there'd be no scene?

Did she really think he'd do that?

No. She didn't. But her heart wasn't as sure.

Looking up, she found Gens staring down at her, worry in the lines of his forehead.

"You okay?"

She headed toward the front door and into the lobby, for once taking no notice of the beautiful space.

"I'm fine."

Or she would be when Tony told them what was going on. If he planned to bail, she planned to get up and walk away. She wouldn't make a scene, wouldn't yell or cry or—

"Ms. Antonoff. Mr. Markov." The receptionist she'd met the day she'd come to check out the space greeted them with a smile in the center of the lobby. "Please come with me. Mr. Blankenship is expecting you."

She glanced up at Gens, puzzled, but Gens just smiled and nodded at the younger woman, who began leading them toward...the elevators?

Had he reserved a room? If he had, why would they need a hotel escort to get to it?

Once the receptionist waved them into the elevator, she took a black keycard from her pocket and passed it over the panel. The button for the fifth floor lit up.

"Mr. Blankenship is waiting for you on five. Have a good evening."

Did she imagine it or did the other woman's smile widen just a little?

What the hell was going on?

Once the elevator door closed and the cage began to rise, she turned to Gens.

"Do you have any idea what's going on?"

He shook his head. "Whatever it is, he didn't tell me."

The elevator stopped a second later, cutting off whatever she would've said. As the doors slid open, she turned to find Tony standing in the hall. In a dark suit. No tie, collar unbuttoned.

He looked mouthwateringly, darkly sexy.

And his gaze burned.

"Thanks for coming. Both of you."

Staring at him with her lips parted, Risa only moved when Gens stepped forward, taking her elbow and prompting her to follow.

"Tony...what's going on?"

"I'll explain in a few. I need you to sign something first."

Okay, now her brain was totally spinning.”

"Could you just please explain what's going on first? I don't—"

Cupping her face in his hands, he put his mouth over hers and kissed her, shutting off her words and causing her spinning brain to pause as he stole her breath.

When he released her seconds later, she had to suck in a deep breath as her eyes blinked open.

"I'd rather show you. But I need you to sign a release first." He looked at Gens. "Both of you."

"What the hell?"

Tony's mouth barely moved but she could tell he wanted to grin.

"Trust me."

An argument rose to the tip of her tongue, but she bit it back because... "I do. Trust you. Let me see what you want me to sign."

Conflicting emotions battled for prominence, but she shoved them down as she reached for the paper he took from his coat pocket.

Fairly standard legal jargon of a non-disclosure form for something called The Salon. She saw nothing that raised a flag and she took the pen he held out without hesitation.

After she'd signed, she passed the pen to Gens, who looked even more suspicious than she felt. But Gens signed, as well.

"Now what?"

Tony withdrew a black piece of cloth from his coat pocket that looked suspiciously like—

Her eyes widened. "You want to blindfold me?"

The look she gave Tony obviously amused him because now he smiled outright.

"Yes. But not immediately. First, I want to say I'm sorry I was an asshole. I know it won't be the last time. I'll apologize then too."

Tony turned to Gens then. "You and I will never see to eye to eye on everything and that's not going to change. But we'll work on it.

"We'll all work on it." He looked back to her. "I'm staying. If I left, I'd realize I'd made the worst mistake of my life a second later. I love you, Risa. I have for a year, but I was too stupid to admit it. I hope to hell you can forgive me for being an ass. I let my bullshit get in my head and fuck with it. That's on me."

He took a step closer and her heart kicked up an even harder pace. Hope was a sweet heat in her blood, one that her first instinct was to guard against, to close off and retreat.

She didn't want to do that anymore. She wanted to reach out and grab both of these men and shout that they were hers. She wanted it to be true so badly, she was willing to risk being hurt so badly she might never recover.

Even now, she was having a hard time getting her lips and tongue to work to form words. She took a deep breath but before she could say anything, he continued.

"Trust me, Risa. Trust us. Tomorrow, we'll talk all you want. But tonight, say yes and I promise you won't regret it."

She didn't hesitate. "Yes."

His smile held so much heat now, she swore she felt it against her skin.

"Thank you." Then he held out the blindfold to Gens, who'd moved slightly behind her.

Gens took the strip of cloth, but before he put it over her eyes, he bent and whispered into her ear. "I love you, too, sweetheart. I always have. And just to be clear, I don't have a clue what the hell's going on either."

Her laughter bubbled out of her a split second before he put the satin strip over her eyes and plunged her into darkness.

Her indrawn breath must have worried her men because Gens wrapped his hand around her right bicep while Tony grabbed her left hand, as if to anchor her.

"I'm fine. I'm also dying to be naked with you so whatever you have planned, it better include a bed."

"There will be a bed. Later." The lust in Tony's voice made her shiver. "First, there's The Salon."

They took several steps forward. She estimated to the end of the hall then they stopped and then moved forward again when she heard a door open in front of her.

After the snick of the door closing behind her, they stopped.

She heard Gens make a noise that was half amazement, half laugh, and she had a second to wonder what the hell was going on when she felt Tony brush his thumb against her cheek, causing a shiver to quake through her.

"Gens is going to undress you. And then we're going to take you. No more asking permission. If you don't want this, say so now. Otherwise, trust us. I promise we won't let you down."

Heart pounding out of control, she nodded. In the next second, Gens released the zipper on the back of her dress and let it fall to the floor. A second later, she felt Tony grip her around the waist and lift her into his arms.

"I changed my mind. Damn, Ris, you look fucking amazing."

She smiled. "I wore it for you. I hoped you'd both get to see it tonight."

She'd purchased the pale pink lace bra and panties set in Italy, praying she'd have the chance to wear it for them.

"And we certainly do appreciate it," Gens said.

"I'm going to put you down now." Tony's voice sounded so close to her ear. "But first…"

He kissed her, hard, total domination in the way his mouth moved over hers. Her arms tightened around his neck as she let him have everything and anything he wanted.

When he pulled away, she gasped, her hands trying to pull him back down. Instead, he laid her out on a soft surface, then tugged her panties down her legs.

"Hate to see them go," Tony said. "But they'll be in the way and I don't want to rip them."

Then he spread her legs wide. Cooler air rushed against her bare sex for a split second before Tony's mouth sealed over her. He made love to her with his mouth, pushing her hard and fast to a climax that had been building since they'd put the blindfold over her eyes.

The loss of her sight had heightened every other sense, especially touch. She very nearly came when he licked over her clit and played with it. She moaned and her back arched as heat rushed through her.

But when Gens grabbed her arms and held them over her head, she practically melted into the cushion.

"Turn to your right, sweetheart," Gens instructed. "Suck me in."

Obeying, she opened her mouth, taking Gen's cock into her mouth and sucking him deep. His groan was kerosene on her desire and she dedicated herself to making him come.

Lost in the dual sensations of giving and receiving, she floated in a haze of sex. When Tony pulled away, she moaned around Gens's shaft as she drew hard on him. But seconds later, Tony returned, this time with his cock.

He filled her fast and so completely, she wanted to cry out, but she couldn't.

Caught between them, she dropped every last wall she had and gave herself up completely.

And as she came, she knew she'd never be able to rebuild those walls against them.

"This place. Oh my god. I had no idea."

Gens just shook his head, his smile as bemused as she felt. "Why the hell did you never tell me about this?"

Tony shrugged, his arms wrapped around Risa, curled against his chest, as they lay on the chaise in front of the fireplace.

"I signed the NDA, just like you."

"And the Goldens use this for what?"

"Parties. I've been to a couple. And before you get pissed off, this was last year."

Risa knew they'd be talking more about that later. For now, she wanted to enjoy being together with her men.

"So what do we do now?" she asked.

"We make our own lives together."

She heard no hesitation in Gens's voice, sitting in the chair next to the chaise, running a hand up and down her legs, while Tony had his arms wrapped around her.

"We'll figure it out." Tony bent down to nip at her ear then kiss the hurt away. "Together."

Risa smiled. "I love you. Both of you. Very much. I only have one complaint."

"What's that?" Gens grinned at her, as if he knew what she was about to say. And maybe he did.

"I want my own damn keycard to this floor."

SEDUCING WHITNEY
WICKED & CHARMING MENAGE ROMANCE

This fairy tale is wickedly charming...

Sheltered heiress Whitney Snowden spent years trying to avoid her powerful father's influence over her life. When he dies suddenly, she finds he had one final hand to play—either she steps in to run his empire or marry a man who will. Otherwise, her calculating stepmother gets everything. Whitney's charitable foundation would be gone. She turns to the only men who have as much to lose as she does, her father's righthand men. If Whitney is to outsmart her stepmother, she has to marry one of them. But she wants both.

Her offer will blow their minds...

Handsome. Sexy. Closer than brothers. Chase Noble and Ryan Delahunt have been groomed by Richard Snowden to run his company, not marry his daughter. But their mentor's death rocks their world, and Whitney's plan could be their salvation, if jealousy doesn't get in the way. Chase and Ryan have both lusted after Whitney for years but inviting the beauty into their lives—and their bed—might put their relationship and the future of Snowden Enterprises at risk.

Can seducing Whitney help her discover the passion and strength to claim her own life? And her own loves?

ALSO BY STEPHANIE JULIAN

WICKED & CHARMING

Seducing Whitney

Claiming Ellie

Sharing Brianna

SCANDALOUS DESIRE

Invite Me In

Reserve My Nights

Expose My Desire

Keep My Secrets

Rock My Heart

INDECENT

An Indecent Proposition

An Indecent Affair

An Indecent Arrangement

An Indecent Longing

An Indecent Desire

LOVERS UNDERCOVER

Lovers & Lies

Sinners & Secrets

Beauty & Brains

OFFSIDE HEARTS

Netting the Goalie

Pucking the Grinder

Falling for the Enforcer

Tempting the Instigator

Desiring the D-Man

Taming the Machine

Gambling on the Ghost

DEVILS HOCKEY

Rowdy Hearts

Rainbow Kisses

Rebel Secrets

Rocky's story (Title TBA)

FAST ICE

Bylines & Blue Lines

Hard Lines & Goal Lines

Deadlines & Red Lines

DARKLY ENCHANTED

Spell Bound

Moon Bound

Twice Bound

MOONLIGHT FANTASIES

Shadow Magic

Enchanted Magic

Dangerous Magic

MOONLIGHT LOVERS

Kiss of Moonlight

Visions of Moonlight

Edge of Moonlight

Temptation in Moonlight

Grace in Moonlight

Shades of Moonlight

DIVINE DESIRES

Dark Desires at Dawn

Rough Caress of Midnight

Double Fantasies at Twilight

Enchanting Temptations in Shadow

REDTAILS HOCKEY

(Third-person OFFSIDE HEARTS)

The Brick Wall

The Grinder

The Enforcer

The Instigator

The Playboy

The D-Man

The Machine

The Ghost

ABOUT THE AUTHOR

Stephanie Julian is a USA Today and New York Times best-selling author of contemporary and paranormal romance. Stay in touch for all new releases and sales. Sign up here.

www.ingramcontent.com/pod-product-compliance
Lightning Source LLC
Chambersburg PA
CBHW070828190726
48292CB00006B/2150